OIL CHANGE
AT RATH'S GARAGE

OIL CHANGE
AT RATH'S GARAGE

SHARI NARINE

thistledown press

Thistledown Press Ltd.
410 2nd Avenue North
Saskatoon, Saskatchewan, S7K 2C3
www.thistledownpress.com

Library and Archives Canada Cataloguing in Publication

Narine, Shari, author
Oil change at Rath's garage / Shari Narine.
Issued in print and electronic formats.
ISBN 978-1-77187-132-7 (softcover).–ISBN 978-1-77187-133-4 (HTML).–
ISBN 978-1-77187-134-1 (PDF)
I. Title.

PS8627.A75O35 2017   C813'.6   C2017-901115-4
C2017-901116-2

Cover and book design by Jackie Forrie
Printed and bound in Canada
Author photo by Rhonda Lemoine

Canada Council
for the Arts
Conseil des Arts
du Canada

SASKATCHEWAN
ARTS BOARD

Canadä

Thistledown Press gratefully acknowledges the financial assistance of the Canada
Council for the Arts, the Saskatchewan Arts Board, and the Government of Canada
for its publishing program.

Acknowledgements

Thank you to my siblings and their partners for all their support: Nandia and Mike; Shaun; and Nandini and Robert.

To my wonderful friends: Cathy; Colleen; Lori; Nancy; Sandy, Ellen and Tammy; and Carol.

To my Daysland school teachers: Mrs. Tylosky, who set me on this path in grade two, and Mrs. McCarroll, who made me feel the power of words.

To my editor Michael Kenyon, who said the words every writer wants to hear: "my changes are only suggestions." Thank you for the fantastic suggestions, Michael. You made this work stronger.

To my mentor Margaret Macpherson, who took a piece of me and helped me finesse it into something of which I am proud. And to the Writers' Guild of Alberta, who brilliantly paired me with Margaret through their mentorship program.

To the wonderful people at Thistledown Press who gave me words of encouragement when I needed them the most and guidance through this sometimes daunting process.

To my mother, who gave me the talent, and my father, who gave me the work ethic.

To my sons: Ethan, whose passion for hockey kept me going in my passion for writing when we both suffered setbacks, and Jonathan, for reminding me that perseverance is an admirable quality.

Arrival

1

THE ATTACK COMES OUT OF nowhere. One minute Matt Humphreys is checking out girls. The next minute he is slammed against a bank of blue lockers.

"Stay away from my girlfriend!"

His eyes swim. The face inches from his is a blur. His head echoes the crash of the hollow steel. He sucks air into his lungs.

"Son of a bitch." He blinks once, twice. The face comes into focus. Who the fuck is this jerkoff?

"You hear me, asshole? Stay away from my girl!" Another quick shove.

Another bounce of his head off the locker and Matt explodes. His fists fly. He clips the prick's chin. He brings his knee up, connects with empty space. "What the fuck?" He plants his feet shoulder-width apart, rubber soles grip linoleum. His hands remain fisted for protection and to keep from exploring the back of his head. He is not going to show weakness. "I don't even *know* you!"

"Now you do." And the guy is back in his face.

This isn't a good thing. He and Ben have been in this school for only two days. *He* is supposed to be knocking guys into lockers, making them understand they need to keep their hands off his little brother. This, right now? Not a good thing.

He throws his shoulders back, collides with the locker, tries not to panic as he pins himself in. The best defense is a good offence. He spits out, "Let's see you try that again, fuckhead."

The guy falters, his sneer slips. The jeers behind him grow louder. Then he is at it again. "I think I will, asshole." And he two hands Matt back into the locker.

"That's the best you can do? Scary," Matt draws out. He steals a quick look around. A crowd has gathered, but no Ben. The kid would have a fit if he saw his big brother getting pummelled. He steps forward, holds his hand out to illustrate his next statement. "I'm shaking."

"Rick, what are you doing?"

It all comes together then. This hot blonde. Lyne. She is the girl he helped yesterday with her biology books. She is this fucktard's girlfriend.

"Nothing, babe," Rick says, pulls Lyne in, kisses the shit out of her. She pastes herself against him, shoves her hands into the waistband of his jeans, and gives right back.

Matt has seen this dance at too many schools. It is show and tell, all for his benefit. Because getting slammed into a locker didn't deliver the message. Now he has a visual to go along with his throbbing back. Life just keeps on rocking.

He walks away, shrugging his shoulders, rotating his neck to work out the stiffness.

"They're always like that."

He stops, stares at the girl beside him. He noticed her yesterday, too, but didn't ask about her. She is not his usual flavour. Lyne is. But this girl, with the short brown hair, wide brown eyes, has a great rack.

"Yeah?" he says.

"Yeah," she says. "I'm Kennedy."

"Matt." Introducing himself is a fucking stupid formality.

"Well, yeah, new boy in grade ten Everybody knows who you are." The corner of Kennedy's red, red lips quirks up. She is hot. A tight little bod and the way she keeps moving closer, fuck, there is potential here.

He smiles, too. "Guess not much excitement in a town this size."

"No," Kennedy says, shaking her perfectly styled hair. "New guy in school and everybody talks. Most excitement we've had in three years."

"Two new guys."

"Two?" Her voice trails off, her carefully plucked eyebrow arches.

He follows her gaze. Rick has Lyne backed up against the wall, is still playing tonsil hockey with her. There is obviously history between these three. He doesn't give a shit. "My kid brother's in grade six. Name's Ben."

Kennedy turns back to him. There is nothing coy about her smile now. "Yeah, us high schoolers, we don't pay much attention to the elementary intake."

He gets that. He wouldn't either if the elementary intake weren't his responsibility.

Kennedy glances back then squares her shoulders to him. "You free tonight? There's a bush party a few miles out of town. Kind of a pre-grad thing."

Oh, yeah. There *is* something here. But he's not sure what this is and any girl who is not a guaranteed lay is not worth Ben bitching him out. And those damned puppy-dog eyes Ben would send his way? So not worth the combo slap-down guilt trip from the kid.

"Gotta pass. Gotta go home and do my Mrs. Doubtfire thing. With school yesterday and today, we have to unpack, get our shit together." Kennedy doesn't need to know that it takes ten seconds to unpack because what they can fit in the back of the BMW hardly breaks a sweat.

She screws her lips up in a pout. "Another time, then," she says and her tongue darts out to touch her top lip. She sashays away, her hips swinging in the tight mini-skirt.

Fuck. Maybe getting bitched out by Ben is worth it if he can get some action. But then again, Dad is still around. So no sweet piece of ass is worth what could happen at home.

Lyne Rutger shoves at Rick. It wasn't the new guy he was performing for. Matt. He didn't stick around. The show was all for Kennedy. Lyne should be pissed royally and part of her is totally annoyed, but another part of her is fully in the take-that-bitch mode. She will work on being angry with Rick now, make him feel guilty. She won't admit to him that that was hot. Incredibly hot. Everyone was watching. Well, with the exception of the new boy. But hell with him. Kennedy and the other rich bitches were drooling, wishing they were with Rick.

"What was that about?" she asks, pulls her shirt down, covers her midriff a little more. The dress code is worse than useless at Delwood Public, but if the principal catches too much skin, he will call home. She doesn't need to hear the that's-what-got-me-into-trouble speech from Mom again. She doesn't need to be reminded that one thing leads to another. And she was the thing it led to with Mom and Dad.

"What, babe?" Rick's grey eyes go wide in feigned innocence. "Can't show my girl I miss her?"

She wards off Rick's advance with her hand to his chest. Holy crap, he is ripped. And all hers. This makeout session is only a taste of what tonight's bush party is going to bring. "I mean, with Matt before that."

"Matt? Oh, that's the dickwad's name." Rick rubs his jaw, a small purple bruise a reminder of where Matt connected. "Fucker needed to know you're taken."

"Whatever!"

"What?" Rick snaps and his eyes spark.

"Taken?" She places her hand on her thrust-out hip. "What is this? Caveman days?"

He pushes her up against the wall, pins her there, hands gripping her arms. There is nothing gentle about his touch. He growls, "What? You don't want to be taken?"

She drops the teasing smile, holds in a gasp. She has seen Rick this way before. All predatory. It is a little scary. But it means he wants her. And she has been fighting for this, for him. She pulls him down, kisses him hard. "I'm all yours."

"Damn right." His sloppy grin reminds her why this boy lusting after her is the catch of the school. "You don't need that jerkwad dicking around after you."

12

She pulls back. That jerkwad dismissed her, walked away, as if she was not good enough. Who the hell is he to judge her like that?

Glory shuffles back before Lyne sees her. As if she would! Her sister is so engrossed in Rick an earthquake wouldn't stop her from swapping spit with him.

Glory has no idea what she has just witnessed. None of it makes sense. Not Rick Jeffries pushing the new boy — Matt — up against the lockers. Or the way Kennedy stood so close to him and then looked flustered as Lyne and Rick made out in the hall. And how could Lyne do that? All those eyes on her, Rick's hands all over her. Doesn't she have any pride? But then again, all Lyne has been about these past few months is Rick, Rick, Rick. Getting Rick. Having Rick. Now it has to be about showing him off, doesn't it? Lyne has always been about boys. She lives and breathes Rick. As if Rick is the answer to the question of life.

Matt hasn't even been here a week and all the girls in Glory's grade nine class — and the entire high school! — are talking about him. She even overheard a couple of Kennedy's friends in the bathroom gushing about how he walked down the halls as if he owned the world, how confident his stride was, how they wouldn't mind slumming it for him. The whole school has gone crazy. Even the boys are talking about Matt, pissed about his swagger, worried about their girlfriends.

But she saw him just now when he threw down with Rick, and Matt wasn't about confidence. He acted like a boy who had nothing to lose. As if one cream-coloured cinder block hallway was the same as any other and he was no more invested in Delwood Public School than he was in the school he came from. Just passing through. He is like the solitary figures she reads about in her novels.

The buzzer sounds.

Ugh! She has run out of time to check the bulletin board for summer jobs. Now she will have to come back after school. She hates being here longer than she needs to be. She turns around and slams into Tina.

"There you are." Tina moves closer as if to share a secret. "Did you see the fight?"

"No, not really," she says.

"Oh." Tina falters, then she flutters her hands in excitement. "You can ask Lyne about it!"

Glory snorts. She is not going to listen to her sister give a blow-by-blow of Rick sticking it to the new guy to protect her virtue. As if Lyne has any virtue left to protect. "Yeah. Not."

"Whatever," Tina says.

Glory walks back to the junior high section of the school, Tina on her heels, chattering. But it is the look on the new boy's face that stays with her until she slides in to her desk. *Of Mice and Men* is propped open, pen between the pages. It irritates her that she wasted so much of her noon hour. Now she will have to wait until after school, after she has looked at the job board, before she can return to her book. She finds George fascinating. This little man with the sharp eyes who cares for Lennie, is so devoted to him. What would drive someone to give so much? Life would be simpler for George on his own. Nobody paints a picture of the complexities of life as well as Steinbeck.

2

JACK HUMPHREYS PUSHES BACK HIS lank dark curls with one hand. With the other, he touches the almost empty bottle of Labatt Blue to his forehead. No relief there. His beer is warm. Benny is clasping a thick book, carefully turning the pages. It is hard to read the kid's face. His damned bangs are a curtain. "You're supposed to be unpacking the books, not reading them."

Benny fumbles the book, drops it. A photograph flutters loose, lands on the stained yellow carpet.

Jack looks at the book now resting at the kid's feet. Thick book. Christ. Is that one of his old textbooks from the University of Alberta? "Where the hell'd you get that?"

"Uh." Benny whips his bangs out of his face with a quick jerk of his head, hesitates a moment to look behind him. Then he tracks the textbook, the photograph, before he lifts his eyes. His words come out in a rush. "It was stuck in a corner of the trunk. I didn't know it was yours. I would have left it if I'd known."

"Put it on the shelf." Jack braces his hip against the yellow and brown plaid couch. He waits a beat or two as the kid shuffles his feet. "Well?"

Benny stares at the book. It lies open, spine facing the ceiling, purple cover no longer glossy. "It has your name in it. But it's not your writing."

"What do you mean it's not my writing?" Sweat runs down his neck, presses the cotton of his shirt tight against his chest. An armoured plate. "Benny?"

"It's a girl's writing," Benny says softly.

15

"Miriam." The name is heavy in the thick air. This is unexpected. One more move to get away, but still she follows.

"Yeah. Mom's." Benny hovers over the book.

Jack's wedding ring clinks on the glass as he waves the bottle. "Pick up the photograph."

Benny moves quickly. His eyes stay firmly on the picture and he swallows convulsively.

"Whatcha got there, dude?"

Benny jumps.

Jack loses his perch on the couch. "Christ, Matt."

Matt grins unrepentantly.

"A photo," Benny says.

"Duh, Einstein." Matt moves in. "Let me see."

"It's a picture. Of you and Dad."

Matt takes it, brushes his fingers softly over the surface. His eyes are gentle. "It's your graduation from university, Dad. When you got your engineering degree."

"Yeah?" Jack says. It is too hot to remember.

"Yeah, Mom took it." Matt's eyes return to the photo. "She called us her two handsome men."

The boy was four and a half, Miriam only just pregnant with Benny. Does Matt really remember that day? It was such a good day. Miriam smiling brightly, one hand constantly resting on the slight swell of her tummy, the other stubbornly twisting Matt's curls into compliance. Jack had wanted that second baby so badly. Miriam did it for him.

"You have matching ties, Matt," Benny whispers.

Jack closes his eyes tightly, can see that June morning like it was yesterday. Sunshine and warmth. Miriam dressing Matt in his little-boy suit, looping the tie around his neck, fussing

16

with him to keep still. She had sewn those matching ties. She said the little flecks of gold in the green silk brought out the hazel that was hidden in their deep brown eyes.

"Yeah. Dad wore a green gown."

"Green?" Benny asks.

"Tinkerbell green, right, Dad?" Matt's smile is strained. He moves, flush side-by-side with Benny.

"What? No!" he says. "Dark green."

Matt toes the book. "Huh. Your engineering textbook."

"Yeah," he says. "Your mom wrote my name in it."

"Huh," Matt says. He doesn't pick up the book.

Jack understands the boy's reluctance. It has been months since Miriam's name has been spoken. But she is always in his head. How can she not be? He looks at Benny and it is Miriam looking back — eyes the colour of the sky on its best summer day, freckles spattered like wildflowers, blonde hair so thick it is a field of hay. That face taunts him, never lets him forget about the life he had. That face keeps him firmly in the past, unable to move on no matter how far he runs.

"You want to see the picture?" Matt asks. But he doesn't close the distance, doesn't hold the picture out.

Jack's fingers cramp from clasping the bottle. "I don't want to see the fucking picture. Get rid of the fucking book, too."

Matt moves now, stands between him and Benny. He stoops, picks up the textbook, slides the photograph between the pages. He drops the book on the coffee table. Then he is shoving Benny back into the hall, away. Getting rid of the face that hurts like hell to see.

"Christ, Matt," he says.

Matt shrugs, stands firm blocking the hallway.

Jack slams his bottle down on the bookshelf. "I'm going out."

Allie Rutger holds a Kokanee in her hand. The beer has lost its chill and its fizz. Just like her. Too damned hot to get excited about anything. But her husband hasn't clued into that yet. He is antsy, prowling from wall to wall in the small living room. The denim of his work jeans swishes with each long stride.

"You want to go out *now*?" she says. "It's late."

Doug stops behind the couch. She swivels to look at him. His face is grizzled, tired, but Lord, he is sexy. After all these years, her body still responds in anticipation. He's been gone for close to a week and the girls are out and she wants to throw down right now on the couch and feel his body pressed against hers, and getting sweaty that way sounds good and . . .

"Jesus, Allie, you an old woman or what?" Doug takes a long swallow from his bottle. This is at least the second beer he has cracked open since getting home an hour ago. His dark blond hair is plastered to his head, the ends sticking out like quills. "It's barely nine. Marples is throwing a party. Got a new job, I heard."

"C'mon, Doug," she says. "I have to shower. You have to shower. It'll be a good hour before we can even leave the house."

"Nothing gets going until after ten anyway," Doug says. He walks back into the kitchen, clanks his empty bottle on the table.

She hears the whir of the refrigerator as the door opens, the smack of it swinging shut. She hangs her head. "Doug."

"What?" he says the word hard and short. He stands behind the couch again, bottle in one hand, the other hand stuck in his pocket.

He hasn't touched her since he got home. She should have taken something from Lyne's closet. Some hot little number that pushes her tits out, offers her body up as a prize. "Let's stay home. Have a party of our own," she says. "You're already on your third beer."

"What the hell is that supposed to mean?" Doug swallows noisily, keeps his washed-out blue eyes on her.

He is looking for an argument. She should have known that. The minute he walked through that door he was at the fridge, bitching that there was only one six-pack in there.

"Okay," she says. She pushes to her knees on the couch, fists his T-shirt and pulls him down for a hard kiss. When he doesn't slip his tongue between her teeth, when he breaks the kiss and turns away, she is left breathless.

Lyne cannot believe what she is seeing. Kennedy is practically sitting on Rick's lap. Her hand is definitely above his knee. Well above his knee.

"The fire is hot, isn't it?" Kennedy says and undoes two more buttons on her shirt, slides her sleeves off her shoulders. She might as well not be wearing a shirt it is so undone. She sure as hell isn't wearing a bra. And Rick's eyes are nowhere near Kennedy's face.

"Little slut," Lyne says. A few heads swing in her direction and then follow her line of sight. There are about thirty kids here tonight and everybody will be talking about how

Kennedy got it on with Rick. And Rick is no longer her fucking boyfriend!

"She is a little slut, isn't she?" Brad Bishop says.

Lyne forces herself to look away from Rick and the bitch. Bishop is flashing white teeth in a face that tries to be understanding.

"I can help you out," he says.

"How?" she challenges. She wants to slap that concern away. Her eyes are back on Rick and Kennedy, Kennedy's hand creeping up his leg, inching her way to his dick.

"Here," Bishop says. He opens his palm, displays little pink pills with stamped-on hearts. "Ecstasy." He drawls out, "The love drug."

"I know what E is," she snaps. She shuffles to look past Bishop. He slides over to give her a better view of the bitch's hand between Rick's legs, rubbing, rubbing, rubbing. "Give me."

"You got cash?"

"What the fuck, Bishop?" Who is this asshole to be toying with her? He's offering her drugs and then pulling them back? She steps into his space, turns her face up to him, spits out fiercely, "What the fuck, Bishop?"

"Okay, okay," he says. "I'll give you one. But I want something for it."

"What?" She needs the hit and she needs it now. Rick is looking all blissed out, eyes closed, Kennedy's hand down his pants, Kennedy's mouth sucking her mark into his neck. If she were to go over there now, he would tell her she's getting worked up over nothing. Over-reacting, he would say.

Kennedy's just servicing him. He's doing nothing. Well, fuck him! "What do you want?"

"I want what the slut is giving your guy," Bishop says. His lips are turned up, half smile, half sneer, his eyes roaming her body. She knows she looks good. Tight denim skirt falling just below her ass, see-through shirt with a lacy purple bra. She looks ten times better than that slut. Any other time, Bishop looking at her that way and she would tell Rick to smack him down. But Rick wants to play this game? She can play it, too.

"You don't touch me. Just me with my hand on your dick. Got it?" She licks her lips, looks over at Rick. She juts her chin to an open space on the log where Rick can see them. She wants him to see this. See what he's making her do. "Give me the pill. Then unzip, sit down, and shut the fuck up."

Bishop swallows, focuses on her lips. "I'll give you two for a blow job."

Jesus! Rick would go ballistic. And it would be too much to come back from. She doesn't want to lose him. She just wants to make a point. "One. A hand job."

"Fuck. Fine," he says. He places a single pink pill in her palm, puts one in his mouth, and shoves the rest back in the pocket of his designer jeans. He unzips, sits on the log and spreads his legs wide, bracing himself with his hands.

Lyne watches him chew and swallow. She chews a little longer, then swallows. The buzz is instaneous, intense. She drops to her knees between his oustretched legs, grasps his dick. He is already half hard. But it doesn't matter. She works him furiously.

"Oh fuck," Bishop says.

She licks her lips. This isn't enough. She needs more. She is about to take him in her mouth, when he is hauled up and she's thumped on her ass.

"That's my girl, you fucking asshole!" Rick says.

Lyne watches the fire, the reds and yellows and oranges climbing higher and higher in the black sky. She listens to the fused sounds of Rick's fists thumping Bishop, of Bishop begging, of boys yelling, of girls screaming. This is a fight over her. The second fight today over her. She is so, so wanted.

"Stupid boy," Jack mutters. Cursing Matt for leaving the book on the table, Benny for finding it in the first place. "Stupid boys."

He falls down on the sofa. The quiet is soothing. The light from the streetlamp shines through the window, spotlights the engineering textbook. He flips open the cover. Miriam's flowing handwriting stands out. It is in the middle of seven or eight darkly printed names. She used to chide him about his scrawl, always erased his name, rewrote it. She made him feel important, that she was proud of him. He shimmies to the edge of the sofa, traces Miriam's handwriting with the tip of his index finger. His hand is surprisingly steady, solid.

The corner of the photo is sticking out from the book. Where the hell is Matt's head at? Why didn't the boy at least put the photo away? Jesus Christ! But he can't stop himself from pulling it out. He lays it down gingerly next to Miriam's writing. How young he was! How little Matty was! Miriam's two handsome men. The three of them. Such a perfect family.

He slams the book shut. He's not drunk enough for this. He should have stayed at the bar longer. Should have taken a bottle of tequila with him into a booth. Hell, should have brought a bottle home with him. Should haves. Way too many of those. Way too many.

3

IT IS SO FUCKING HOT that all Matt wants to do is take off his shirt. He would, but Lyne's mother just joined her in the window. And while he is all for sticking it to that asshole Jeffries, stripping in front of someone's mother is not his thing. He is not his father.

So he throws the ball to Ben and feels his shirt paste to his body with the swing of his arm. He hopes Ben hasn't noticed their audience. The kid is still tense from last night. He thought he had hidden that book, that photo. But somehow Ben found them. And Dad? Fuck. He never knows what Dad will do. He can't ever remember being so relieved to have Dad head to the bar.

Ben catches the ball. "She's still watching, you know? And now her mom's there."

Okay, so much for Ben not noticing.

"I saw them." He shrugs it off, catches Ben's perfect throw. They have precision gleaned from playing catch in too-small spaces.

"Why are they watching us?"

"Dunno, Benny."

"Ben." The boy snarks the single syllable. It is hot but not too hot for Ben to complain about the baby name. Never too hot — too cold, too late, too early — for that.

Matt pauses. "I think they're watching you, actually." Then he throws.

"What?" Ben bobbles the ball.

He laughs, deep and rich. "Why wouldn't they be? You're cute and smart and well, cute."

Ben snorts. His bangs, damp and heavy, still rise in the breeze he creates. He shields his eyes with his glove hand. With his other hand, he grips the ball as Matt has shown him with seam and fingers just right, and throws.

Matt catches it easily. "Should have worn your hat, bro." He lifts the brim of his Oilers cap to sweep his sweaty hair back.

"Forgot."

"Go in and get it."

Ben eyes the door to their townhouse, shifts from foot to foot. "Nah. That's okay."

"Ben," he says softly.

Ben slaps his glove. "Have you spoken to her yet?"

"We've only been in school two days! Not even *I* move that fast," he huffs. But that's not true. Fast *is* how he operates because there is never any guarantee from one day to the next. Because Dad always keeps them moving.

"Well, she's totally your type."

His hand freezes over his glove. "I have a type?"

Ben squints into the sun. "Well, every time I've caught you, you know, with a girl, she's always blonde-haired and blue-eyed."

"How many times has that been?"

He feels listless, energy zapped by the heat and stark reality of a little brother who knows too much. He has been doing it since grade nine, other things since grade six. Ben

24

only stumbled on him, naked and going at it in their bedroom earlier this year. The look on Ben's face was the same look the kid gets when they catch their father. It killed him. The guy who gets it on with girls is not who he wants to be to his little brother.

"Okay, just once. But I've seen you enough times making out with a girl and they're, you know, stacked." Ben emphasizes his words with his hands. The gesture is funny, but not so funny because the kid is referring to him.

He laughs but it is on the edge only, empty in the middle. The heat beats down. Ben's words beat down. There are days he feels the weight of everything he has done — and not done. But feeling sorry for himself, for his poor decisions has never gotten him anywhere. Teasing Ben, though, that always helps. He smirks. "How do you know she has blue eyes, Benny? You've been checking her out?"

"What? No!" Ben screeches.

"Uh huh." He winks at his little brother. Lyne does have blue eyes. Very nice blue eyes.

"I haven't looked!" Ben stomps his feet, sticks out his bottom lip.

Matt laughs. The full sound.

"So that's the boy Rick got into a fight with yesterday," Allie says. She steps closer to her oldest daughter to get a better look out the dusty picture window. A crack runs through the inside pane, splits the scene in two, the boys on one side, the rest of the street on the other.

"How'd you know about that?" Lyne regards her fleetingly.

25

Allie keeps her eyes on the boys, keeps her tone casual. "Heard Glory talking to Becca."

"Of course," Lyne says, throws up her arms.

She hates having to drag the full story out of her daughter. There was a time when Lyne couldn't wait to tell her what was happening at school. When did that change? Probably when she discovered boys. Or maybe when boys discovered Lyne. Now Allie counts herself lucky if her eldest raises half-hooded eyes in her direction. Well, at least one of her girls still tells her everything. If she had waited long enough, Becca would have shared Glory's story, embellished as only Becca can. Glory, though. Well, that girl stopped speaking to her about anything almost the moment Allie taught her to sound out words. Replaced by a book.

"Well, anyway, it wasn't much of a fight." Lyne taps a slow rhythm with her red-painted nails on the window pane, works her way along the length of the crack.

Allie clenches her teeth. It is a toss up which she hates more, that tone of voice or the silence Lyne uses to block her out.

"Rick had Matt pinned against the locker and then I came and Rick found something better to do," Lyne says.

"And what was that?"

"He started kissing me. Showed Matt I was taken," Lyne says.

She should have seen that one coming. Rick is like Doug was at that age. Always working hard to mark what he believed was his, always feeling threatened. "You need to be careful, Lyne."

26

Lyne whips around, eyes flashing. "I know, Mom! Jesus, I know!"

Allie steps back, stares at her daughter. Where did that come from? "Watch your language, young lady!" And crap, where did *that* come from? She is sounding like her mother more and more every day. Something she swore she would never do.

"I know. You keep telling me not to screw up. Hell, not to screw, period." Lyne grits her teeth. "I'm not going to."

Is that what she keeps saying? Has she been so obvious with her fear? It terrifies her that Lyne will make the same mistakes. She turns away. She massages her neck, feels the dampness that has become a part of her body for the past few weeks. This far north in Alberta and mid-May, it shouldn't be this hot. This hot, this early, it is never a good thing.

"Look, Mom," Lyne's voice is softer now, but determined. "I know, okay? I know."

Allie swallows her sigh. This will get them nowhere. "What is that boy like anyway?"

"Matt?" Lyne returns to the window. "He's full of himself. He thinks he's hot."

"Is that you talking or Rick?" Okay, so much for letting things slide.

"What's that supposed to mean?" Lyne stares at her.

"It just seems that Rick is awfully quick to let Matt know you're his girlfriend. It's like Rick's worried about him. You said the boy hasn't even been here a week."

"You don't know what you're talking about." Lyne turns back to the window, clicks her nails against the pane. "Just look at him. He acts as if he owns the street!"

27

Allie looks. But that isn't what she sees. She sees a boy wrapped up in his little brother, a boy not hungry for attention. It is Lyne who is hungry for attention, Lyne who wants it all. And she remembers that feeling from high school, too.

Matt tosses the ball up, catches it easily. "Jesus, it's hot." He pinches the ball in his glove, pulls both off his hand. "Come on, Benny, let's get a drink."

"Ben, Ben, Ben," the kid mutters, trails behind.

Lyne and her mom are still in the window. Matt pulls down the visor on his hat, takes a moment to study them. They are almost the same height, same slim bodies, but the mom is slightly heavier in the hips, her hair slightly shorter. They are dressed similarly in cutoffs and cropped shirts, but Lyne's clothes are tighter all the way around. Just the way he likes it. There is no denying Lyne is a hottie. And she knows it. She had no problem giving him extra attention when he was handing back her biology books. But yesterday? She didn't even bother with him when Jeffries pushed him up against the locker. Yeah, she's a bitch. So what the hell? Let her see what she's giving up for her Neanderthal boyfriend. He drops his hat, slowly peels off his T-shirt. He is careful not to catch the ring on his leather-braided necklace.

He twists on the outside tap, soaks his shirt under the cold water. He presses the wet shirt against the back of his neck, runs it along his chest, his stomach, up and down his arms. He won't take another guy's girl but he can fuck with her in other ways.

"What are you doing?" Ben's eyes go wide and the question comes out high.

28

"She wants a show. I'll give her a show."

"Her mother is there!" Ben's voice pitches even higher.

Upsetting his little brother isn't what he had in mind. So maybe this wasn't such a good idea. But he can salvage it. He twists his wet shirt, snaps it at Ben's bare legs.

"Ow!" Ben screams, jumps back.

Matt grins.

"You're so dead." Ben snatches the discarded hat, races for the spigot. He fills the hat, flings the water at Matt.

"Already wet, Benny." He flicks his little brother again. Ben jumps out of the way. He pulls his shirt back on, revels in the cool. "Get a drink. Too fucking hot out here."

Ben puts his head under the spigot, mouth open wide, drinks the cold water in sideways. Then he twists his head, soaks his hair. His wet T-shirt pastes to his body and Matt tries not to fret, but the kid is so freaking skinny. All arms and legs. And hair. And big blue eyes and dimples. Jesus. Even when Ben was still in Mom's stomach being a big brother meant everything. And now. The way Ben looks at him? He couldn't breathe if Ben weren't here.

"Yeah, that feels good," Ben mutters. He shakes his head like a dog.

Matt swipes his Oilers hat from the ground, plops it on Ben's wild hair. He draws the kid down beside him on the cracked two-step concrete stoop in front of their townhouse. The stucco on the small rental is dirty and brown, rust-stained from broken eavestroughs. He leans back on his elbows. The concrete is hot, but the sting feels good against his wet skin. He closes his eyes, turns his face to the sun. He feels the warmth of his little brother.

Ben mimics him, rubs his shoulder against his big brother's. "Do you think we'll finish school here, Matty?"

His breath hitches. Ben always trots out the nickname when he feels displaced. He cracks an eye open. "Why? Some hot chick in your class you're into?"

Ben whacks him, dislodges his elbow and he nearly brains himself on the step. But he is laughing too hard to care about the close mishap.

"Seriously." Ben pokes him in the side.

"Six weeks left, bro. Good chance we'll hang in at least that long." His words take on a lazy drawl as he turns his face back to the sun.

"I hope so," Ben says.

He hopes so, too. He waits a few minutes to see if Ben needs more reassurance. The kid remains silent. "After lunch we'll hit up some places around here. Grass is growing. Summer's coming. We can line up some mowing jobs. Maybe even get some late spring cleaning."

"You should put that on a poster," Ben says.

"What?"

"'Grass is growing. Summer is coming.'" Ben grins, darts away from Matt's quick strike.

"Ha ha, dumbass. I've already got my poster boy. All you have to do is flash your dimples. Maybe we'll even be able to do some work today."

He laughs when Ben snorts. But the kid has dimples that dig a hole down to China. He knows the power those dimples have on him, has seen those dimples tweak the hearts of moms and grandmas alike. But they never work on Dad.

He knocks the ball cap off Ben's head, gives him a noogie. Ben strikes out with long arms, clocks him in the face.

"Fuck!" he growls, rubs his chin.

Ben answers with a grin, grabs the fallen hat, scampers away.

He launches himself at Ben and the boys go down, roll on the ground, crunch dead grass, green grass, pebbles. He ends up on top, Ben flat on the ground, his shirt wet again from the puddle formed by the dripping tap. He straddles Ben, digs his knees into the boy's sides.

Ben gasps for air, yells out, "Okay, okay. I'm sorry!"

He rolls off, catches Lyne's eye for a moment then joins Ben on the wet ground, flat on his back.

He has dismissed her! Again! What an asshole!

"Did you see that?" Lyne asks. She squeezes her hand and her fingernails dig into her palm.

"See what?" Mom asks.

"That! What he just did! How did you not see that?"

"See what?" Becca pushes against Lyne, sneaks in under her elbow. "Oh, hey, there's Ben!"

"The little boy?" Mom asks, tugs Becca in front of her.

"He's not little, Mama! He's in my grade!"

"Oh, you're right. He's not little!"

"Well, he is a year younger than me." Becca drops her voice. "I know because Amy saw his file on the counter in the office. He must have started school early."

"Oh," Mom whispers. She makes more room for Becca at the window. The grade sixer giggles at the antics of the brothers.

31

The whispering and giggling annoy Lyne. Who the hell ordered a family conference?

"What are you doing here, Becca?" Stupid girl should be in the bedroom, playing with her loser dolls or whatever else lame shit she gets up to these days.

"I didn't know it was your window," Becca says.

She wants to pinch Becca, but she can't do that in front of Mom. Mom has already snapped at her for swearing. Mom and her screwed up Pentecostal ways, her stupid hang-up over using Jesus Christ in any other way than Praise-the-Lord. There are times Mom totally channels Grandma. She doesn't get grounded often, but Mom has been in a snit lately and she can't take the chance. Not after last night. She needs to make it up to Rick and quick. She worked too hard to get to this place. She has everything to lose. She doesn't want to go back to asshats like Matt. He thinks he's such a stud. He can't even bother looking at her. She should have let Rick beat the shit out of him. Next time.

"What are you looking at?"

Three heads swivel at Glory's voice. The girl has her index finger pinched between the pages of a thin paperback.

"The new boys," Becca says. She motions for Glory to join them. "You must have seen them at school already."

"Course she hasn't seen them. She'd have to take her nose out of her book to see them," Lyne says.

Glory juts her chin out then she ducks her head. "I have seen them. All the girls are talking about Matt."

"Do you think he's hot, Glory?" Becca asks.

Glory blinks. "I suppose."

Lyne stares at Glory, but her sister is scrunching her book, not even looking at the boy they are talking about. Since when did Glory start noticing boys anyways? And this one has only been in school two days. Duh. Her sorry, sorry sister. Doesn't Glory know not to crush on the guy all the girls are talking about? Don't any of her idiot books tell her that? Lyne turns her attention back to Matt. He is still fooling around with his little brother. She mentally flashes him the finger.

"Did you see the look she just gave me?" Matt sits up, runs his hand through his hair. What the fuck is wrong with that girl?

"What are you talking about?" Ben shifts his gaze from the cloud formation Matt has claimed is a pole dancer. Ben swears it is a monkey climbing a tree.

Matt stands up. "Come on. Let's go in."

"What?"

He shifts his eyes back to the window across the street, clenches his fists. "Fuck."

Ben looks up, eyes wide. "What happened?"

Matt scans the road. The trees here are skinny. The grass is patchy brown. It has all been planted and forgotten, abandoned like much of the neighbourhood on the east side of Main Street. Five doors down a small cat take refuge under a forgotten Toyota up on blocks. The gravel road would stir dust if the wind blew. He fixes a smile on his face, turns back to Ben. "Nothing." He offers his hand to his little brother. "Hey. I'm hungry. Let's go eat."

After a moment's hesitation, Ben clasps his wrist and he hauls the kid to his feet in one swift motion.

"How about hot dogs? I know we have wieners and buns."

Ben giggles.

"You are such a girl, Benny!" He slaps his brother on his arm, pushes him ahead to the house, nabs the gloves and baseball as he passes. He found them abandoned on a ball diamond a couple of towns back. Ben didn't ask how the gloves had made it into their belongings. The kid has learned to accept the gifts that appear.

Matt looks down the townhouse complex. The Humphreys' door is yellow, the next door is red. The second row of townhouses dead-ends the street at an awkward angle. That door, the one with the girls and their mother in the window, is blue. It is the same blue the sky is now, no longer brilliant. The clouds are heavy and grey.

Allie saw *that* look. But the boy, Matt, seemed more upset than anything else. What is happening between this boy and Lyne? The anger is rolling off of Lyne. Glory slinks out of the room. Becca stays put. She envies Becca's willingness to take on her oldest sister.

"He sort of reminds me of your father." She throws out the comment, needs to say something, anything to break the tension.

"What? No way. He doesn't look like Dad at all!" Lyne shrills. The girl's vehemence is surprising.

"I didn't say he *looked* like Dad."

No, Matt is a head-turning boy. He is all dark Hollywood good looks: wavy hair, long lashes, chiseled chin, chocolate eyes. It is in the way he moves. There is a practiced ease in his actions. That is what it is. A not-quite-comfortable-in-your-skin look. Doug still has that. Her own comfort has always been full, like the comfort Lyne has, like the comfort Glory has never had. It is still too early to tell about Becca.

"What do you mean, Mama?" Becca asks, her back to the window, her face turned up.

"Oh, Matt just looks like a guy who wants to have fun. Your dad is like that." Geez! Who is she? Cyndi Lauper?

"Fun? When was the last time Dad had fun?" Lyne challenges.

Allie wonders when this became a competition. And a competition for what exactly? Between who exactly? "Your dad and I like to have fun. We've always liked to have fun."

"You mean the fun that led to me?" Lyne asks. Her voice is cold.

Allie shivers. "Geez, Lyne." Is this how she was with her mother? No wonder Mother walked around with that woe-is-me face when she wasn't quoting Bible verses like a good Pentecostal church lady. It was that or a quick slap. Yes, Mother was a firm believer in the Old Testament.

"Mama and Dad had fun last night. They went to a party," Becca says.

Fun. Fun isn't the word Allie would use. Doug was halfway cut before they even left home. He was overly possessive and then belligerent at the party. But when they got home, Oh Lord, the sex was incredible. Doug has been distracted these past few weeks but last night! He would have taken her on the couch if she hadn't forced him into the bedroom! He even had some new moves. It was like their first years together all over again, when he used to rock her world.

Why is she standing here arguing with Lyne when he is still in bed? Tomorrow he is back on the road. She cups Becca's chin, kisses her on the forehead. "Yes, Lyne, your father and I still have fun." She itches to walk away. She will give herself a minute or two, not be as obvious. Although right now all she wants to do is flash Lyne the smile that says fuck-you-I'll-do-what-I-want. The smile Lyne so often gives her. Yes, just one more thing she recognizes from when she drove her own mother crazy.

Glory throws herself down on Lyne's bed, closes her eyes tightly. Why can't she ever find the words to be snitty back? Why does she let Lyne walk all over her? Of course she knows who Matt is! She would have to be blind and dumb and deaf not to have noticed him. Does Lyne think she is blind and dumb and deaf? No. Lyne doesn't spend any time thinking about her — except to get a rise out of her. And she is stupid enough to give Lyne exactly what she wants.

"Oh!" She needs to learn to swear.

Everybody swears. Why can't she swear?

She opens her eyes, searches out the worn spot on the ceiling above Becca's bed. She and Becca share bunk beds. When Becca lies on her bunk and reads, she wedges her feet on that single spot on the ceiling. She has rubbed a raw patch into the stippling.

Mom and Dad haven't even noticed the damage. But then again, what difference would it make? It doesn't matter how much Mom rags on Dad, Dad hasn't fixed the screen in the window. And Lyne just keeps sneaking in and out most nights. A worn patch on the ceiling means nothing.

Glory clenches the blanket that covers Lyne's bed. The sunflower-pattern is wilted. Lyne never makes her bed. And

Becca's bed is always crisp. Becca pulls the bright orange and blue quilt tightly along the top mattress, tucks it in at the sides and bottom. Her own bed is more like Becca's, but without the military precision.

She hoped Becca would have followed her in by now. But, no, Becca hates being left out. She would rather stick with Mom and Lyne, even though Lyne has made it clear she doesn't want Becca there. Lyne is sometimes forgiving of Becca but never forgiving of her, and that feeling of always being judged wears her down. Is it her fault she isn't pretty like Lyne or Mom? Or is shy around boys? Or doesn't want to hang out and gossip with girls? Why can't Lyne just leave her alone?

Or why can't she be like Becca? Nothing is worth getting upset about according to the youngest Rutger sister.

4

THE BRISTLES ON THE TAMPED-DOWN welcome mat sting his bare feet as he rubs them dry. Ben barges past, his damp footprints disappearing from the warm linoleum almost as quickly as they mark the path from the mudroom into the kitchen.

Matt follows slowly, listening carefully. Nothing. Good. That's good. He heard Dad come home last night, stay in the living room for too long. He is always vigilant on nights when Dad is battling memories, when he has been drinking.

He pulls the plug on the sink, the water gurgles past the cereal bowls and glasses. "Stop farting, bro. That's disgusting."

"That's not me!" Ben says but his flashing dimples do nothing to reinforce his indignation.

"Do the breakfast dishes while I start lunch, will you?"

"Aye aye, captain." Ben salutes and dodges to avoid the fist aimed at his shoulder.

Matt opens the freezer on the top of the avocado green fridge, digs out the package of wieners. He breathes in the cool air as he watches Ben slowly, meticulously run the washcloth around the edge of a bowl. He has no idea where Ben gets that level of precision. Mom maybe? Dad has never been like that.

He puts the hot dog buns on the table, turns around for the pot and is blinded by a beam of light. "What the fuck?" Ben is reflecting the sun off a shiny stainless steel spoon. He bows. "Spotlight on perfection."

Ben giggles. Kid is full of giggles today.

"Hey, Matt, do you think we can have mac and cheese for supper tonight?"

"What the fuck, bro? We haven't even had lunch yet!" He laughs. "Yeah, we can have mac and cheese. Chicken nuggets, too. If we can do a lawn today maybe we can stop by the store, pick up stuff for a salad. Fight off the scurvy."

The kid has hit a growth spurt these last couple of months, ankles and wrists poking through clothes. He is grateful for the hot weather. It means shorts and T-shirts. It means he doesn't have to bother Dad for money to buy new clothes for Ben. It means having more time to earn the money himself.

"Are you making extra hot dogs for Dad?" Ben asks.

"Yup. Don't know if he'll be up to eat with us, but they'll be ready when he gets out of bed."

Ben sets three plates beside the buns. Freshly dried glasses go on next. He fills two glasses with milk, slurps from the jug before he returns it to the fridge.

"Hey, get the ketchup and mustard packages. They're in that cupboard right above the sink."

Ben clambers onto the counter, fists the packages, dumps them in the centre of the scarred yellow Formica table. The chairs are metal frame, have psychedelic yellow and green patterns on the vinyl that covers both the seats and backs. The kitchen is perfectly coordinated in a style older than Matt.

"Hey, there's some relish here," Ben says as the packets scatter across the table.

"Awesome." He drains the water from the pot then sets it on the table. "Dig in."

Ben fixes two hot dogs, slathers each liberally in ketchup.

Matt does the calculations. There was a time when a dozen wieners fed them both for four meals. Not any more. He holds back, makes only one hotdog. When Ben starts to labour through his second dog, Matt reaches for another wiener and bun. Three meals now. That's all they're going to get. Soon it'll be two. He needs to find a job. Right-the-fuck-now. "You up to door-knocking this afternoon?"

"Sure," Ben says. "The usual signs, right?"

The kid sounds like a veteran and Matt is equal parts pissed and proud. "Yeah, the secret code of old people." He talks through a full mouth, rubs mustard from his lower lip with his thumb. In the five years he's been mowing lawns and shoveling walks, he has perfected his hunt for willing clients. Older-style homes, older cars parked in the driveway, uncluttered front lawns, half-planted gardens.

"Where should we look?" Ben asks.

"Still not ready to lead, young grasshopper?" He takes a big chomp of wiener and bun, wets his mouth with milk, swishes it around. Ben throws a disgusted look his way. "I noticed a few houses on the other side of the school we can hit up."

"Sounds good." Ben pushes back his chair.

He grips Ben's arm, stops the kid from standing. He tips his chin at the doorway. "Hey, Dad. There are a couple of dogs here for you. I can nuke them if you want."

"No, that's fine." Dad's voice is scratchy. He tucks his yellow golf shirt into his opened jeans, cinches his belt. The crest for Rath's Garage stands out in electric blue on the bright yellow. Dad's eyes are red-rimmed, his face covered in three-day-old whiskers, the purple bruise on his jaw fading. He hangs in the entryway a moment, keeps his eyes on the boys. Matt holds Dad's gaze. He is brazen. It is Dad who ducks his head. He shuffles to the fridge, pulls on the stainless steel handle, lingers. He retrieves a Blue, twists the cap, flicks it into the sink. A loud clatter.

Matt slackens his hold on Ben's arm.

"Hey, Dad," Ben says, eyes cast down.

"Benny." Dad makes his way over, drops into the chair next to Matt. He draws his plate across the table. The glass remains untouched. He pinches both wieners from the pot.

"There's some relish here, Dad." Ben fishes two packets out of the mess of ketchup and mustard.

Dad takes the packets, smiles briefly at the boy. Ben's dimples show and Matt's throat tightens. Making Dad happy with packets of relish shouldn't bring on a full-fledged smile from the kid. It just shouldn't. In Ben's world that small smile fills the Dad-quota for at least a month. Matt keeps his face carefully blank.

"What are your plans for the afternoon?" Dad takes a long pull from his bottle, almost empties it. "Grab me another, Benny."

Matt lifts his chin at Ben's glance. Ben takes another beer from the fridge, twists off the cap, flicks it into the sink. He places the opened bottle on the table.

"Thought we'd check out the neighbourhood a little." He never tells Dad about the work he tries to line up. Dad sees it as a personal affront. "It's nice out. Almost summer weather and it's only May."

"Did you need us to do something?" Ben asks, slides his chair closer to Matt.

"No." Dad moves on to his second beer. "I've got a shift later at the gas station. Starts at six. I'll work through until midnight."

"You want me to make supper early? We can eat at five." He hopes his tone passes for eager.

"Nah. I'll pick something up there. Easy enough to do. And it's free." Dad pushes his chair back, stretches his long legs under the table. "I can probably get you a shift or two at the station. You interested?"

Ben clutches the back of Matt's shirt, pulls hard.

He slouches to relieve the pressure. "Would I work the same times as you?"

"Probably not. The shifts I work, Cal's already on them. The usual guy. You'd probably get a Saturday or Sunday. Even a couple morning shifts before school starts." Dad straightens

41

up, rests his elbows on the edge of the table. "Then you can work there through the summer."

"Sure. Ask." Matt grasps Ben's arm, rubs his thumb over the smooth flesh on his wrist. The kid's breathing slows down, his death grip loosens.

There is no danger of Dad getting him a shift. Dad just needs to offer. Matt knows that, but he doesn't know why. It is as if Dad is hungry to do more, tells himself he can do more. But he never delivers.

"Come on, bro. The dishes are calling your name." He will explain to the kid later why he doesn't have to worry about being alone with the old man.

The cold bitter liquid goes down smoothly. It is the only thing that goes down smoothly in his life. It stings to hear the need in Benny's voice, see the spark of anger in Matt's eyes. But he gave up a long time ago figuring out how to do anything about either. He is too tired. Too tired to make an effort. Too tired to care enough. This is who he has become and he can't be anybody else. He gave up on that possibility a decade ago.

He leans back in his chair, takes another swig, holds it in his mouth, swallows it slowly, slowly. He rubs his hand along his jaw, flinches when his thumb brushes against the bruise. Goddamned asshole. The man wasn't supposed to be home for a couple more days. He'd had it planned. He didn't want to be moving the boys, not with less than two months left in the school year. Denise said her husband was working a two-week-in, one-week-out shift. It used to be a game, fucking another man's wife. How long he could make it last without being found out, without getting his ass kicked. It was the excitement that drove him. Teetering on the edge made him remember what it meant to live, to feel. Now, it is only about forgetting.

A thunk on the counter as Benny sets down a glass brings him back to now. He shifts in his chair, watches the boys move around the kitchen. They are quiet. They are never this quiet when they think he is gone, when they think he is not listening. They dance easily around each other, a push here, a tug there, Matt's top lip raised in a half-sneer, the corners of Benny's eyes crinkling in suppressed laughter.

He pushes his chair away from the table suddenly, a harsh sound cutting through the boys' camaraderie. He tightens his grip on the nearly empty beer bottle. Matt and Ben stop. Frozen in domesticity. But this is no fucking Norman Rockwell painting.

"Everything okay, Dad?" And just like last night, Matt is moving, positioning himself in front of the younger boy.

"Yeah." He clears his throat wetly.

Matt watches him, Benny peeks out.

Jack pinches the bridge of his nose as an ache builds behind his eyes. This throbbing, this emptiness, this loss, this is what he knows. This is what keeps him from going on. And there is no going back.

5

GLORY SAVOURS THE SUN ON her face, the warmth on her skin. She loves the feel, can't understand why people are fretting about this heat wave. How quickly they forget about winter, about the cold, the snow, the ice! No, give her heat and sunshine any day over frigid winter temperatures.

She sinks further into the bleached wooden bench, untucks her shirt, unbuttons it to expose her midriff. She rests her head on the back of the bench, stares into the sun until spots fill her vision. She used to love doing this as a child then Dad said it would blind her and Mom said she wouldn't be able to read any more. She squeezes her eyes tightly. Spots dance on her eyelids then fade. The noise from the playground filters in. She tracks Becca's movements, her rubber soles squeaking as she mounts the steps, her denim shorts swishing down the metal slide, her feet thumping on the gravel. The girl can be an elephant sometimes.

Then there is a shadow, solid darkness, but not cooling.

Glory opens one eye, then the other. Lyne.

The older girl slides her cellphone into her knock-off Gucci bag. "You keep staring into the sun, you'll go blind," she says after a moment.

And just like that, Glory is five years old again. She closes her eyes. Lyne already thinks she is blind, unaware of things around her, so what does it matter?

"Rick will be here soon."

And of course. That was why Lyne hung back. To phone the handsy boyfriend.

"Figured if Mom and Dad can have some afternoon fun, I can, too."

How long will it take Lyne to realize that she is the only one talking?

"I mean, Jesus. What's wrong with them? They're screwing all the time." Lyne nudges her knee. "What's wrong with *you*?"

That didn't take long. Glory mumbles, "Nothing." God! Why does Lyne have this effect on her? Why can't she be the confident person she wants to be?

Lyne keeps going, as if she hasn't heard the answer. She is on a roll. "Doesn't it bug you? Mom and Dad, going at it all the time?"

But she isn't on a roll. She isn't just complaining. There is concern in her voice.

"Well, doesn't it?" Lyne peers around the playground, stops on Becca. "She's got to be burning her legs on that slide. Silly girl."

Glory tries to find the right words. Why can't she think faster? "I don't know."

Lyne snaps. "Of course you don't. You and your frigging books." And just like that she is cool again, dismissive. "Well, you might as well be useful." She reaches behind her back, unclasps her bra, pulls her straps down one at a time through her sleeves. She folds in the underwire cups, passes the bra to Glory. "Stick it in your pocket."

"Uh, no. Stick it in your bag."

Lyne heaves a put-out sigh, shoves her bra in her bag.

Glory stands up, blocks the view from the street as Lyne slips her arms out of the sleeves of her tight orange shirt. She rolls the sleeves in under her armpits, rolls the top of her shirt down to reveal cleavage, rolls up the bottom. She creates her own version of a tube top.

When Lyne is finished, Glory sits down, pastes her back against the bench, warms herself again. "Well, it's not as if you and Rick aren't doing it."

"What are you talking about?" Lyne pulls lipstick from her purse, dabs three spots on her bottom lip with the brush, smacks her lips together.

"You're complaining about Mom and Dad doing it," she says. "But you'll be getting some with Rick."

"No, I won't," Lyne says. Her voice softens. "Rick wants to do it, but I won't let him."

"Really?"

"Is that so hard to believe?" Once more she hears the change in Lyne's voice. "I don't want to be like Mom. But I want to have fun, you know, and what's wrong with having it with Rick?"

Glory stares. Her stomach clenches and her throat constricts. What if she says the wrong thing? And once more that split second of connection is lost.

"I mean, Jesus. He's the hottest guy in school. He's got money and toys. And he wants me. What more is there?"

Is Lyne reassuring herself? That can't be. Lyne never wavers. She knows what she wants and she always goes for it. But this morning she has been all over the board. And yesterday at school, when Rick dug his fingers into her arms and Glory saw that flicker — what was it? fear? — cross her face.

Before Glory can choose her words, a deep-throated engine fills the void.

Lyne turns in the direction of the red Camaro. Her voice grows hard. "Don't say anything to Mom."

This is the sister she knows. This is the sister who gets her back up. "I never tell Mom when you sneak out of the room. Why would I tell her now?"

Rick pulls up, leans across the seat to rest his arm on the opened passenger window. "Coming, babe?"

Glory wants to claw his eyes out. Doesn't she warrant at least a nod?

Lyne slides into the car, doesn't look back as Rick peels out.

Glory needs something she can understand. She opens the Steinbeck book she abandoned on the bench. She tunes into a world that is beautiful and tragic, a world that has symmetry.

Matt lucks out at the second door they knock on. A frail, white-haired woman in a faded flower housedress answers. He slips into his used-car-salesman persona. "You have a nice yard. Bet you could use some help keeping it that way, getting it ready for the summer."

The woman's eyes move slowly from the Oilers cap on his head down to his well-worn Pumas. He nudges Ben forward. Ben smiles at the old lady. Matt has always joked to Ben — much to the kid's disgust — that his smile will soon have the girls lining up for him. Matt has a smile that attracts girls, too, but his is slow and sexy and speaks of seduction and good, good times. It is a smile he does not use on moms and grandmas. It is a smile he has seen his father use on married women. Always successfully.

The old woman's eyes soften, remain on Ben's face. Matt is thankful Ben has lost his baby fat otherwise this grandma would be pinching his little brother's cheek. She has that fond, absent look on her face.

"I could certainly use some help, young man." Her voice is raw. "I'm Mrs. Boychuk."

She comes out in blue flip-flop slippers, leads them along the narrow footpath to the back of the house. She wrestles with the large door on the metal shed, mutters, "My grandson promised to oil this for me."

"Here." He waits for Mrs. Boychuk to drop her hands. He pushes the door in, slides it on the sticky runners.

"Thank you." Mrs. Boychuk smiles. "Everything you need is in here." She points to her glistening weed-eater and too-clean lawn mower, battered rubber-grip rake and hoe.

"So," he says, working his way into the shed, standing amidst the clutter of old garden pots and little rusted steel fences, "because you're our first customer for the season, we're offering a special deal. I'll weed-eat and mow and Ben here will work in the garden, break up the lumps, get it ready for spring seeding."

"If you boys do a good job, I'll hire you for the summer. And I have friends who are always in need of dependable young men," Mrs. Boychuk says, her voice clearer now. "Does fifty dollars for today sound fair?"

Matt places his hand on Ben's shoulder. The kid is ready to jump out of his battered Nikes. "Sounds fair, Mrs. Boychuk."

The old woman slip-slaps her way to the back porch.

"Here." He smacks Ben in the chest with the hoe.

Ben scowls, eyes the lawn mower.

"Next year, Arnold Schwarzenegger, you can mow."

Ben grins, waltzes away with the hoe.

"Fuck." Matt shakes his head. He wrestles the lawn mower through the junk in the shed, down the footpath. He yanks the pull cord. It snaps back, bashes his knuckles. "Fuck! Fucking stupid mower. Brand new and no fucking push start!"

He's careful the second time around and the mower roars to life. It glides along the grass. An iPod would be great right now. He could get lost in Sam Roberts and Our Lady Peace.

But an iPod is just one more thing he can't afford. Fuck it. He breathes out, clears his mind, pushes on.

When he finishes in the front yard, he guides the mower to the back. He leans against the house, watches Ben. The kid is elbow-deep in mounds of dirt piled high in last year's dead vegetable stalks. The garden is framed by thick railway ties that still smell slightly of creosote.

Mrs. Boychuk comes out. She has traded her dressing gown for pale green polyester slacks, a striped cotton shirt. Her hair is brushed and her cheeks are tinted with pink. She passes each boy a tall plastic glass of lemonade.

"Thanks, Mrs. B.," Matt says. He is grateful for wayward grandsons. And pissed that Mrs. B.'s grandchildren don't care enough to help. But he stifles the anger. He needs the money.

She titters, fans herself with an open hand, steps lighter on her way back inside.

He swallows his lemonade in successive gulps. "Remember when you used to bring me drinks, Alfred?"

Ben gulps, too, needs to take a large breath before he answers. "Yeah, you made me think you were dying and I had to bring you lemonade like right now."

"And you did, dumbass!"

"Yeah, because I really thought you were dying. I was a kid, you know!"

Matt sucks back his reply. Ben is still a kid.

It takes the rest of the afternoon to finish the job. Waiting at the back door to collect their pay and return the glasses, Matt motions to Ben to wipe his forehead. Ben swipes at his face with the bottom of his T-shirt and leaves a streak of dirt.

Mrs. B. answers the door. "Oh. One minute," she says.

The boys stand on the screened-in porch. Matt nudges Ben, points to the shuffleboard table with the junk piled high.

Mrs. B. returns with two damp face cloths.

"Thanks," he says, chucks a cloth to Ben. He rubs the soft fabric on his neck and it feels good, but a cold shower right now would be even better. "Maybe next time we can clean out your porch, Mrs. B."

She nods, presses two twenty-dollar bills and three tens into his hand. He stares, uncertain whether to correct her math or assume she is paying them extra. He says nothing. She counts five loonies into Ben's hand, each shiny coin causing Ben's dimples to dig deeper. Then she gives them Häagen-Dazs ice cream bars and Ben's face glows. Is this what grandmas are all about? Matt remembers his, but only in glimpses.

"Can you come back next Saturday to mow the lawn? Maybe even plant the garden?" Mrs. B. asks.

Matt nods.

"And by then I'll have a couple of names and phone numbers of people who can use your help," she says, shows two rows of clean dentures.

He nods again. The relief that floods through him almost takes him to his knees. Having work lined up so quickly rarely happens. Now he doesn't have to worry about Dad and money. He waves, steers Ben down the sidewalk. They are too busy licking Häagen-Dazs to gloat.

Lyne is up on her knees sucking on Rick's neck the moment he pulls his Camaro into the stand of trees behind the school.

"So that asshole lives a couple doors down from you, huh?" Rick says, hands still on the steering wheel.

Lyne stops. She has her hand between Rick's legs and he's asking about another guy? What the hell? She picks up her pace, works on branding him with a hickey.

"Humphreys," Rick says. He pulls away, presses his back against the driver's door.

She slides down into her seat, knees tucked under her. "What are you talking about?"

"Humphreys," Rick snaps. "He lives near you."

"I guess," she says. What does that asshole have to do with any of this? Rick can't be worried. What happened with Bishop won't happen again — and not ever with Matt. She is sure she gave Rick the blow job of all blows jobs last night. At least she thinks she did. But she doesn't want to bring it up. Not after Kennedy with her hands down Rick's pants. Not after Bishop. What she needs to do is give Rick an instant replay of the good part of last night. She shimmies closer, slides her hand under the hem of his cargo shorts.

He stares at her hand and she stops her exploration. But she won't pull back. If she pulls away now, it could be over. And they have only been together since April. It took her months to get him to dump Kennedy. She has worked too hard to lose now.

"What does it matter, Rick?" she pleads, inches her fingers up. "What does that have to do with anything?"

Rick remains silent, his gaze travelling to her face. His grey eyes are slate cold. She refuses to flinch. She tucks two fingers inside his boxer briefs. His breath hitches and his eyes blink shut for a second. He still says nothing but she knows she has him. She crawls her fingers up higher.

"Look, I wouldn't have done Bishop last night. I mean he's nothing. He's nothing compared to you, Rick. But he gave me that hit of X," she says.

Rick's mouth twists into a mean line. "That's why I beat the shit out of him."

He grips her wrist and panic builds in her. He is going to make her stop. He is going to tell her it is over. God, she'll do anything. Anything. But he doesn't speak. He shoves her hand further up his leg.

She grasps his balls, breathes softly, licks her lips. "Got no X now, but I don't need X to be with you."

"Yeah?" he says.

"Yeah," she says. She uses her free hand to unzip him. His eyes are closed, head resting on the door frame, quick gasps parting his lips. She has him.

Jack works his hands along the worn leather steering wheel. These days steering wheels come heated. Not that he needs more heat in this stifling weather. Air conditioning would be good, though.

He's parked three cars down from the door of the Delwood bar. He's not thinking about going in to get a drink. Even if it takes more than a couple of beer to give him the slightest buzz, showing up at work with alcohol on his breath, well, that would be stupid. And that kind of stupid would get him fired. Worse, it would get him Matt's sharp tongue, bitching him out for having done poorly by Benny.

He twists his hands on the wheel. The squeak from the sweat on his palms is grating.

Every time he moves to a town without a liquor store he tells himself never again. A bottle of tequila in the bar will cost twice as much as it would in the liquor store.

"Goddamnit."

But that sharp taste on his tongue, that burn in his throat. God, how he needs that.

His boys and their perfect synchronicity. "Goddamnit."

No place for him in their lives. "Goddamnit."

How could Miriam leave him with this mess? "Goddamnit."

His head is too clear. "Goddamnit."

There is nothing to muffle his thoughts. "Goddamnit."

He slams his palms on the steering wheel. The thud fills the air around him. "What the fuck?"

Jack shoves himself out of the Beemer, slams the door. Another air-filling thud. He craves the cool, the dark. He craves the need to disappear, if only for an hour or two. The metal handle on the bar entrance burns his hand. He throws the battered door open and the gloom embraces him.

6

THE HEAVY PLASTIC BAG SLIDES down Matt's arm, catches on his wrist. Delwood Grocers was hot as hell. Just like it is outside.

He didn't even have to spend all the extra money Mrs. B. gave them. The rest of the cash will go into the Dempster's bread bag stuffed under his mattress. He already has $120 in there, money earned and saved from shoveling snow in Alix. Money for emergencies.

"We heading home?" Ben blows his sweaty bangs out of his eyes.

Matt looks at his watch. It's five. Another hour and Dad will be gone. "No. Let's hit the playground."

"Sure." Ben's face opens up like he has another Häagen-Dazs stashed in his pocket.

"Go ahead."

"Hey, there's Becca!"

Matt scans the playground, spots Lyne's sisters. The youngest girl is swinging on the monkey bars. "Huh. Do you know the other girl's name?"

"Nope," Ben says.

This could be awkward. But she was only in the window for a minute. Maybe she didn't get the full view of him working his shirt. He has *got* to start thinking these things through.

"You okay?" Ben says.

"Yeah, go. I've got the groceries. I'm sure as fuck not running."

Ben offers a quick wave and then he is gone. His smile still comes so easily. How much longer will that last?

Matt ambles across the street, swings the grocery bag, tracks Ben's movements. The kid is already chicken fighting with Becca on the monkey bars that have been worn dull red and polished to bare steel in some spots. The other sister is reading. He clears his throat. "Hey." He tucks the bag of vegetables and Thousand Island salad dressing under the bench in the small patch of shade. He shoves his hands into his pockets. His clothes are dirty. Fuck. He hopes he doesn't stink. Not too much, anyway.

The girl looks up. Her eyes are blue, not as striking as Ben's, but still brilliant. "Hey."

"I'm Matt."

"Glory." She adds, "Rutger."

Those unblinking eyes make him feel exposed. Maybe she did see him with his shirt off. Yeah, this is all kinds of awkward. "That's my brother, Ben, over there, with your sister. They, uh, they're in the same grade."

"That's what Becca said."

Okay. Matt scrubs his hand through his hair. "Good book?"

"*Of Mice and Men.*" Glory sounds so much like Ben that he relaxes a little.

"I read *Grapes of Wrath.* That was really good." It was for an advanced school project last semester but he doesn't have to tell her.

Glory closes her book with her finger pressed between the pages. "Yeah?"

That is the same look he gets from Ben when the kid is impressed. It makes him nervous and it keeps him talking. "Yeah. I like Steinbeck. That book in particular."

Glory tilts her head and he recognizes that look, too. She wants to hear more.

"There is just something about the Joad family," he says. "They keep moving, keep searching for that Promised Land, keep believing that it's going to be better. Better than what they've left behind."

"It's about hope and perseverance," she says.

He blinks. "Even when each place they come to is shittier than the one before. They never consider going back. They keep starting over, keep moving forward."

"Yes, they do," Glory says. Her eyes are locked on his.

He looks away, fingers the ring on the leather strap. He is more self-conscious about this free flow of words than he is about his grass-stained jeans. He barks a sharp laugh. "But, hey, if you really want to talk books, you need to talk to Ben. He's a regular Hermione Granger."

Glory's eyes linger on him before she turns to look at Ben.

He takes that moment to study her. She has worked the elastic low in her sloppy ponytail. He has never seen hair done like that. How does the elastic even stay in? She wears no make up. Her look is natural, inviting, with a dusting of freckles. She is pretty in a way he has never noticed before in a girl.

She turns back to him, raises the thin book to shield her eyes against the sun, her index finger still pinched between the pages. "But you read, too." It should be a question, but she says it as if she knows him, knows him deep inside.

He examines the parched grass at the base of the bench. "Yeah, but not as much as Ben. Maybe you can lend him some books. He had to choose his favourites when we moved and he left a lot behind. I couldn't fit them all in my box."

Fuck! What is wrong with him? He can't stop talking to this fresh-faced girl with the intense stare.

"Your box?" she asks.

"We move a lot and we can only bring one box each." He drops his eyes again.

"How do you know who you are?" she asks and it is so heartfelt.

He looks up. "What?"

"If you have to leave so much of yourself behind?"

"I take the most important part with me," he says and his eyes stray to Ben. He feels raw in his openness. "Anyway, it's Ben it really sucks for, having to leave half his books behind. I'm not a geek like him."

Glory snorts, covers her face with her book. "Can't believe I just did that."

"Ben does that all the time," he laughs.

They turn to watch Ben and Becca. Ben's legs are firmly wrapped around Becca's waist. The young girl shrieks, swings, twists to break away. Ben tugs and chants, "I've got you. I've got you." One last tug and Becca's hands loosen. She falls, lands awkwardly in the sand that is more gravel.

"Oh!" Glory breathes and is off the bench in an instant. Matt is close on her heels.

"Matt!" Ben yells.

Glory sinks down next to Becca, cradles her little sister. "Where does it hurt?"

"My ankle," Becca whimpers.

Matt squeezes Ben's shoulder. The kid is shaking.

The loud growl of an engine swallows Becca's tiny hitches. The Camaro slides to a stop.

Rick's look is smug when he pulls Lyne in for the parting round. She gets out and Rick flashes Matt the finger then does a U-turn, pebbles and dirt flying.

"Dick," Matt says under his breath.

"What the hell?" Lyne asks, bites back a sigh. Perfect. Just perfect. This prick and his stupid kid brother and her snivelling little sister.

"I didn't mean to hurt her. We play this all the time at school," the boy says.

"Maybe you shouldn't be so rough," Lyne says harshly.

The kid flinches.

Matt pulls his brother away. "Back off."

And she does because that is the tone her mother uses when she is pushed to the limit.

Matt turns to Becca, his voice soothing. "How about I give you a piggyback ride home?"

And there he goes again. Dismissing her. What is up with this asshat? Her make-out session was less than satisfying. All Rick did was fixate on Humphreys. And now this. She just can't win.

Becca wipes her face with the back of her hand, nods her head. Matt squats and Glory and the boy take Becca by her elbows, settle her on his back. She wraps her arms around his neck and he grabs her legs, stays clear of her sprained ankle. He turns to the boy, "Hey, bro, I left our groceries under the bench. Could you get them? And Glory's book is still there."

The boy takes off without a word. If she were to order Becca around like that, Becca would bitch non-stop. And damn it. She forgot to pick up grapefruits from Delwood Grocers. So much for breakfast again tomorrow morning. This stupid diet has been harder than she expected.

The boy smiles when he hands the book to Glory.

Great. Another book freak.

Glory walks beside Matt, her hand settled on Becca's uninjured ankle. Matt keeps looking at Glory and she keeps smiling up at him.

What is this? Lyne follows a step behind, undoes her makeshift tube top. She will have to go braless. She watches as Matt carefully picks his way along the sidewalk. *Step on a crack, break your mother's back* springs into her head and she swallows a wild laugh.

Matt glances back at her then turns to his brother. He speaks too softly for her to hear. The younger boy squeezes out a smile.

"Do you need to rest?" Glory asks.

God! It's not as if Becca weighs a ton! And then there is Matt with that damned smile again, all soft and, what is that? Caring? Understanding? Prick!

"Naw, I'm fine. She's as heavy as a twig," he says. Becca giggles.

What is wrong with him? Lyne takes a couple deep breaths. This guy might be all kinds of hot — and yeah, she's big enough to admit it — but there's something twisted about him. This sickeningly sweet picture is going to make her gag. She hustles past them, wants to say something snide to Glory about crushing on the new guy. It would put a quick end to all this sweetness. It would be perfect. And it would be mean. Like the cold glare in Rick's eyes this afternoon when he toyed with her, made her think it was over. Made her desperate enough to believe she would do anything to keep him. And then she stops short when they reach the row of townhouses. Mom and Dad are sitting on the front stoop, sharing a cigarette. She squeezes her eyes shut. Dad is shirtless in the heat, jeans unbuttoned. Mom is wearing Dad's shirt, the essentials barely covered. Jeez. Now everybody is going to know exactly what Mom and Dad were doing. Why does God hate her?

Allie uses Doug's shoulder to lever herself up. "What happened?"

Doug stands slowly, crushes the cigarette into the step with his heel. He lifts his chin. "Who's that?"

"He just moved here. Matt, I think."

Glory gives the younger boy's arm a quick squeeze, says, "Becca fell off the monkey bars at the playground."

Doug picks his way down the hot concrete steps, rests his hand on Becca's arm. "Give her to me."

The older boy holds tighter. "Why don't I put her down somewhere? That'll be easier."

"*Who* are you?" Doug snarls. He steps in, grips Becca.

Allie moves quickly. The only time Doug bristles is when his youngest is hurt. He was protective of Lyne and Glory, too. She used to envy that special relationship he had with each daughter in turn. But time put a natural end to it.

Her fingers wrap around Doug's wrist, rest on his pulse point. His heart is beating fast. She waits until his eyes slide from Matt to her. "They live just down the street."

"This is Ben," Glory says, "and that's Matt."

"Oh yeah?" Doug drops his hand, flexes his fingers.

Matt heaves Becca farther up his back, stays silent, hunched over. This is not the same boy Allie watched this morning, teasing his brother mercilessly, flinging water. Lord. What must this boy think of her, hanging in the window, staring at him? Peeping Mom, that's what she is.

She swallows her discomfort. "Take her to our bedroom."

Glory leads the way. Doug scowls, steps back only enough to let Matt pass. He shoves his hands deep into his pockets, drags his still-unbuttoned jeans down low on his hips. Allie rakes her eyes over him. His shoulders are stiff and he rolls his head from side to side. What does he see when he looks at the boy who so casually rejected his help with Becca? The boy obviously doesn't know better than to get between a father and his child.

Doug takes the steps two at a time, almost pastes himself to Matt's back.

Movement from behind stops Allie from following. She turns around, catches Lyne pocketing cigarettes from the half-full pack of Export A Doug left on the stoop. Lyne arches an eyebrow, the challenge clear.

She will not take on her daughter. She is about to close the door, make her way to the bedroom, when Matt and Ben push past her. She hangs back, watches as Matt stops in front of Lyne.

"Keep walking," Lyne says.

"Fuck you," Matt says. He gives Ben a little shove and they drag their feet across the street.

What the hell? Allie shakes her head. She has Becca to worry about. Lyne and her moods can wait until later. Or not at all.

7

GLORY STANDS OUTSIDE THE YELLOW door, plate of chocolate chip cookies in her hands.

"Knock," Becca says.

Glory doesn't move. Her face heats up and the plate slides in her suddenly wet palms. How could Mom have talked her into doing this? She isn't ready for this. She will never be ready. She is not Delwood's Welcome Wagon!

"Fine," Becca says. She leans on her crutch, knocks on the door.

"Becca!"

The door opens wide, reveals Matt. Shirtless. "Uh," he says. "Uh, one minute."

Glory stares after his retreating back.

"Hey." Matt returns rolling a blue Diesel shirt down his stomach, Ben in tow.

"Hey!" Ben says, eyes the cookies. "Those for us?"

"Stand down, cookie monster!" Matt shoves the boy.

Ben's answering grin is so cheeky, Matt responds in kind.

Glory is mesmerized.

"Mom says the best way to a man's heart is through his stomach," Becca says.

"Well, Becca." A slow grin spreads across Matt's face. "You're a little young for me. And, sweetheart, let me tell you, Ben's not really a man."

"What?" Becca screeches.

Glory laughs, ends with a full snort. Oh, mortification!

Matt's grin swallows his face. "Like I said yesterday, Ben does that all the time."

"I do not!" Ben delivers a two-handed shove, sends his big brother stumbling forward.

Glory wards Matt off, a hand on his chest, her other hand cradling the plate. Touching him burns. She drops her hand, drops her eyes. Why can't this be a book? The floor would open up, swallow her whole.

Matt takes a step back, runs his hand through his hair, perfects his bedhead.

She shoves the plate at him. "Mom had us bake these this morning to say thanks for bringing Becca home."

"It was my fault," Ben says, hiding behind his bangs. "If I hadn't yanked her off the monkey bars . . . "

"It was an accident, Ben." Glory and Matt speak at the same time.

Glory tears her eyes from Matt. It is safer to focus on the younger boy. "It was an accident, Ben. No big."

Ben looks up.

Becca pokes him with her crutch. "No big. But could I sit down now?"

"Right. Head into the living room." Matt passes the plate to Ben, rubs his hands together. "Can't have cookies without milk. Be right back."

Glory follows Ben. The room is dark even though the faded velour drapes are pulled wide open. She stops short at the sight of the obnoxious brown and yellow plaid couch. The back is woven and the front is brown vinyl. There's a wretched orange armchair and an ancient three-shaded pole lamp in the corner. Her eyes roam the two book shelves. She itches to run her fingers down the spines of the books, to see if *The Grapes of Wrath* is there.

Matt returns with a jug of milk settled in the crook of his arm, a mug hanging from one finger, three plastic glasses pinched in his other hand. "Sorry. Don't have a lot of dishes."

"You should do some garage-saling," Becca says.

"That's a good idea," Matt says quickly, drops the milk jug into Ben's lap. The boy jumps. "Gotta do something to make this ugly-ass furniture look better."

"This place had furniture?" Glory asks.

Matt slaps his hand against the sticky vinyl. "Do you think I'd let my dad get this fugly couch?" He pours the milk, Ben holding out the glasses and mug in turn.

"That's a huge jug," Becca says.

"Cheaper when it's four litres," Ben says.

The plastic jug groans in Matt's hand. "No," he says, has eyes only for his brother. He holds up the jug in a mock salute and says, "Milk. It's the only beverage Justin Bieber doesn't drink."

Becca giggles.

Then the younger boy laughs, taps his glass to the jug Matt still holds. Matt's shoulders drop and he smiles broadly.

Glory can't look away. Matt's face is as pale as the milk. And the smile does not reach his eyes.

School Days

8

MATT TRAILS BEHIND THE OTHER three kids. Glory and Becca are listening intently to Ben spout off about *Owls in the Family* and he hates to admit it but he is, too. When did he become such a geek? He looks forward to these morning walks to school, him and Ben, Glory and Becca. Yeah, his little brother is rubbing off on him. And as that thought begins to feel a little less repulsive, Jeffries drives by, Lyne pasted to his side, flashes him the finger.

"Asshole!" he shouts after the Camaro. "It really pisses me off when he does that!"

"That's why he does it," Glory says.

"The guy's a dick!"

"He doesn't like you. And he wants to make sure you know that."

He hears Glory's unspoken "duh" in the words she says so coolly.

"What the fuck have I ever done to him? Jesus. I don't even *talk* to him."

He quickens his steps. Jeffries hasn't been in his face since the first week in school. It is just these drive-by one-finger salutes now. Every fucking day. And Lyne hanging off of Jeffries reminds him that it has been a long time since he hooked up. A hell of a long time.

Glory shakes her head. "You don't have to talk to him for him to hate you. He feels threatened by you. You've come to his town and now all the girls are talking about you."

"Yeah? And what are they saying?"

"Oh, jeez." Ben rolls his eyes.

Matt ignores the kid, focuses on Glory.

The girl's cheeks pinken and she drops her eyes to her Tevas. "They all think you're hot."

"Because he really needs to hear that, Glory," Ben says.

"Shut it, dumbass," he says.

"Yeah, because the girls never say you're hot. Doesn't matter what school we go to! You've never heard *that* one before!"

"Can't hear it too much, Benny," he says.

"Ben," the kid snaps.

"Whatever."

"Anyway, Glory thinks you're fugly," Ben says.

"No, she doesn't!" he says.

Ben and Becca burst out laughing and he wants to knock their heads together. Fuck! Why did he say that? He sounds desperate. He stops abruptly. "I, uh, I forgot my homework."

"What?" Ben breaks his laughter with the single word.

"I need to go home. Get my biology." He is already turned around.

"Matt," Ben says.

"Just go on. I'll see you after school."

9

SHE IS SUPPOSED TO BE rocking the Camaro with Rick. Instead, she is sitting on the hood of his car in the parking lot of the school at noon hour listening to him obsess about Matt Humphreys. Maybe if he were bitching to her, she wouldn't feel like a hood ornament. Her knees are hugging his hips and he is sounding off to a handful of boys from his old Midget AA hockey team. Rick wants to be the big man. He says Humphreys walks the halls like he is King Shit. That is his position. She swallows her laugh. It wouldn't do her any good to put an undignified end to his tirade. Not that she will defend Humphreys. He is an asshole.

"Fucking jerkoff comes to our school, thinks he can have whatever girl he wants," Rick says.

That is her cue. "He can't have me, boo." She digs her hands into the front pockets of his jeans. "I'm all yours."

"Damn straight." He leans against her, sucks in her lips. At times putting out in front of his friends is more important than putting out in the backseat.

"Fuck, Rick, just do her right here," Tony says, grabs his balls. The other boys hoot.

She pulls away. Tony McMasters could pass as Rick's best friend. They were the top point-getters on the hockey team. Tony makes her feel like sleaze. He watches her when she and Rick are making out. Once she called him on it and Rick told her she was a fucking princess, that she had nothing all the guys hadn't seen before. And a lot of the guys had seen it on her. Now, she tries to avoid doing anything with Tony around.

"You think Rick beat the shit out of Bishop?" he says. "That's nothing compared to what he'd do if Humphreys laid a hand on you."

"Bet your ass," Rick says.

10

"HEY. WHATCHA DOING?"

Matt jumps, spills the plastic margarine container of nuts and screws.

Glory sucks back her laughter. He has the deer-in-the-headlights look. But there is no way he would be rifling through their garden shed without having asked Mom or Dad. He is not forward like that. Except the way he walks the halls at school.

"Looking," he says. He drops to his knees, picks up the scattered metal pieces. "I need to find a tip for the bicycle pump so we can put some air in the basketball."

"Oh," she says. She joins him on the floor made of rough-hewn wooden planks. He inches away, shoulders tightening, movements rigid. "Is it in this pile of stuff?"

"Stuff?" He sounds as if he has swallowed half the bolts in the container.

"The, the pump adapter, I guess."

"Becca said your dad said it was in one of these plastic containers."

She tries to catch his eye, to smile at him, but he keeps his back to her. What is with him? He must still be hung up on what Ben said. But he has got to know nobody thinks he is fugly. She doesn't think he is fugly. She backs away. "I'm surprised we even have one," she says and drops the last two screws into the container. "It's not as if we play basketball. I don't think we even own a basketball."

He stands, pushes the small plastic tub back on the shelf, starts going through another one.

She debates leaving but she is drawn to this sullen boy. She moves to a different work bench, surveys the contents. Who knew they had this much junk? She rattles a glass jar full of bits. "You're sure she said a plastic container?"

"What? Yeah, plastic she said. A margarine tub or Cool Whip."

She can be cool, just like Cool Whip. "So you guys have a basketball?" Duh. Maybe not so cool.

"A couple of birthdays ago, Ben bought me a Raptors ball," Matt says. "He used to walk this lady's dog, saved up his money from that. He really liked that dog. Name was Bandit."

If she could stop breathing, she would. If she makes a noise he will stop rambling and she wants to know more about him.

"It takes too much room to keep the basketball full when we're travelling, so we deflate it." He takes another margarine tub. "We left it blown up once and Ben was playing with it in the back seat. He was throwing it from hand to hand. He wasn't trying to piss Dad off. But still, Dad got pissed."

She keeps her attention on the Becel container. "So, your basketball and books, that's what you bring?"

"Clothes, too. And Ben brings an assload of school work." Matt pauses, smiles a little. "I guess that's how he knows who he is."

She pictures Matt smoothing out Ben's report cards, special assignments, drawings, placing them between pages of books to keep them flat. Putting those books in his own box. That is who Matt is.

"We've lived here forever," she says. "I can't imagine what I'd take with me if I had to choose."

Matt does a slow three-sixty of the shed. "Not really that difficult."

"What?"

"Nothing."

The heat in the tin shed is stifling even though the doors are open. She heard what Matt said. But everything that surrounds her, defines her. Her friends, her family, her home, her town. She can't imagine being without them. But everything in here? Do they have too much? "I never realized we ate so much Cool Whip."

Matt grunts, continues sorting through his collection of metal.

"My mom likes to bake pies. You should have some of her pie."

He looks at her. It is the first time since she entered the shed that he has kept his eyes on her for more than a split second. She offers a tentative smile.

"She rivals Sara Lee, huh?" he says.

"Yup."

"What's going on in here?" Her father stands stiffly on the step of the shed, his eyes settled on Matt. "What are you doing here?"

Matt stands mute, hands shoved deep in his pockets as if he had never held the container.

"We're looking for an adapter for the bicycle pump," she says quickly. "Matt and Ben have a basketball that needs to be pumped up." The only time she has seen Dad like this, hard, rude, is when he talks to Rick. He says Rick is a waste of skin. "You remember Matt?"

"You're the kid who brought Becca home," Dad says.

Matt straightens up. "Got it in one."

"Your brother yanked Becca off the monkey bars at the playground."

"It was an accident, Dad."

"So Becca said."

"My brother wouldn't deliberately hurt Becca."

"Uh huh."

"Listen." Matt pulls his hands out of his pockets.

Dad cuts him off. "Check in the corner to your right. It's in a pickle jar." He walks away, unhurried.

She glares after him, mad like she hasn't been in a long time. How could he treat Matt like that? As if he were a nobody? She wants to apologize, but Matt has moved to the corner, is already emptying the contents of the pickle jar. He flexes his fingers before he starts picking through the pieces.

"Matt."

"Here it is," he says, sets it aside, refills the jar.

"Matt?" Why is it she can never find the vocabulary she is so proud of in the moments it matters the most?

"I'm going to fill the basketball now." He brushes past her, his head down.

11

JACK CHECKS THE CLOCK ON the stove. The boys are late coming home from school. They're probably hanging out with friends or Matt is shooting hoops and Benny is watching. Jack hasn't played one-on-one with Matt for a while. Now that the basketball is pumped up, he should take the boy on. The kitchen is too quiet. He needs a radio. He and Miriam . . . he needs a radio.

Then he hears them. But there are girls' voices, too. He must be wrong. Then silence. What the hell? He slides the frying pan from the burner, heads to the open door. Oh, yes. They have noticed the Beemer parked at the curb. The first thing Matt would have seen, because that boy notices everything, would have been the opened door. Then he would have scanned the street for the car. Matt stands at the BMW, his shoulders move slightly, Benny gestures wildly. They are arguing. But he still can't pick out their words. His boys have mastered the art of disagreeing in fierce whispers. He retreats to the kitchen. By the time they come in, he is back to pushing ground hamburger around the pan.

"Dad?" It is Matt and his voice is faked happiness and edgy caution.

He hates that goddamned chilling combination. "In here, Matt." He tries to pull off casual. He doesn't have to turn around to know that Matt is standing in front of Benny. But he turns anyway. It is his penance for being such a shitty father. Ah, Miriam, if she could see him now she would have some choice words for him. She used to chew him out when she thought he could do better. She would push him. Make him want to be better. This never-ending road trip has made him bitter, cruel. Miriam would be so disappointed in him. But she would not be disappointed in Matt. She would be proud of how he has become so kind, so caring. Miriam said if they had to have two children, she would want two boys, two brothers who could be close to each other. They didn't *have* to have two children. She agreed to it.

"Benny." When the younger boy takes a step out from Matt's shadow, Jack feels lighter.

But Benny remains close enough to brush Matt's arm. "Hey, Dad," he says and rocks back on his bare heels. He cranes his neck, doesn't leave his safe spot. "That smells good."

How he has grown this year! His T-shirt is tight and if he weren't wearing cut-offs, his ankles would be poking out from below the hems of his jeans. After this summer's growth spurt, the kid will need a whole new wardrobe. He can't remember the last time he bought Benny clothes. That has become Matt's job. Just one more way he has failed. It takes everything he has not to hurl the cast iron frying pan against the pukey green tiles, to add tomato paste and brown meat and little flecks of yellow onion to the disgusting colour scheme.

He turns back to the pan, pushes the onions to the side so they don't burn to a crisp. He doesn't cook often. "I was going to make hamburgers, but damned things fell apart. How do you feel about Sloppy Joes? I kind of have a craving for them."

"Sloppy Joes are better," Benny says, voice too bright, too eager.

It stabs through him and he grips the stove for balance, the heat from the burner warms his fingertips.

"Should I grate some cheese?" Benny says.

"Grated cheese is an excellent idea," he says. "If we don't have cheddar, find the tiger cheese."

Benny snickers at the slang name for the marbled cheddar and mozzarella cheese. He has never told the kid that "tiger" is the term Miriam used. Does Matt remember that?

He hears the clink of the brown bottles as Benny rearranges the bottom shelf in search of the cheese. He would kill for a beer. Or a shot of tequila from the bottle stashed in his bedroom closet. But he promised himself when he came home early today he wouldn't drink.

"Craving Sloppy Joes, Dad?" Matt says. "Is there something you're not telling us?"

Jack arches an eyebrow.

"You pregnant?"

Sassy little shit. "Yeah, dude, I'm pregnant. Slipped my mind."

Benny laughs and Matt grins stupidly. Why can't there be more moments like these? But he is the one who doesn't know how to be this way.

"Well, hell, if this is what pregnancy does to you, I'll take it," Matt says.

Jack makes to swat Matt across the head but the boy ducks.

"Pass me a plate, Matt," Benny says. He has already liberated the cheese grater and is setting up on a corner of the counter. If the boys were working side-by-side, they would be jostling elbows. But now, Benny has his arms tucked in firmly as he starts to grate.

"Do you remember your mother used to call that cheese tiger cheese?" he asks. The surprise on Matt's face easily mirrors his own. Why the hell did he say that out loud? The heat is frying his brain. A Labatt Blue would cool him down nicely. But he doesn't touch the fridge.

"I remember," Matt says softly.

Benny has stopped grating. His blue eyes are shining and wide. "I never knew that."

There is a lot the kid doesn't know about his mother. Matt knows a bit more but still there are too many blanks. He has done a piss poor job of keeping Miriam's memory alive with his two boys. He forgets he should talk about her. Because every time he sees his boys, all he thinks about is Miriam: Matt with her spirit, Benny with her looks. He doesn't want to be reminded of the small things she did, the way she tilted her head when she listened, or how she would blow her bangs out of her eyes instead of moving them with her hand, or how happy she was counting down the days until Benny was born.

The tension in the kitchen ratchets up in the sizzling heat.

"Yeah," he says. "She had some peculiar names for things."

"Like what?" Benny whispers, all awe and small boy.

"Well, let's see." He turns to face Benny, rubs his suddenly damp palms down the front of his jeans. "The little paring knife she would call the chopper. The colander was always the spaghetti drainer."

Matt speaks slowly. "She called the drying towel the wiper."

"You remember that, son?"

"I guess I do," Matt says softly.

"That's cool," Benny says and his eyes are firmly on his brother and in them is a deep sadness he didn't think Benny could possibly possess. After all, the kid never knew his mother, how could he miss her?

A beer. Christ, he needs a beer.

"Benny, grab me a . . . " and he sees the look that passes between his boys and he should be angry because he has the right to do what he damned well pleases, doesn't he? Instead he finds himself sharing Benny's deep sadness " . . . Coke, would ya?"

Benny's lips turn up slowly. "Sure, Dad. You want one too, Matt?"

Matt takes a moment to answer. The older boy is studying him. He feels the warmth of his approval. "Yeah, bro, a Coke's good."

Benny pulls out three. He leaves Jack's on the counter next to the stove, hands Matt his, and then cracks the tab on his own. He takes a long sip.

"Cheater!" Matt says, cracks the tab on his can.

He cracks his, too, and the boys stare at him. And then the chugging race begins.

Deep, painful belches will follow those downed colas, but he sinks into the sudden camaraderie that fills the sun-dappled room. Miriam would approve of this.

12

ALLIE LEANS AGAINST THE ARCHWAY leading into the kitchen, watches Lyne thrust her spoon into the pink grapefruit. The girl shoves pulp into her mouth and doesn't even grimace. "How can you eat that without sugar?"

"Jeez, Mom."

She twists an elastic band into her hair. A few strands fall out. While Lyne can turn those loose pieces into an appealing look, on her it is only untidy. She pads barefoot across the kitchen, automatically goes through the steps of making coffee.

"The same way you can drink coffee when it's so frigging hot outside," Lyne says.

"What?" She turns slowly. Her eldest is wearing a lime green Lululemon shirt that hugs her nicely. She used to dress this way for Doug when they were dating. But her tight clothes were worn under baggy jeans and sweatshirts. She would take off her outer layer two blocks from the house on her way to school, shove them in a plastic bag, stash them under a bush. That worked for months. Not even a dog peed on the bag. "What are you talking about?"

"Mom! You asked me how I could eat grapefruit. The same way you can have coffee when it's so hot out." Lyne wraps her long fingers around the grapefruit husk, digs for gold with the spoon.

"If you're that hungry you should eat a real breakfast." She uses her nail to follow the white swirled pattern on the brown countertop as she waits for the coffee. Can't it perk a little faster? Everybody has those specialty Keurigs now. Ah yes, welcome to the Rutgers' kitchen where nothing has changed. Forever.

"I read up on the grapefruit diet. It's a very low calorie diet."

"Yum."

"Whatever."

"I just don't know how it can be enough."

Lyne stands up. Her grey skirt is short. Very short. "Look at this body." She does her best Vanna White imitation, runs her hands inches away from her figure, curves in all the right places. "Not a gram of fat." She picks up her dishes, throws the grapefruit husk in the garbage, sets her plate and spoon in the sink. "And Rick loves my body."

Doesn't that damned school have a dress code? This is not something she wants to be fighting about at 7:45 in the morning. Too damned early for this. She soaks in the heat from her coffee cup. The girl knows how to push her buttons.

13

GLORY STOPS IN THE DOORWAY of the bedroom she shares with her two sisters.

Mom and Dad have talked for years about getting a townhouse with three bedrooms. Well, Mom has talked about it. Dad has listened. Sort of.

She would probably end up sharing a bedroom with Becca. Lyne would use Oldest Sister Rule, call trump and get a bedroom to herself. The same way she called trump years ago and had Dad paint the walls Pepto-Bismol pink. Definitely puke-inducing now.

This bedroom is crammed full. Of the things that define them? She is not so sure. Books. Makeup. Stuffed animals. Dolls. Candles.

One side of the room has Lyne's double bed. On the other side, the bunkbeds are pushed up against the wall. The little dressing table is near the window.

There's no way to tell who belongs to what in this room. Sure, Lyne has the makeup. And the candles. But the candles could be swapped out next week with whatever is her newest fad. And Becca has the stuffed animals and the dolls. And they both read the novels. But Lyne has a shelf and a half of self-help books and beauty magazines. And they all share the secret of Lyne sneaking in and out the screenless window.

Glory throws herself down on her bed, studies the wooden slats on the bottom of Becca's bunk, takes in the faded yellow of Lyne's comforter, all of it bordered by pink pink walls. She is intertwined with her sisters in this room.

14

LYNE'S EYES ARE DRAWN TO Matt as he sinks another basket. He is shirtless, the sweat rolling down his back between his shoulder blades, disappearing into the waistband of his snug Levis. He high-fives a teammate, acts as if he sank a three-pointer instead of a simple lay-up. If Rick were here, he would stuff that ball down Humphreys' throat. Where the hell is Rick?

"Jesus, what an ass," Lyne says.

"You like his ass?" Kennedy says. "Aren't you still with Rick?"

You know it, bitch. Lyne ignores the little slut, pictures Kennedy bristling with indignation. She notches one for herself. Those mental tallies of strikes sure can make her day.

"Whatever. Matt has a good ass." Kennedy's voice rises. Matt turns to look at her. She twists her hair in one hand, stares back. He tips his chin at her.

"Bitch," Lyne says under her breath.

Kennedy's head snaps around, eyes narrowed. "What?"

"Nothing," Lyne says sweetly. Matt is going to get his balls served to him. Boy doesn't know his place. Kennedy is just messing with him. There's no way she thinks he is worthy of her. Lyne cants her head, peeks at the other girl. Her eyes are locked on Matt on the court and Lyne recognizes that look. It is the same look Rick gave her, said the merchandise was worth slumming for. Kennedy wants to be doing Matt? That is all kinds of disgusting. Matt is nothing. What is wrong with the little hussy?

Two damp hands slide up under her shirt to rest flat on her stomach.

"Jesus."

"What's that, babe?" Rick sounds smug.

"Where were you?" She feels Kennedy's eyes on her and leans into him. His hands climb higher, cup her boobs.

Rick breaks off. "Missed me?"

"Missed you, boo," she says loud enough to keep Kennedy's attention.

Rick struts to the front of the bleachers and she slides down, meets him halfway. She pulls him in between her legs, rubs up against him. Her eyes slip to Kennedy's face. The girl is livid. Matt may be hot, but Rick used to fuck Kenndy and the bitch still wants him. Lyne purrs her satisfaction. Her mental tally board is full. This is a good day. A very good day.

15

MATT STEPS INTO THE LIBRARY, stops abruptly. Ben and Becca are at a back table sorting through paperbacks. There is a shit-ton of books next to Ben's elbow and his eyes are gleaming. What is the kid planning to do with all of those books? There is no fucking way they can pack even half of them when Dad decides to pull out of town in the next month or two.

He works his way behind the bookshelves, as few as they are. He is almost at Ben's table when he picks up on the conversation.

"I don't know, Ben, that's an awful lot of books," Becca says.

"Matt'll have a cow." Ben lets out a long breath, bangs fly up. He picks up the novel on the top of the pile. "There's no way I'm going to be able to take even a quarter of these when we move. But whatever books I can't take, you and Glory can have, right?"

Matt sinks to the floor, rests his back against the shelving that runs under the window. The urge to cry is so sudden it is overwhelming. Sometimes he forgets how smart Ben is. His little brother understands the reality of their lives. God, why is he never able to protect Ben?

"Hey, Humphreys, you have an aneurysm?"

He hops up. "Big word there, Bishop."

"Matt!" Ben stands. Becca, at his side, offers a wide smile.

Bishop whooshes his long blond bangs out of his eyes with a well-practiced flick of his head. "Well, if it isn't Lyne's little sister."

"Lay off, Bishop." Matt pivots, partially blocks Becca. He knows about the party and Lyne, and Jeffries beating the shit out of Bishop.

"What the fuck, Humphreys?" The grade twelve student is a couple inches taller, twenty pounds heavier. His face is still mottled from the beat down he took.

Matt plants his feet. "Don't be a dick. She's in grade six, for fuck's sake."

"So?" Bishop shoves him hard against the wall. Then he flips his middle finger and stalks away.

"You should have taken him down," Ben says, voice tight.

"Not worth the effort, Hulk Hogan." He shrugs his shoulders to loosen up. He flicks his hand at the neatly stacked books. No doubt Becca's doing. The girl is OCD. "What you got there?"

"The library is selling their old books. They're only a quarter a piece," Ben says.

"Choose whatever you want. But stay away from the how-to-crossdressing ones, okay?"

"Matt!" Ben huffs.

"Tell Ms. Cardinal to hold them for you. I'll meet you after school. We'll pay for them then and haul them back, okay?"

"You sure?" Ben says.

"Summer's coming. Gotta find some way to keep you out of my porn stash."

Becca giggles and Ben turns cherry red.

Matt sidesteps Ben's fist. "Later, 'gator."

16

ALLIE BITES HER TONGUE, CAUGHT between saying, "This is incredible" and "How can you waste money like this?"

"Well?" Marcie asks. She waves her hand at her brand new washing machine and dryer, both bright red, both perched on stainless steel pedestals. She looks like a model from *The Price is Right*, complete with her high heels and deep purple pencil skirt. Except for that slight bulge her silky shirt doesn't quite hide.

Allie should have kept walking past the post office. She should have run past the post office. Instead, she stopped when her sister waved at her through the window. So this is what she gets, another example of this-is-what-I-have-and-you-don't-have, poor-unfortunate-little-sis. Endless parading. This time it's a renovated laundry room, amazing with its fresh new paint and red tulip paper-lined shelves, the Tide and Febreeze and Shout all in a neat row.

"It's nice," she says. Understatements piss Marcie off.

"Nice?" Marcie's model-like smile dips.

"Really nice." The inflection in her voice almost turns her statement into a question. Being in Marcie's or Tracy's company puts her firmly in the role of little sister, either the pushy, teasing brat or the child seeking approval and acceptance. Thank God Becca isn't like that!

"This is a laundry room out of the *Canadian House and Home* magazine," Marcie says. She leans against the side-loading dryer, clicks her purple painted nails on the red steel lid. Allie wants to tell her that purple and red clash.

Marcie's entire house is out of the *Canadian House and Home* magazine. It is a surprise the photographers haven't come and shot a spread and . . . would they do perfect family, too? As Allie remains silent, Marcie's face starts to fit in nicely with the colour-scheme of the laundry room. It does not suit her neatly curled blonde hair or gold dangling earrings.

Of the little sister personas Allie takes on, she finds it easier to slip into the snark. "Yes, Marcie, really nice."

Marcie heaves a deep put-upon sigh. She avoids confrontation like she is riding her stationary bike through an obstacle course. "Come on," she says. "Thomas had a craving for Jell-O and made some this morning. I thought it was a pretty crazy thing for him to do. But, well, you know how twenty-year-old boys can be?"

No, actually, she hasn't a clue how twenty-year-old boys can be. Not perfect ones, anyway. The twenty-year-old boy she was most familiar with never would have made Jell-O. Jell-O shots maybe.

"It should have set by now," Marcie says. She glances back. "He has your taste for lime so it's nice and green. I think we even have Cool Whip."

Allie nods, pauses before she steps out of the laundry room. It is gorgeous. She wishes she could tell Marcie that but little-sister belligerence doesn't allow it. Neither does envy.

Lyne rounds Rick's car, stops suddenly when Matt walks out of Delwood Grocers. He flaps the bottom of his T-shirt in the non-existent breeze. Showing off his six-pack. What an asshole. "You're not as hot as you think you are."

Matt almost tumbles down the four peeling wooden steps.

She smirks, slouches against the passenger car door. She starts another running tally in her head.

"What the fuck?" He gives her the once over, jerks his eyes back to her face.

"You're nothing."

"What the fuck?" This time he stresses each word.

She tucks her thumbs into the front belt loops of her low-riding denim shorts, makes sure her belly-button stud gleams in the sunlight. "Truth hurts, doesn't it?"

"Fuck you." Matt leans against the railing on the stairs, crosses his arms.

The mocking gesture grates at her. Who is this boy to come to her town and figure he is hot shit? He hits on her and then dismisses her? He cannot begin to compete at the same level as Rick. He hasn't earned a thing. But she has. She has earned the right to be with Rick. She has put in her time. This is why she despises him. He doesn't care about how things work in Delwood.

"You're dreaming if you think Kennedy will spread her legs for you."

Matt's cocky grin falters.

Chalk one more on her tally board!

Then he pastes on the expression that makes her want to knee him in the balls. He tips his chin at her ride. "Not like you with the rich boyfriend?"

"Take a good look at that car because it doesn't matter how many lawns you mow, you'll never own a Camaro."

Hurt flashes across his face and she tallies another point before his features harden.

The bell chimes on the glass door. Glory steps out, a white plastic bag clasped in her hand. "Matt? What are you doing out here?"

"It was fucking hot in there and Ben was taking too fucking long figuring out what the fuck he wanted. He was driving me fucking nuts."

"Oh," Glory says.

His knuckles blanch white on the railing.

Lyne smiles. Mr. Suave isn't so suave. Another mark for her. Go Team Lyne!

Matt looks at Glory. "Sorry. It's just hot."

Oh, God. Another sappy scene. "You're boring, Matt." She swings Rick's car keys on her finger. Becca and Ben are now with Glory on the steps. "You're all boring little kids."

"We're not little kids," Becca says.

"Oh, just go mow a lawn, Matt," she says, gripping the handle on the driver's door.

"Fuck you, Lyne," he says.

"If wishing made it so." She laughs, high and rich, slides into the driver's seat and peels out. Screw her grapefruit. She looks in the rear-view mirror. Matt is flanked by Ben. Glory and Becca are two steps behind them. There is something sad about that way the boys stand alone. Then she turns the corner and the picture is gone.

"Christ!" Jack slams on his brakes, prides himself in missing the hockey stick that came flying into the street. He's not so lucky with the puck. It thunks off his passenger-side door.

He pulls into the first spot he finds. What a perfect way to end a perfect day. If Tanya Rathenburg doesn't start delivering on all the goods she's been dangling in front of his face — with her tub of a husband right in the garage, for Chrissakes — he is going to tell her to fuck off and he's going to find someone else to put his efforts into.

With the number of small towns he and the boys have lived in after criss-crossing Alberta for years — Christ, almost an entire decade — it doesn't surprise him any more how easy it is to bed married women. God knows there are enough women casting the scent, who stop in at the garage regularly. Most of them are teases. But Tanya, the way she is acting, not looking for promises, that's his kind of woman. Christ. He should have had her by now! He slams his car door, stalks back to the house with the opened garage. There is hockey gear strewn over the driveway next to a well-cared-for red Camaro.

"What the hell?"

"Sorry, man!" yells a kid, about Matt's age. The kid stares hard, a twinge of recognition in his face.

Jack sure as shit doesn't know this kid. "'Sorry, man?' That's all you have to say? You about put your stick through my windshield. Dent my door with your puck! And 'sorry, man' is what you say?"

The kid rubs his hand over his head. It's a crewcut that has gotten out of control. His grey eyes are desperate now. "Look, my dad's not in a good mood."

"Your dad threw your equipment out into the street?" He can't believe it. The little piss-ant is lying.

"If you're not going to play hockey, you might as well get rid of all this crap." The voice booms from a dark corner of the garage.

The kid holds Jack's eye, pleads with him to walk away. But he is worked up over Tanya, worked up from this heat, worked up over another dead-end crap job, worked up over dodging fucking hockey equipment.

He picks his way through the shoulder pads and hockey socks to the back of the garage. "Yeah, get rid of the equipment, but don't throw it at passing cars."

"Passing cars?" The man steps out from the shadows. He's the kid's old man, no doubt about it. Same face, same build, but Jack is man enough to admit he wouldn't want to throw down with this guy. His hands are beefsteaks, wrapped around a glass of clear brown liquid. Bourbon. Neat.

Jack straightens to his full six-foot-two height. The guy is still a good four inches taller. "The hockey stick just missed my car. The puck wasn't so lucky."

"Sorry 'bout that," the man says gruffly. "My kid just told me he isn't playing hockey when he goes to Edmonton this fall."

"I didn't say that, Dad!" The kid is right behind Jack and Jack jumps.

"Shut the fuck up! I'm not talking to you." His mouth is a mean slash when he turns to Jack. "You give up all your time, your weekends, Christ, all your fucking money for this equipment and all the camps and all the hockey fees. And then he wants to piss it all away?"

The guy's grey eyes, just like his kid's, bore into Jack. "Fucking ungrateful kids," the man steamrolls on. "Going to school — going to NAIT — and he figures all he'll do is study."

"Dad," the kid whines.

"If you're not going to play hockey, then you better be showing the girls a good time," the guy says. "No Jeffries is just about studying."

"I didn't say I wouldn't play hockey. I said I didn't know. But showing the girls a good time, I can do that." The kid's smile is wicked.

"Christ," Jack mutters. He scrubs his face, walks away wearily. He pauses on the passenger side of his car, pulls at the bottom of his garage shirt. He wipes at the puck mark. It is only a smudge. He looks back up the driveway. The kid is picking up the equipment. The old man is nowhere in sight.

So, the kid is a couple years older than Matt, going on to trade school. Jack has no idea what Matt wants to do when he graduates. The boy is smart. Matt might push Benny as the geek, but he gets good report cards, too. The boy could do anything.

Jack stops cold. If Matt goes to university, he will be alone with Benny. That face. Those eyes. The constant reminder. Christ. Tanya better put out tomorrow. He needs a damned good lay. He doesn't want to think about Matt leaving him.

17

WHEN GLORY HEARS MATT'S NAME, she pastes her back against the cool wall, peeks around the corner. Kennedy is primping in front of the mirror glued inside the door of her locker. She is flanked by three girls.

"Have you heard if Matt's getting it on with anyone?"

"I heard Lyne's got a thing for him," Marly says.

Glory muffles a snort.

"No fucking way!" Kennedy's voice rises sharply. "Bitch has got Rick. Why the hell would she want Matt? I mean, Jesus. She made Rick beat the shit out of Bishop."

"Hello? Have you seen Matt?" Jacey says, combs her fingers through her dark hair, blonde and red streaked. "Rick doesn't even begin to compare to Matt."

"C'mon, Rick's no dog."

"We're not saying he's a dog, Kennedy." Jeannette sneaks a quick look in the mirror before Kennedy slams the door. "We all know you don't do dogs, but, Jesus, girlfriend, you got to admit Matt is one fine-looking boy."

Kennedy sticks her bottom lip out. "Rick's got money and he's got moves."

"Moves?" Jacey says. "You've seen Matt play basketball at noon hour. That boy's got moves. You wouldn't want to have those hands all over you?"

"Not just his hands," Marly says and the girls laugh wildly.

Glory has heard enough. She turns the corner and spots Matt strutting toward the group. She hurls herself back around the wall.

"Hey," Matt says. His voice is smooth, a hint of invitation in the single word.

"Hey," Marly says. "We were just talking about new, uh, things."

Glory can't make out Kennedy's voice in the abrupt laughter. She needs to see what is happening. She takes a deep breath, pokes her head around the corner. Kennedy, close to Matt, is scraping her red-lacquered nails down his arm. Matt's eyes are dark. His lip slides upward as he slowly leans in to cup the back of the girl's neck with his hand and whispers.

"Any time, Matt," Kennedy says, curling her hand around his arm. "Any time."

He laughs, a guttural sound. He turns sharply on his heel, walks away.

"I'll take those hands and whatever else he wants to give," Kennedy says, her eyes firmly on his retreating form. "Yeah, I can slum for that."

The bile rises in Glory's throat. Kennedy treated Matt like a piece of meat. And the way he touched her just now, smiled at her? This is the boy she walks to school with. She doesn't know him. Not at all.

18

MATT LIFTS BEN'S BARE LEGS, plops down on the couch, drops Ben's feet onto his lap, groans.

Ben raises his eyes from *Shoeless Joe*. "What?" He doesn't even tilt his head, simply stares up through too-long bangs. That move is impressive.

"You need a visit from Edward Scissorhands."

That makes the kid move. Quickly. He covers his head with his book.

"You're looking like a sasquatch, bro. Should give you a buzz cut."

"No way. You're not touching my hair," Ben says. "And, anyways, that's not what you were going to say." Ben squeaks his bare back along the vinyl couch as he gets comfortable, book now laid open on his sticky chest. Neither of them have a shirt on. Too fucking hot for that.

Matt groans again, squeezes Ben's toes. He shouldn't have come into the living room. He can't share this with the kid. Dad has been MIA too long and the money is almost gone. With this heat, yardwork is practically non-existent and he has been dipping into the bread bag. "What? You a mind reader now? Dial 1-900-PSYCHIC BOY?"

Ben pulls his foot from Matt's lap, nudges him.

He lunges for Ben's foot and *Shoeless Joe* hits the floor with a light thud. A heavy thud follows and they jump.

"Boys?" Dad's voice is alcohol hoarse, too loud.

Ben shifts quickly, pushes his back into Matt's chest.

"Dad?" Matt says. The word comes out soft, too soft. He clears his throat, calls out again. He rests his hand on the back of Ben's neck, feels the shiver that glides through the kid.

Dad appears in the entryway. He braces his shoulder against the wall, tucks his hands into his front pockets. His yellow garage shirt is wrinkled, sweat-stained under the arms. His gaze rests on the boys huddled on a single cushion on the couch.

"Dad, hey." He can't tell if Dad is in the middle of his latest binge or riding the tail end. His face is covered with days-old stubble, distorts a purplish bruise along his cheek bone. Matt slides out from behind Ben, grips the back of the couch with one hand. Silence always makes him nervous. This Dad, quiet and hungover, home in the middle of the afternoon, is a wounded dog. "You want me to make you something to eat? Lunch maybe? It's, uh," he eyes the starburst clock above the TV, "two, I guess. You hungry?"

"No," Dad says, pushes off the wall. He stops behind the couch. "Not hungry. Thought I'd grab a couple hours of sleep. Maybe a shower. Got a shift at five."

"Oh," he says. Dad still has a job. There is still money coming in. He loosens his grip on Ben's shoulder. The red marks from his fingers fade pink.

"But, hey," Dad heaves his hip on to the top of the couch, "the boss says he can give you a shift or two."

"At the garage?" he asks.

"That's where I work, isn't it?"

"Well, yeah." He plants his feet a little firmer on the floor as Ben pushes his weight back. "I just wasn't sure that was going to happen."

"Told you it would, didn't I?"

Ben tenses and Matt's grip tightens again. "Yes, you did." He prays gratitude is coming through and not uneasiness.

"Matt doesn't need a job at the garage," Ben says. The kid's voice rings clear in the hot air.

"What's that, boy?"

"Matt doesn't need a job at the garage," Ben says, voice still firm but not as loud.

"Working in a garage is good enough for your old man but not good enough for your brother?"

"No, that's not what I mean," Ben says quickly.

"That's not what he's saying," Matt speaks over his brother.

Ben rushes on. "We're cutting lawns now. We're busy with that."

"Yeah," he says. "We've got a few houses we're — "

Dad strikes out, pulls Ben by his hair. Ben is over the couch before Matt can move. Skin hitting skin spurs him into action.

"Dad! What are you doing?" He vaults the couch, stands between his father and a fallen Ben. The whiskey is strong on Dad's breath.

"Get out of the way, Matt. Gotta teach this boy not to be so proud."

"Dad." He pushes his father away.

Dad kicks out, his toes grazing Ben's hip. The boy gasps then crawls on his feet and hands, back pedals to the wall.

"Stupid fucking kid!" Dad's face is red, the purple bruise a dark shade of eggplant.

"Ben." He doesn't dare look at his little brother. "Go to the bedroom."

The boy pushes himself up the wall, stands unsteadily.

"Now," he says and Ben is gone.

"What the fuck, Matt?" Dad tries to shoulder past him.

But he fists his hands in his father's work shirt and won't move. "He didn't mean anything by it. Just wanted to let you know we were working. Jesus. That's it."

"Stupid fucking kid." Dad deflates with each word. He leans his head on Matt's shoulder then straightens up almost at once.

He lets go of his father's shirt, but still doesn't move.

Dad takes a step back, sways. He swipes a hand across his mouth. "What do you need?"

He carefully schools his features. He needs to go to Ben. But even more, he needs his father to leave. He weighs feeding Ben, keeping a roof over Ben's head against consoling the kid right-the-fuck-now. "Power bill's coming due. And I need money for groceries."

Dad pulls his worn leather wallet from his back pocket. He folds twenties and fifties into Matt's palm, closes the boy's fingers around the money. He keeps his hand there a moment longer. Then he turns and leaves. The door slams shut.

Jesus fucking Christ. Just when he is lulled into a comfortable state of being, everything changes. Or nothing changes. That's what it is. They keep moving, but nothing changes, it never gets better.

He runs his fingers through his hair. He can't take this. He can't fucking take this. He needs something. He thinks about Kennedy in the school hallway, Kennedy in the bleachers at noon hour. How she looks at him. He thinks about pushing her up against the wall and fucking her senseless. Ten minutes of nothing but pure bliss. It has been too long since he has been able to forget it all.

19

ALLISON CHECKS HER REFLECTION IN the glass door of Patterson's Hardware store. Her ass looks good in these yoga pants. She almost helped herself to the matching crop top. But if Mother is inside, or any of the ladies from the Evangelical Pentecostal Assembly, she would receive a sermon. She is not up to asking for God's forgiveness today.

The yoga pants are Lyne's. She should feel guilty about wearing Lyne's clothes when she is not doing it for Doug. But turning heads other than Doug's when she is wearing her seventeen-year-old daughter's fashions feels pretty damned good.

Allison hesitates, her hand on the door of her father's hardware store. She hates coming here. But Doug forgot to take in his receipts for his expense account and they are already hurting for money. Listening to her sisters talk about their RSPs and college funds makes her laugh. She barely has enough money to pay for school field trips. And thank God the girls aren't into sports. But Becca, monkey that she is, will probably break that pattern once she hits grade seven. Lord. This September her baby starts junior high!

She wishes she had Doug's thick skin. Then she wouldn't have to worry about being a Patterson girl, could get a job anywhere. She could join Molly Maid. They're advertising for help. But she can't do that to her parents. She is still doing penance for getting pregnant in high school.

But Doug isn't without pride. He demanded that she not ask her parents for anything. When the storm blew over after he knocked her up, he told Daddy he wouldn't take a managerial position at Patterson's Hardware. He insisted he would start as a grunt. And now, almost twenty years later, he is still in the trenches, travelling northern Alberta making sure Patterson-custom bathrooms are properly installed. If he were a plumber, they would be better off, would be able to afford to buy the dump they live in, fix it up, have something to put their name to. But he refused Daddy's offer to pay for trade school. Instead, he swings a hammer, installs tubs, spreads grout, makes sure the stainless steel showerheads match the faucets for the bathroom sink. He said labour was good enough for his old man.

The bell chimes when she pushes through. There isn't a store in Delwood that doesn't have that stupid bell.

The air conditioner is a low whir. Paint cans are lined up on the front shelves, brushes hung in neat rows according to size. The green Frog tape is stacked in two towers of identical height. Patterson's Hardware is clean and almost empty. But damn it. There is Mrs. Bailey. Allison ducks behind the display of tiles.

"Oh, Allison, dear." Mrs. Bailey rolls her portly self over. She is as meticulously turned out as the store. Her snow-white hair is in pin curls and her button earrings match the gaudy pattern on her polyester dress. "Oh, are you putting new tiles in your kitchen? Or your bathroom? I know they give long-term tenants a chance to buy. Have you bought? No, I imagine you haven't bought or your mother would have told me. I haven't seen you in such a long time. Step out, dear."

Mrs. Bailey lives four doors down from Allison's parents. When she was in high school, Mrs. Bailey would promptly report to Mother whenever she saw her get into a boy's car.

Allison steps out.

"Oh," Mrs. Bailey tuts. "Oh. I see you still like the tight clothes."

And she is in high school all over again. All because Doug forgot to bring in his damned receipts!

"And makeup," Mrs. Bailey says, tuts after that statement, too.

"We can all do with a little pick-me-up," Allison says. And decides she will blame her boldness on Lyne's clothes. "And I'm not talking about a drop or two of cooking sherry."

Mrs. Bailey does not tut then.

"Of course, tight clothes and makeup aren't as hard on the heart," she says. And that feels damned good! What is the word

Glory would use? Yes, liberating. Until Mrs. Bailey's eyelids flutter. Oh God! Has she given the woman a heart attack?

Mrs. Bailey reaches for a shelf, knocks off a can of Clay Beige paint.

Daddy rushes to her side. "Penelope! What's wrong?"

"Roland, oh," Mrs. Bailey clutches tightly to Daddy's arm.

Well, if the woman can speak, she is not having a heart attack.

"Oh, nothing is wrong, Daddy," she says. "Mrs. Bailey and I were just catching up." She recognizes Lyne's snark in her voice. Perhaps snark and boldness came with the clothes?

Roland Patterson stops short.

She has not seen her father for three months. Mother visits semi-regularly, but Daddy rarely comes to the townhouse. He is still distinguished looking, smoky grey hair with white brushed in his temples. He is gaining weight, a small roll of flesh covers the buckle of his belt.

"Why are you here, Allison?"

There is no warmth in his voice. Never has been. Even as children he made it clear Mother was the one to love and keep discipline. All Daddy was responsible for was paying the bills. And arranging the shotgun wedding that almost ruined his family's reputation because Mother had failed at her job. It took until Glory was born for Mother to go back to hosting her regular Pentecostal Women's Fellowship afternoon teas.

"Doug forgot to bring his receipts," she says.

"They could have waited until he was back from his road trip," Daddy says.

"No, they couldn't have." After all these years, her father still does not get it.

20

IT IS ALL WEIGHING ON him and he is about to implode. Anger at Dad. Guilt over Ben. Shame from Lyne's accurate dissection of his life. Nothing fucking changes.

Now all of those feelings have rolled into rage and a noon hour of basketball is not cutting it. Fighting for the ball, dribbling full speed down the court, rimming the ball around the basket with hard shots, going up for his own rebounds have only left him exhausted. The rage still smoulders. Walking off the court, he plucks his shirt from the pile, wipes the cool cotton across his forehead.

"Fuck." He has to wear this shirt for the rest of the day. He needs to bring a towel tomorrow. The days are so hot.

He is itching for a hookup. It is the only way to take the edge off. He can't think straight. He is desperate for a release. He had a farewell fuck before he left the other school over a month ago. It is the longest he has gone without sex since he did it for the first time in grade nine, a quick introduction courtesy of a grade eleven girl in the back seat of her father's Buick.

He slips the damp shirt over his head, hears his name. He scans the bleachers, stops on Lyne. Obviously not her. The bitch and Jeffries are hot and heavy on the top bench.

"Matt."

Definitely Kennedy. He drops his gaze from her face to the dip in her shirt, the thin fabric stretched taut over her chest. Jesus fucking Christ! Is that a nipple ring?

"Too fucking long," he mutters. He is vibrating. He lifts his chin.

Kennedy purses her full lips, licks them slowly.

He has been in the game long enough to know what that means. He shifts his feet to relieve the tension already filling his jeans. He tunes into the words coming from Kennedy's friends. They are chiding her about slumming it. Who gives a fuck? He is out of here in three months tops. It doesn't matter what anybody else thinks. And fuck it, he needs this.

Kennedy pats the seat next to her.

He saunters across the hot asphalt, slides into the vacant space on the bleacher. "Hey," he says. For a pick up line, it barely registers, but when he parts his lips and gives her the slow, sexy smile and her eyes glaze over, he knows how this is going to end. He leans back on his elbows. "Fucking hot, huh?"

"God, yes." She pulls the shoulders of her sleeves down, shows more curve.

He is growing hard, worries he is going to shoot his load right here if they don't do something right the fuck now. There is no more than fifteen minutes left in the noon hour. He does a quick search of the grounds. No Ben. He doesn't like advertising his hookups to the kid.

"Don't you think lemonade would taste just heavenly?" Kennedy asks. Her voice is low, sing-song. Her friends snigger.

What the fuck?

"I live only a block from here," she says. "Want to go home and get some lemonade?"

Delwood code for an actual bed. That doesn't happen often. "I sure am fucking thirsty," he says. He stretches out, brushes a hand across Kennedy's bare shoulder, tucks his finger under her bra strap. "Your mom not home?" He has heard Kennedy's dad is no longer in the picture.

"No, she's off planning a, uh, fundraiser," she says. The girls behind her cackle. She shoots them a sharp look and they go silent. Then she curls up her lips sweetly at him.

"Look, we only have fifteen minutes," he says. "Five minutes to your house, five minutes back, only leaves five minutes. I'm too fucking good for you to only have five minutes with me."

Kennedy says nothing.

Fuck! Blew it! He dares to look at her. She is looking back.

"You're that fucking good?" she asks.

"That fucking good," he says.

"My mom's gone all afternoon. And it's so late in the school year, Mrs. Murphy doesn't remember to phone home when students are missing, especially after lunch. You want to skip the afternoon?"

"Fuck, yeah." He slips the leather braid with the ring off his neck, pockets it. He stands, flicks his hand. "Lead on."

The girls titter behind them as he follows Kennedy down.

They walk in silence, not touching. He is humming like a tuning fork. As soon as they step into the bungalow, he kicks the door closed, pushes Kennedy up against it. There is no room in his brain to ease her into this gently. His mouth claims hers, his tongue probing. His hands move expertly to rid her of her clothes. Kennedy wraps her legs around his hips, directs him toward the back of the house.

"Fuck," Matt says when he sees the king-sized bed. This must be her mother's bedroom. Space and time. It doesn't get better than this. He pulls off his T-shirt, slips the condoms out of his wallet before he drops his jeans. Kennedy's nipple ring tells him exactly where he is going to start his exploration. But that will come after he fucks her.

An hour later, used condoms in the waste basket beside the bed, Matt lays next to Kennedy, plays with her nipple ring. Breaking his drought like this, in a bed, no rush, is almost worth the shit that has led up to this moment. Now he needs to leave, while his body is still thrumming, his head in that space that says life is good.

"God, you're fucking awesome," Kennedy says. She twists to face him. "You're ten times better then Rick."

"Lyne's Rick? You've been with that prick?"

"Not a lot of girls in high school haven't. But he's all about him. It's all about getting him off. Not like you. Not like what you're doing. Jesus, Matt, Jesus." She gasps as he moves his hands down her body.

Jeffries pisses him off all over again, pushes him further, giving more to Kennedy. She will get the word out, fuck with Jeffries' reputation. She moans loudly and that is all the encouragement he needs to go another round.

When her eyelids flutter shut, he kisses her hard. He feels boneless, could easily doze off. But he can't. He searches the floor for his clothes, sits on the edge of the bed as he pulls on his boxers, jeans. "Got to get going. Kid brother to pick up."

Kennedy tucks her hand into the waistband of his jeans, scratches a sharp fingernail down his spine.

"Kennedy," he says, tightly.

She drops her hand. "We going to do this again?"

He runs his fingers through his hair. Fuck. He got carried away, didn't set the ground rules. He always sets the ground rules. Fuck, fuck.

"Matt?" she asks, still speaking to his back. There is uncertainty in her voice.

He has never been about stringing girls along. Fuck. He turns around, keeps his eyes on his hands. "I can't promise anything," he says. "We move a lot. But I should be good until the end of June."

She is quiet.

Fuck. Nothing kills the buzz better than this. He shoves his hands in his pockets, studies the blue streaks on the white area rug. It's a frenetic pattern.

"We can do this again before the end of June. This works for me," she says.

He looks at her. "Yeah? It's only about hooking up. No boyfriend-girlfriend shit."

"I get that," she says, but the uncertainty is still in her voice. "I don't want that. Just you. Just this."

He pulls her up, kisses her. It starts off soft then builds. He pushes her back on the bed, works his way down her body, keeps the intensity going until she pants his name. His tongue is magic. Every girl shows him that.

He climbs off the bed, tugs on his shirt. He tucks his socks into his pocket, slips on his Pumas. Kennedy's eyes droop. She is blissed out. Nearly a month, but he still has it. He is loose-limbed, at ease. There is nothing he loves more than the feeling that follows perfect sex. Well, except for the perfect sex itself.

21

JACK STANDS IN THE ARCHWAY of the living room, watches Benny slowly, slowly tent two cards as the peak of a castle. He is on his knees on the old carpet, hovering above the coffee table. Christ. Is the kid using Uno cards?

"We don't have a single deck of cards?" Jack's voice is gruff.

"Uh!" Benny yells. His hand jerks and the castle tumbles. All of it. The kid swings around and delivers a death glare. Then his face slides into contrition.

Jack wonders if that look would have been accompanied by a string of words if it had been Matt that had caused the castle to fall. No doubt very colourful words. He slumps against the wall. "No real cards?"

"No," Benny says and he crawls up onto the couch.

"Didn't know we had Uno cards."

"Had them for a while," Benny says. He is still clutching the top two cards. And he is all kinds of jittery. The jittery that says Matt's not around. The jittery that makes him feel like a shit father.

"Did you hear about the man who was found dead on the floor with fifty-three Bicycles in the room?" he says.

"What?" Benny squeaks.

"It's a riddle. Detective walks into a room, finds a man dead on the floor. And there are fifty-three Bicycles lying around the room."

Benny's mouth is open in a perfect little "o."

"What happened?" he says. Why can't the kid run with this? Why can't he ever make things easy? Where the hell is Matt?

"Fifty-three Bicycles," Benny says slowly and he rubs together the two Uno cards. "Fifty-three Bicycles."

"It's a play on words," he says.

"Fifty-three Bicycles." Benny stares at the Uno cards and his eyes sparkle blue. The sun off of lake water on a beautiful summer day. Exactly like Miriam's when she pieced the puzzle together. "He was playing cards and cheating and he got shot."

He smiles grudgingly. "Pretty damn good, kid."

Benny beams. And that is so, so Miriam. God, it hurts. It still hurts so much.

"I'll, uh, I'll get you some cards," he says, and he turns around and leaves.

22

GLORY'S EYES SKITTER FROM THE textbook balanced on her knees to the groan of the door opening on Matt's house. He steps out. Maybe he won't look her way, see her studying on her front stoop. She has heard the rumours, what Kennedy has said about him. It is nothing but sex. She wishes she could duck back inside, but any sudden movement would draw his attention. Then he looks, catches her staring. He smiles fully.

"Hey," he calls across the yards.

"Hey," Glory breathes out.

"What have you got there?" He slouches against the jamb of the open door, crosses his ankles. He is wearing knee-length cotton shorts, the drawstring hanging untied. His green American Eagle T-shirt matches the stripes on his shorts. He only needs canvas boat shoes and he would be a *GQ* model.

"Oh, an assignment." She can do this. He is still her friend. The way he smiled at her just now wasn't made up. "The class was fooling around today and Bruns got pissy. She gave us a whole bunch of questions to answer from the textbook. It's due tomorrow."

"Bruns seems like a tightass." Matt shuffles to fit more snugly into the door frame. "Why are you doing your work out there?"

"Same reason Becca's in your house," she says. "Well, not quite the same."

"What do you mean?"

"Becca's over there because Mom and Dad were giving each other the cold shoulder. Now, well, they're, well, you know. Making up." Glory scrunches her nose.

"Your mom and dad are a couple of Energizer bunnies." Matt's eyes sparkle bronze.

"That's not funny!"

"Okay, okay." He holds his hands up in submission, but there is nothing apologetic in his face.

She can't think of her parents that way. But she can think of Matt with Kennedy. She shakes her head. A strand of hair falls lose from her ponytail and she tucks it behind her ear. She looks up to see Matt still watching her.

"Hey, can I join you?"

"Really?" Her voice goes high.

"If it's okay?" He hooks his thumbs into his pockets. "I have a bit of review to do. Some stuff we didn't quite get around to covering at my last school. Figure your brains might rub off on me."

"Whatever!" She smiles. At least she hopes she smiles because her stomach is making it difficult for her lips not to grimace.

Matt ducks into his townhouse. His voice carries on the air and she imagines him telling Becca and Ben where he is going. She closes her eyes and his voice takes over, a combination of deep and soft. She startles back when the door slams. Matt hops across the scratchy grass and loose pebbles, still barefoot.

"Here," he says, hands her an ice cream cone. His textbook is tucked against his body with his elbow. "Ben, dumbass that he is, left the ice cream on the counter. Figured I better use it before it spoiled." Matt settles on a lower step, bumps her knees. "'Course, I gave him hell for not putting the ice cream back in the freezer."

"'Course you did," she laughs.

"What?"

"I can't see you giving Ben hell for anything and meaning it."

"Okay, busted." He licks the chocolate, chases a drip down the side of his cone. "But I got to keep up my image, right?"

The door swings open behind them and Lyne comes out. Matt shifts on the step, sits taller. Lyne's eyes are heavy with liner and her lips plump with dark red. Her clothes hug her.

"Hey," Glory says, suddenly conscious of her jean shorts and pink tank top.

Lyne's eyes flit from Glory to Matt. "What? No ice cream for me?"

"Go to hell," Matt says.

Glory almost drops her cone. Matt's voice is hard. This is nothing like the light-hearted banter they've been sharing.

"This is my house, asshole," Lyne says.

"Yeah, well, Glory invited me. So piss off." He presses his back against Glory's legs and she wonders if he is protecting her or getting protection from her.

"Matt came over to study with me."

Lyne looks at her. "Really?"

"Yeah, really. So fuck off," Matt says.

This is a tennis match. Volleys of hatred hit and returned.

"Rude much?" Lyne asks.

"Fuck off," Matt says, each word distinct.

This is going to get ugly. Very ugly. Glory is sure of it. She can't get Dad. He and Mom are still . . . doing it. Oh God, oh God. When the roar of a familiar engine fills the air, she can't ever remember being so happy to have Rick come to the house.

The Camaro skids to a stop but Lyne doesn't move. Her eyes remain on Matt, her hands digging into her hips.

Rick cuts the engine, steps out of the car. "Hey, babe. What's going on?"

"This asshole," Lyne says.

"Lyne," Glory whispers.

In three quick strides Rick is at the bottom of the stairs. Matt is standing now, ice-cream cone gripped like a weapon.

Glory steps down between the two boys. They tower over her.

"Glory," Matt says. "What are you doing?"

"What's going on?"

They all turn. Dad is in the open doorway, jeans slung low on his hips. His hair is tousled. Relief washes through Glory. "You going out, Lyne?"

Lyne nods.

"Then go."

Lyne grabs Rick's arm, pulls him away.

"You," Dad says to Matt. "Head home."

"I'm sorry," Matt says to Glory. He picks up his textbook. His shoulders are hunched as he walks away.

23

"MATT," BEN WHISPERS.

"Just leave it alone, Benny." His voice comes out gravelly.

"Is it Dad?" The question is tight, desperate.

"Who else would it be?"

"Should we check?" Ben makes no move to get up. "What if we forgot to lock the door and somebody came in and is stealing our stuff?"

He sighs. "Yeah, Ben, they broke in to take the ten gold bars I stashed in the freezer."

"I don't know, but what if it isn't Dad?"

"Shh," he says sharply. He shifts on to his side, faces his brother. The street lamp outside is bright, lights up the small bedroom through the wide crack in the drapes. They can see each other clearly.

Ben turns away, focuses on the ceiling. He bunches the sheets under his fists.

"It's Dad," he says.

"But how do you know it's Dad?" Ben whispers fiercely. "How do you know?"

When did the kid become so fucking paranoid? "I've been awake long enough, Ben."

"And?"

"I got up and checked." He wants the discussion to end right the fuck now. He is exhausted. But it's not enough for Ben to back down. It never is.

"And?"

"Jesus, fuck, give it a rest." He spits out the words, all hard-edged and as close to a shout as he can get without raising his voice.

Ben presses his face into his pillow.

Fuck! He waits for Ben's breathing to grow shallow. He digs his nails into his palms. "He's brought someone home with him, Benny."

"Oh. Did you see them?"

"Yeah. I got my own personal peep show. They're doing it in the living room."

"Oh," Ben says.

"She's blonde. Stacked. You know, the usual."

"Do you know who she is?"

"No. Didn't really see her face."

"Oh."

"Yeah, 'oh.'" He forces out a laugh.

"But he didn't see you, right?" Ben's voice is barely there.

"No, Benny, he didn't see me." When he hears his brother take a breath to ask another question, he bolts upright. "No, Ben, he was too busy fucking the hot blonde. She was saying, 'More, Jack,' and he was saying, 'Like this?' And then he was ramming it in. And in a week or maybe two, her husband is going to bust through our door and beat the shit out of him. And then we're gone again."

Ben gives into tears which turn into hitches and then into deep sobs.

Fuck. Fuck. Fuck. Matt slams back onto his bed, scrubs his hand down his face. He doesn't understand why being angry and scared and so, so tired also make him mean. "I'm sorry, Benny. I'm sorry."

"It's okay, Matty."

He wants to reach between the beds, to wrap his hand around Ben's wrist, to say things will get better. But he stays still and silent.

24

"WHAT DO YOU MEAN YOU'RE not coming home today?" She locks her fingers around the phone receiver.

"This custom shower fitting is a bitch, Allie," Doug says. "Nothing is working. It'll take at least another day."

She sucks in a deep breath, leans over the sink where 500 grams of hamburger meat is defrosting. She had planned to cook something special for Doug, let him know she was tired of fighting. He left in a fit. But now.

"Doug . . . "

"Look, Allie. There's nothing I can do about this. You know that. It's my job." His voice is hard. It is as if he is giving her permission to fight some more, to keep pushing him. It has become a habit of his lately.

She won't do it. "I know it's your job."

"I have bills to pay," he says and his voice is still hard.

"I know you do." She pokes at the meat through the cellophane wrap, beats it into submission with a wooden spoon. A thin stream of blood runs toward the drain.

"So, I'll see you in a couple of days, okay?" Now he sounds apologetic.

"Yeah, okay." She keeps the phone to her ear, doesn't hang up until the buzzing is replaced by voices. The girls are home. She pulls a battered recipe book from the shelf, sinks down at the table. The pages are grease-splotched, scribbled-on, corners folded. She has these recipes memorized. Family favourites. The familiar feel of the book is as comforting as the food it contains. She brushes her fingertips along the bottom of her eyes, pushes away moisture.

The chatter in the living room is punctuated with a slight tenor. That is Ben. She doesn't hear the deeper bass. Matt is not here. Becca and Ben are inseparable. She has never seen Becca take to a child — a boy, especially — the way she has taken to him. When will the platonic relationship break down? When will one of them want more than a friend to confide in? She wishes they could stay children forever.

"Isn't Dad supposed to be home today?" Becca asks.

Glory's voice is more difficult to hear. "Obviously not. It's too quiet."

"Not yet," Becca says.

"Not at all today," Glory says.

"What do you mean?" That's Ben.

"If Dad was coming home, Mom would be flitting around," Glory says. "I don't know. Nervous energy, I guess."

"Huh," Ben says.

"Huh," Allie says. Is she really that way? Flitting around, perhaps. But not nervous energy. She got rid of her nerves with Doug before she got pregnant with Lyne. No, it took a lot of nerves to go against her parents' wishes. She was a Patterson girl after all. And Doug's father was a drunkard, hit his wife, his kids. Doug was shy in school, but he was a catch. It was rumoured he stood up to his father and Old Man Rutger was one of the ugliest drunks in town. The rich bitches didn't mind slumming it for Doug. And she was the rich bitch who got him. And everything else that came with him. She was young, stupid. He was handsome, gentle, considerate. She never figured she would get pregnant. Didn't realize that getting pregnant meant judging looks from the church women. Where was the forgiveness then? The Pentecostal Women's Fellowship probably gathered around their kitchen tables, wrung their hands, consoled her mother, "Oh, poor Theresa, you did all you could. That one has the devil in her."

She jumps her fingernail along the coil of the cookbook. She hates fighting with Doug especially when there are so many days in between, so many days before they can figure things out. Not that they ever talk things through. It is either sex or sweep it under the rug, unspoken code for it has been dealt with.

She smooths a smile across her lips and calls out, "Come get a snack, kids. I baked a strawberry-rhubarb pie." It was supposed to be for dessert tonight but that doesn't matter any more.

"Hey, Mom." Glory leads Becca and Ben into the sunny kitchen. Becca slides the warm pie from the counter and Ben snatches the milk from the fridge. Glory stands still, hands gripping the back of a kitchen chair, eyes resting on the phone next to the cookbook. Her eyes go dark with pity.

Allie worries her daughter will understand that at this very moment, she wants to be pitied. Glory needs to realize that this is their life. Hard work and dreams do not make things better. Not in Delwood. No, this is all they will have.

Allie forces cheerfulness into her voice. "I'll get the glasses and the plates."

She reaches for the plastic tumblers. Her hands falter. What kind of mother is she that she feels it is wrong for her daughter to have hope? It is not that she wants Glory beaten down at so young an age. She only wants her to understand that there is no escaping this life. But she can't tell the girl that. Glory won't believe her. Glory needs to read it in the pages of her books.

25

MATT FOLLOWED KENNEDY HOME AT noon hour because of anger and the desperate need to be in control. He doesn't know why life in Delwood is so hard. Delwood is no different than any other stop in any other small Alberta town. But his anger here has been simmering, slow burning. In Delwood, sex has become a weapon.

"Jesus, Matt," Kennedy says, "don't stop."

He doesn't. Even when she whimpers, even when she tenses up. He is not ready to release yet and this fuck is all about him.

"Jesus, Matt." This time Kennedy is pleading, her fingernails dig into his back, draw blood.

The sudden sting stops him. Fuck. Fuck. What is he doing? This is not him. He gentles his motions, pushes himself, releases his need in a final shudder. He rolls off of Kennedy, covers his eyes with his arm. His head fills with images of Dad in the living room, the way Dad moved with the blonde bimbo, the way Dad controlled her, the way she took it.

"Fuck!" He sits up suddenly.

Kennedy pushes away. "What?"

Her absence is a splash of cold water. He has frightened her. He fists his hands tightly, reins himself in. He is not his father. He is not. "I didn't mean to hurt you."

"What? No." She drops her eyes a moment, blinks rapidly before looking up at him again. "Jesus, Matt, no. You didn't hurt me. That was incredible."

Why is she saying that? He knows he hurt her. Why doesn't she tell him the truth?

"You want something even more incredible?" she says.

He tips his chin.

"A clit stud. They're supposed to be fucking incredible — for the girl and the guy."

"Yeah?" Jesus. He hurt her. But she would do that for him? Why?

She slides her hand up Matt's leg. "If I did that, if I got one, would you be the first to try it out?"

How can she still want him? "You would do that? Get a clit stud?"

"For you," she says.

He is not his father.

"I'm probably going to be gone by the end of this month, July for sure, right?" he says. She has got to understand. It is only about sex. He can't give her any more than that.

Her hand stills and she says softly, "I know."

"We're not boyfriend-girlfriend. You know that, too?"

"I know that," Kennedy says. Then her smile turns feral and she is straddling him. "But what the fuck, right?"

"Jesus," he says. "What the fuck."

26

LYNE ANGLES HER FACE A little more to get out of the glare. The afternoon sun is screwing with her reflection in the small table-top mirror. She can't gauge the depth of her blush, the glimmer of her lipstick. She has been telling Mom forever about needing a pull-down blind, but Mom hates to go to the hardware store and Dad always forgets.

"I'll have to do it myself," she says, shudders at the thought.

She slots the Ruby Red lipstick in with the other tubes of red. Becca and her OCD have colour-coded her lipsticks. This used to drive her crazy, but when she is in a rush, it is a life saver. Not that she will ever tell Becca.

Rick will be here soon. They are heading out to an afternoon bush party, which will last until midnight. Too bad tomorrow is school. She loves bush parties. Everybody is a little wilder, alcohol flows freer, and drugs are easier. She won't be hitting the E — never again — but that doesn't mean she can't take advantage of the high Rick gets off of the pot and alcohol. He has been so tense lately, always mouthing off about Humphreys. Why is he so caught up with Matt? Rick has it all. Matt has nothing. It will be good for Rick to loosen up. Good for her, too. Tension makes him harsh, demanding. And that makes her uneasy.

She twists her white belt a little more to the side on her red Baby Phat shorts. Incredibly hot. Rick bought them for her after the run-in with Humphreys on her front stoop. She was so pissed that day. If he had tried to console her a different way, she is sure she would have done it with him. She was that pissed.

"What an idiot." She laughs, high and nervous. She came *that* close.

She is wearing a little white zip top with her lacy red bra peeking out. One more pull on the zipper when she gets into the car. Maybe she and Rick can stop before they hit the party, have an early matinee. She glances one last time in the mirror. Perfect!

She slides into her Flojos at the front door, stops when she hears Becca talking.

"You have beer in your fridge."

What the hell? She fingers the screen door open a notch. Oh yes. It's the *Suite Life of Zach and Cody.*

Ben, braced on his elbows on the hot concrete stoop, cocks his head in Becca's direction. "You want one?"

Lyne lets out a "humph," covers her mouth and jumps back from the door.

"No!" Becca says, "No! I hate the taste of beer."

"You've drank beer?" Respect colours Ben's voice.

"You haven't?"

"Are you kidding? Matt would beat the crap out of me if I even looked at a bottle."

Holier than shit Matt Humphreys. Lyne watches Ben finger a cigarette butt then throw it. She tracks its short path.

"When did you have beer?" he asks.

"Daddy gave me a drink once. Well, a couple of times. Every time I try it, I think I might like it better, but I don't. I don't know how he can drink that stuff."

"My dad gets drunk on beer. Other stuff, too. He likes tequila." Ben picks up another cigarette butt, squishes it between his fingers. "Actually, I think my dad would drink anything. He's not picky."

The lost expression on Becca's face convinces Lyne that Ben doesn't talk much about his father.

"Where does your dad go when he takes off?" Becca asks.

"Around," Ben says, drops the butt, rolls his hand in the air. "He gets around."

The Humphreys have lived in Delwood over a month and Lyne hasn't seen Jack Humphreys once. She has heard that he is fucking the garage owner's wife. There are also rumours that link him to one or two of the town's more willing housewives.

"How come Matt doesn't drink?" Becca asks.

"He's only sixteen!" Ben's voice rises in indignation.

"Doesn't matter. Lots of guys — and girls — drink underage. Lyne does. She goes to parties all the time and drinks," Becca says the last bit quietly.

Lyne hates beer, drinks it only because the guys think it is hot to see a girl slug back a bottle.

"Matt doesn't do parties," Ben says.

"How come?" Becca asks.

"Huh." Ben is quiet a moment. "Probably because we're never in a school long enough for anybody to invite him."

"I don't think it would take much for someone to invite a guy like Matt to a party," Becca says.

"I guess. But he sticks around. Just in case Dad comes home."

What the hell does that mean? But Becca doesn't ask. And Lyne can't. But it doesn't matter. Matt is an asshole. But still . . . no, she doesn't care. All that matters is Matt won't be there today to ruin her fun and Rick won't be obsessing about Humphreys. Just as she is ready to blow past the annoying twosome, Matt crosses the space in cut-off jeans, wifebeater, bare feet.

"Hey, heads up," he says. He has an ice cream float in each hand, spoons sticking up from each plastic cup. "Figured I'd come see what you two little nerds were up to."

Ben ignores the bait, but takes the treat. He scoots over for his brother. Matt passes the second cup to Becca.

Lyne tucks back behind the wall before Matt can see her.

"Your sister not home from doing her project yet?" he says.

She swears he sounds disappointed.

"Glory? No," Becca says. "Probably another couple of hours. Tina likes to talk."

Matt laughs. His ease with the two kids is a surprise. Rick has never spent time with Becca. Not that Lyne has asked him to, but still . . . Jesus. Where are these thoughts coming from? She *hates* Matt Humphreys.

Shit! She is not ruining her perfect afternoon by Rick being in a mood when he comes here and sees Matt. She heads inside, pulls out her iPhone, thumbs to the first name on her menu.

120

"Hey, Rick, I'm running late. Give me another half hour, okay?"

27

MATT SPOTS GLORY AT HER locker, threads his way through the junior high kids.

"Hey," he says, breathes out the word a little weaker than he intended.

Glory turns around. Her eyes are wide then they are sparkling sapphires. And then they dull a little. "Hey to you, too," she says softly.

"So, uh, how did your presentation go?" His smile falters. He doesn't understand why she has turned off so suddenly. He leans up next to her locker, lets the cool steel calm him.

"It wasn't bad." She turns away, struggles with her combination lock. She slams her palm on the locker. "Oh! I hate this thing! All year it's done this!"

He laughs, releases his tension. This he can fix. "Here." He moves in, gently clasps her hand. She is soft, warm. Fuck. "These things are always tricky. What's your combo?"

Glory pulls her hands away and Kennedy's voice, a booming siren, drowns out her reply. "There you are! I've been looking all over for you."

Matt swallows. "Yeah, the school is so fucking big."

"Seriously, Matt, why are you slumming it with the junior highs?"

He hears Glory's sharp intake of breath, shifts closer to her. "What do you want?"

"Jesus, Matt," Kennedy says, "who pissed in your cornflakes?"

"What do you want, Kennedy?"

"Some of the guys are making a liquor store run. Want to know if you want anything." Kennedy's lips are stuck out in what he has come to recognize as her pissed-off face. It has never been directed at him before.

"I don't drink."

"Maybe you should. You're pretty fucking uptight right now."

"Whatever," he says. But she is right. He is tense. He runs his fingers through his hair, plasters on a smile.

"Yeah, whatever." Kennedy smiles back, splays her hand across his chest, plays with the ring that dangles there.

He squeezes her fingers away, tucks the ring inside his shirt. She knows better. He firms up his smile to lessen the sting. "Thanks for the offer. I'll take my chances on the next sale."

Kennedy leans in. "Sales prices are negotiable."

"Don't want to have to sue for false advertising," he says.

"I'm sure we can work something out for later," she says.

"Well then, later, yeah." He steps back to let her pass. Her cowboy boots click on the floor. He watches her hips sway in her tight jean skirt. Her offer of later does not stir his body.

"It's twelve, around twice twenty-five, and forty-seven," Glory says.

Fuck, fuck, fuck. He shuffles in front of the locker, doesn't look at her. He doesn't want to read the disgust in her eyes. He twirls the dial carefully and the lock snicks open. He pulls it off the door, holds on to it as she shelves her books. When she shuts the door, he passes the lock back. She pulls her hand away before their fingers brush and he feels the absence of her touch.

Glory clips the lock on. "Why don't you drink?"

"I never know when Dad's going to come home, if he's going to be drunk, if he's going to be mad or depressed. Someone's got to take care of our family." He keeps doing this. He doesn't understand why this girl has the power to make him share parts of himself he doesn't even know he has.

"Oh," she says, wraps her arms around her body.

He watches her go, too, quiet in her Tevas.

28

ALLIE LOWERS HERSELF CAREFULLY ONTO the front stoop, a cold beer in hand. Her muscles burn but in the good way. She and Doug had one night and almost two full days in bed before he had to hit the road again. There was no talking. She didn't even ask him about the scratches on his back.

She takes a long swallow, loses herself in the bitter, cool liquid as it slides down her throat. The engine of the Camaro brings her back to her senses. Rick pulls up in a spray of gravel, one hand on the wheel. It doesn't take long for her to figure out where the other hand is. Lyne leans back against the seat, her mouth forming a soundless moan. Music blares from the open window. Rick cuts the engine, but the two of them stay at it. She watches. She should stop this. But embarrassing Lyne won't help their already strained relationship.

Laughter coming from down the street announces Glory and Becca walking with Ben. Matt is a few steps behind. Ben's hands are flying frantically, punctuating whatever story he is telling. Becca is laughing, but Glory is . . . not there. Glory has not been there for a while now. She doesn't need an in-depth conversation with the girl — as if that would ever happen! — to know that she has discovered boys. One boy in particular. Matt's deep brown eyes are lit up, intense, and he is focused solely on Glory. Yet he walks behind her. His face is soft, but worry lines crease his forehead. He is a troubled boy. Whatever this thing is that Glory has or does not have with Matt Humphreys is getting out of control. He is not the kind of boy to be any girl's first crush.

The kids stop outside the Humphreys' door while Ben finishes his story. Glory laughs. Well, she must have been listening to the tale after all. Matt steps up to the group and says something. All three move in close. Ben grins, Becca laughs and Glory . . . Glory drinks him in.

"Oh God," she mutters. The girl has it bad.

And Lyne and Rick are still making out in the car.

One girl all about sex, one girl falling in love.

Sex is bad enough, the consequences could be longlasting, but love — well, love could do more damage than sex. She finishes her beer in one deep swallow, lets the rush of the alcohol take her away. She is not going to worry about any of this today.

29

LATE IN THE EVENING JACK finds Matt at the basketball court shooting hoops. The Raptors' ball goes up, swooshes through without hitting metal or twine. Matt snags the rebound, dribbles back. Then goes in for a lay-up. There was a time when he did his own play-by-play.

"Still got it," Jack says.

The ball rounds the rim, flies wide.

"Hey, Dad!" Matt grins, grabs the ball, one-hops it to him.

"Yeah?" He drops his coat on the bottom row of the bleachers. When the air conditioning kicks in at Rath's Garage it gets damned cold in there.

"Yeah," Matt says, wipes his forehead with his bare arm, crouches, palms up.

And then it is on.

Jack is stiff from changing one too many tires today, but he has the moves. Or he remembers having the moves. Matt is unrelenting. He dekes and the boy stays with him. He goes up and Matt stuffs him. He sinks two points and Matt tags up and gets three points. At the end of twenty minutes, with every muscle aching, he understands that all the points he managed were courtesy of Matt's goodwill.

"Christ, you're fast," he says and slumps on the bleacher. He is breathing hard, sweat stinging his eyes.

Matt tucks the ball under his arm. Boy is barely panting.

"Here, old man, have a drink before you pass out." Matt removes the cap, taps the half-full bottle of lukewarm water on his shoulder.

"I call rematch," he says. He polishes off the rest of the water, passes the empty bottle back. Damn. He should have saved some for the boy. Oh well. Matt is young. He will recover from water deprivation far faster than his old man. "But not today."

This is the first time he has been to the school grounds. He doesn't usually head this way but he heard the rhythmic bouncing of the ball, needed to check it out. Needed to know it if was his boy.

"This isn't a bad court," he says.

Matt laughs, settles next to him. He screws the lid back on the bottle. "In the daylight it sucks," he says. "We play ball out here most noon hours. The high school guys."

"Yeah, I played ball all the time in high school."

"I watched you play basketball with the Golden Bears, didn't I?" Matt asks.

"You remember that?" He keeps his eyes on the rusted red hoop. Those university days were a long, long time ago. Eons.

"Vaguely," Matt says. "Me and Mom."

"She was a pretty passionate fan before you were born. When we had you, she said she had to dial it back. She figured she couldn't yell the same way because she didn't want you growing up thinking she was some kind of displaced sailor." He is surprised the words flow so easily.

Matt's jaw drops.

"Yeah, your mom had a mouth on her."

"I don't remember that."

"She cleaned up good, your mom." He leans back, his elbows on the row behind him. Matt follows. He looks away quickly. It has been a long time since his boy has mimicked him.

"Ben's good at basketball," Matt says.

"Hm?" He doesn't want to hear it. It has been good sitting here, connecting with Matt, remembering Miriam so easily. But the boy can't let it alone.

"The three of us, we should come shoot hoops sometime." He grunts.

"We should. You'd be impressed by how good Ben is."

"Where *is* your brother?"

"Oh, he's hanging with Becca. They've got their own little book club. Kid's a geek."

Matt's tone hits him hard, takes him back years and years when Miriam would speak so lovingly of Matt. Even when the little monster left painted handprints on the walls. Too many memories. Too many goddamned memories.

He gets up suddenly. Matt flinches. "I'm heading off," he says.

30

"HERE, BEN." ALLIE PASSES THE boy a bag of white chocolate chips.

"Really?" Ben's voice breaks.

Becca snickers.

"Becca," she gently admonishes.

It is nice having a boy around the house to add to the mix of girls and their hormonal swings. She doesn't want to scare Ben off. The boy is here a lot, almost her fourth child these days. He seems to crave her company. She wants to ask him about his mother, but she can't bring herself to do it. It doesn't matter. It is only morbid curiosity. She'll ask Becca sometime. The girl must know. But right now, she enjoys providing that mother's touch for the boy.

It is hot outside, hotter in the kitchen with the oven warming up for a few dozen cookies, a special order for the grade six class. Both she and Becca are wearing shirts tied in knots at their midriffs.

"Is that a belly ring?" Ben stutters out when the sunlight glints off the tiny bit of gold in her stomach.

She swallows back a laugh at the horror that covers his face. She went out of town to get it done. There was no need to invite the gossip which would have accompanied the piercing if she had done it at Marge's Miracle Makeovers. She had wanted to do something sexy for Doug. After all, he had expanded on his lovemaking techniques.

"Mama just got a belly ring," Becca says. "Lyne's had one for a while." Then she stage whispers, "I think Lyne even has a ring somewhere else."

Ben chokes.

"No, she doesn't, Becca! You know that. Stop teasing." She brushes her hand down Ben's arm. The boy leans into her touch.

"What are you all so noisy about?" Glory asks, stops at the table to observe the mess.

"Baking cookies for school tomorrow," Becca says.

"Matt doesn't bake cookies, huh?" Glory asks Ben.

"Matt is cookie-challenged. He always burns them," Ben says. "He's an expert at making Rice Krispie squares in the microwave. And he always bakes my birthday cake. And he makes lunches and suppers."

My God! Allie almost says. She takes the bag of chocolate chips from Ben, tags it, stuffs it into the cupboard, slams the door before the rest of the baking goods falls out. She has seen Jack Humphreys at the gas station, never in his yard. She doubts he knows she is the mother of the two girls his boys spend most of their time with. That man is hot. He sends shivers through her when he looks her way. She notices. She is not dead.

"Your dad doesn't cook?" she asks.

"Dad's not around much. Works lots." The words come out smoothly. Ben keeps his focus on the beaten-down batter. "Hey, Becca, pass a cookie sheet."

Becca puts a blackened sheet between her and Ben. Ben stares at the sheet, stares at Becca. She shrugs and he does, too. Allie smiles. He probably thinks her household is "cookie-challenged," too!

Ben spoons rounded chunks of dough on to the sheet. Becca uses a spatula to flatten the rounds and move them closer to each other. She gets her precision from her father. Allie is certain that it is Matt who influences Ben.

Glory grabs a spoon, scoops raw cookie dough from the bowl.

Ben watches as she savours her mouthful. He blows his bangs out of his eyes. "Matt likes raw cookie dough, too."

Glory flushes, finishes chewing. "Where is he?"

"Studying for his biology final," Ben says. "But he can use a break."

"Yeah?" Glory says.

"Yeah. He's done *studying* studying, he's just reviewing right now."

"He gets good marks?" Glory asks.

"He's smart." Ben stops spooning dough on to the cookie sheet. "Doesn't get to do real good on all his assignments and tests because he has other stuff he has to do, too."

"Other stuff?" Allie keeps her voice soft. Being gentle gets answers from Becca. Maybe it will work with Ben, too.

"It's because Dad's not around much." Ben fidgets with the cookie sheet. "Right now we're mowing a whole bunch of lawns. I help, but still. Matt wants to get more lawns to do in the summer."

It takes a minute to read the boy's tone. It is a combination of pride and guilt, anxiety and relief. She has never heard that quality in her daughters' voices, in any of the voices of their friends. She cups Ben's neck. The boy leans into her touch again, presses her hand firmly between his cheek and shoulder. It is as if he doesn't want to let go, as if he has never experienced mother-love, maybe not even father-love. Maybe only big brother-love. She saw that the first day she watched Matt and him on the front lawn of their townhouse, hears it in the words Glory and Becca speak about the boys.

Her eyes shift to Glory. Her daughter is watching. Becca is, too. Ben is not aware of the attention he has garnered. She wraps her arm around the boy's shoulder. She wants to pull Glory in, too. The girl's face is open, wanting. She feels heartbreak all around her. Ben backs into her, stays that way for a heartbeat then shakes her off. She feels the loss of his small body.

Ben taps his spoon on the counter. "You should go get him, Glory. Matt loves cookie dough."

Glory leads Matt into the kitchen. His hand is warm on her back, brushing just above her waistline, on the strip of skin between her shorts and cropped top. Her skin feels raw where his fingers touch.

"Hey, Mrs. R.," Matt says. He pulls out a wooden chair, twists it around to straddle it. "You look like a regular Rachael Ray, Ben."

"Huh?" The younger boy turns.

"That freshly baked look suits you."

"What are you talking about?"

Glory laughs. "You've got flour all over your face!"

Ben scowls and brushes at his face, streaks the flour farther down his cheek.

Matt laughs hard, rocks his chair back on two legs.

"Becca! Get rid of the flour!" Ben demands.

Becca pinches Ben's chin, wipes a damp towel across his face. "There." She surveys her work. "Good as new."

Glory snags an unbaked cookie from the sheet, waves half in front of Matt. He takes her offering, shoves the dough into his mouth. He pulls out the chair next to him and she sits down. When he nudges his knee against hers, she doesn't move. She wants his touch. Then he reaches over and fingers her ponytail.

"I've always wondered how you manage to keep the elastic in."

She carefully turns to face him, wills herself to keep breathing. "You've *always* wondered?"

"Yeah. The first time I saw you at the playground, when Becca did her Catwoman impersonation, you had your hair like this," Matt says.

"You remember that from the *first* time you met her?" Becca asks.

Glory feels the pull on her ponytail as Matt's attention snaps to Becca. All eyes are on them. And he is still holding her hair. As if the realization hits him, too, he drops her ponytail.

Mom turns to the cookie-makers. "Ready to put a tray in the oven yet?"

Ben nods. His eyes linger on his brother, his face uncertain.

Matt grins wickedly, makes a play for another cookie.

Ben slaps his hand away. "Hey. Stop stealing the cookies. They taste better baked!"

"No way, Benny. Better raw," Matt says.

"Yeah, Benny," Glory chimes in, but her head is not in the little game. She wants Matt to touch her again, to have his hand on her back, his knee against hers. She wants to ask him what it means that he remembers so clearly the first time they met.

"It's Ben!"

"Oh, chill, bro." Matt swipes at his brother's head.

Ben ducks, knocks into Lyne. She steadies him, a hand on each shoulder.

Lyne's sudden appearance puts Glory on edge. She moves her chair closer to Matt, revels in his attention when he pushes his knee stronger against hers.

Lyne steps back, fingers her belly button stud. "So. Matt. I heard Kennedy got a special piercing just for you. A new stud for her new stud?"

Glory feels Matt stiffen. She looks between him and Lyne, their eyes locked on each other. What is this mutual hatred they have?

"What?" Ben says.

"Never mind, Ben," Matt says, voice low.

"Lyne," Mom says. "What's going on?"

"Kennedy and Matt, that's all," Lyne says.

"Tell her she doesn't know what she's talking about," Ben says.

"Leave it alone, Ben," Matt says.

"Glory's golden boy over there has been getting it on with Kennedy Larson," Lyne says. "He's banging her almost every noon hour."

"That's enough!" Mom says.

"Tell her." Ben's voice is tight and full of tears. "Tell her Kennedy means nothing."

"Ben," Matt says.

"He's not *my* golden boy, Lyne." Glory stands, waits for Matt to notice she has moved away. But he is only about Ben. And when the younger boy crosses the kitchen, he stands, rests his hand on Ben's shoulder, steers the boy out.

She waits for Matt to turn around, to say something, anything. To smile, wave two fingers. But he has forgotten all about her.

31

JACK LOOKS AROUND FOR CAL when the RCMP cruiser pulls up to the gas pump.

Rath's Garage is a self-service station, but Rath has made it clear that cops and old ladies and mothers with a carload of kids get their gas pumped. A somewhat odd combination. Cal told Jack that Rath always has them pump for old ladies and crazed mothers, but cops were added to the short list after 9/11. It made no sense. Patriotism is great but 9/11 didn't happen in Canada. Maybe Rath is originally American?

Jack rubs his hands down the front of his jeans. Cal is nowhere in sight. As usual. The little prick spends more time toking up than working. If he weren't Rath's nephew, Cal would be out on his ass so fast he would have tar burn.

"Shit." Making the acquaintance of the local RCMP is not his favourite pastime.

The scrape of the sagging door draws the cop's attention. He remains at the cruiser, arms folded on the roof.

"Fill 'er up?" Jack asks.

"Yes," the cop says. He shifts slightly but Jack still has to crowd him to get to the pump.

"Premium?"

"No, regular's fine." The cop's voice is gruff, but his manner is friendly enough.

Jack flips the switch on the pump, shoves the nozzle in the tank of the car. He jams the lid from the cruiser's gas tank into the hose handle to keep the gas pumping then he picks up the squeegee. He isn't much for small talk, even less when it involves cops. The white cruiser reflects the hot sun and heat comes off the tarred surface in visible waves.

He starts on the passenger side of the windshield. The cop watches baldly. It is unnerving. He cannot remember the last time he was in such an uncomfortable position when it didn't involve another man's wife. Or more accurately, the other man.

"New here," the cops says and it doesn't come out as a question.

Jack knows to answer, though. "Yes, sir," he says, glances up. "Been a month or so."

"Delwood's a nice little town," the cop says.

"Yes, sir, it is." Jack works the edge of the squeegee on a stubborn bug splat.

"Name's Constable McDermott."

A couple of drinks in him and he would say that McDermott's mother must have been high on the pain killers to have named him Constable. But he is unenviably sober. "Constable," he nods. "Jack Humphreys."

The pump clicks off. McDermott moves slowly to the end of the Crown Victoria, removes the cap from the nozzle, squeezes a few more drops into the tank. He is tall, not bulky but solid. Jack pegs him to be about ten years older. He looks like a no-nonsense kind of cop. Jack hustles around the front of the car to finish off the windshield.

McDermott hooks the nozzle back. "Can't believe Rath hasn't replaced these pumps." He runs a hand along the old-fashioned pump, flakes off more of the red paint. "Used to be you could see these things from miles away."

Jack flicks down the second wiper on the windshield. "You grew up in Delwood?"

"No," McDermott says, "a couple towns over. Used to play hockey here, though. This gas station was the meeting point for parents because of the bright red pumps. Well, they were bright red back in the day."

"Makes sense." Jack rocks back on his heels. He has wondered when the garage became a falling-down mess. The paint is stripped on the building and the tin roof is peeling off. "You're supposed to sign, right?"

McDermott nods and follows him to the station.

Sweat courses down his back, pastes on his Rath's Garage shirt. He yanks open the door and the air conditioning slams him like a solid wall of ice. "Christ," he says.

McDermott chuckles. "Surprised you came out to pump my gas."

"Rules of the establishment," he says. From next to the register he pulls out a kid's school notebook marked "RCMP." He leans around McDermott to read the pump, records it on the blue line. He passes the book over and the cop scrawls his name.

"Nice meeting you, Mr. Humphreys." McDermott pauses at the door, maybe bracing himself for the onslaught of heat. "I'm sure I'll be seeing you around."

Jack smiles tightly. Don't count on it.

32

MATT STARTLES WHEN KENNEDY LAYS her head on his chest. He is sweaty and spent and should tell her he has to go. But his muscles don't agree. He's loose-limbed, loose-brained, loose-lipped.

"Where *is* your mom?" he asks as if they are halfway through a conversation.

"Hm?" She snuggles in.

"Your mom. I mean, we almost always do it in her bed. Where is she?" He doesn't look at Kennedy. He's learned that questions about parents are easier answered when nobody is staring, cataloguing facial expressions, trying to figure out what to say to minimize the damage when the answer comes out more shocking than expected.

"Not here," she says.

"No shit," he says. But he takes the hint. "She's got a great collection of rubbers. Those ribbed ones are fucking awesome."

Kennedy stretches across him, pulls the box of Trojans from the still-open night table drawer. "There's only a few left."

"We going to have to buy her some more?"

"No, she's always got plenty of condoms around." Kennedy sounds bitter, tosses the box into the drawer. She lies next to him, not touching.

"She brings guys home, huh?" he says. Kennedy says nothing. "My dad brings women home."

"I've heard about your dad." She is studying him, doesn't subscribe to his don't-look-too-closely philosophy.

"Doesn't take long for my old man to get a reputation," he says.

She fits herself under his arm, draws circles on his chest with her index finger. It is the only nail that is not perfect. She chipped it, eager to get his zipper down. She says quietly, "My dad left when I was five. Just walked out one day. Mom says he left for work and never came back. She took it pretty hard."

Matt grunts. "Imagine she would."

"But he sends child support, you know? No return address, but every month a cheque comes. Keeps us in this house." She pauses in her spiral pattern. "I've never told anybody that."

It is because they are lying here naked. A combination of vulnerability and trust. Nothing to hide behind. That is why her secrets are spilling out. It has always been quick fucks for him, not this. They are too naked.

"It isn't enough to just get money. Does he write you letters, too?" he asks. As fucked up as their lives are, at least Dad is part of it.

"Does your mom?" Kennedy challenges. She starts drawing again, more a scratch than a tickle.

He stays silent, turns his attention to the room. Would his mom decorate with white flowers and sky-blue paint like Kennedy's mom? Would she have a million cushions on the bed? Would her walls be so bare? No family photos, no paintings, nothing that adds that personal touch. This is nothing but a room to fuck in. It is not a room to share secrets in. "Got to go."

"What?"

"Just, just got to go." He has already pushed her off, already has his feet on the plush throw rug, already scanning the room for his boxers. This is too much. He can share his body with her, not his life. Not Mom. He doesn't want this with Kennedy. "Ben said he has an early day today."

Kennedy braces on her elbow.

He feels her judgment. What-the-fuck-ever. She is just a lay. "I don't want to hook up any more."

"What?" This time she sits up, hugs a cushion to her chest. Protection. From him? He sees the confusion in her face and hears something in her voice. Fear. Fear that he doesn't want her. Fear that it is over. Fear that he will tell her secrets.

"I just . . . " Just what? He doesn't want to be with her. He doesn't want to share with the girl he fucks. Jesus. "I don't know. I've got to go."

He finishes dressing, shoves his feet into his Pumas. He pauses in the doorway, listens to the soft rustling of sheets, her stuttering breath. He fingers the ring in his pocket, leaves without looking back.

33

GLORY PUTS DOWN *THE CHRYSANTHEMUMS*, wipes her eyes. How can she be crying over a boy? A boy like Matt. Is she like Elisa? So desperately lonely she thinks the Tinker is so much more than he is? Matt only wants one thing from girls. Kennedy walks around school like she is everything because she and Matt are doing it. Maybe that is why Lyne hates Matt so much. Because he uses girls.

She sits on the warm concrete step, her back against the hot metal screen door. Becca took off with Matt and Ben about half an hour ago. If she knew her place in Matt's life, if she wasn't hoping for more, she would have tagged along, too. The brothers were going to mow one of their yards. Matt has lined up five yards to do on a weekly basis. That Matt works so hard, loves Ben so much, she cannot reconcile with the boy who spends noon hours with Kennedy. How can he be all of these things?

Lyne is off with Rick, and Dad and Mom have gone to a party. When Dad came home unexpectedly, Mom was beyond pleased in a way that she cannot remember seeing before.

If it were cooler in the house, she would take advantage of having the place to herself. But Dad still hasn't talked to the landlord about putting in air conditioning. There is a long list of things he hasn't done. So it is better outside. A faint breeze stirs the air, not enough to raise dust. She opens her book and tries to read. But all she can think about is Matt. His stricken face when Lyne lit into him, not denying anything. And not saying anything to *her* although only moments before he had been touching her, looking at her.

God! How can she be so stupid, so needy? There was a time when the words on the pages filled her with wonder and excitement, when she experienced life through the books she read. But now everything about her is wrapped up in a boy who doesn't even want her. How did she turn into this girl whose life has exploded beyond the pages she reads?

Matt spots Glory the moment he and Ben and Becca turn down their street. She is the main character in a tableau, frozen against the sun, lost in the book that rests in her lap. *This* girl makes him reveal his secrets. She terrifies him. And he can't stop thinking about her.

As they near her, he draws in a deep breath. Mrs. Boychuk asked if he had a girlfriend. There must have been something in his face because she patted him on the arm and said no more.

"Hey," Becca calls out.

Glory looks up, waves the book, her fingers firmly pinched between the pages.

"Why are you outside? The bugs are getting bad," Ben yells.

"Too hot inside," Glory says.

"Hey." Matt sits down next to her. She slides away and his fingers twitch to pull her back. He has missed her, felt her absence keenly. It has forced his decision. He shares an openness with her he has only experienced with Ben and, on very, very good days, with Dad. He cannot imagine staying in Delwood and not being with her.

"Mama and Daddy still out?" Becca asks.

"Yeah, and Lyne took off with Rick just after you left," Glory says.

"Hey, why don't you guys come over for ice cream?" Ben says. "We still have ice cream, right, Matt?"

"Unless you left it on the counter again, dumbass, and it's now vanilla soup." He needs to get the lightness back, the easy feeling the four of them once shared. Before Lyne screwed it up. He turns to Glory. "Going to join us?"

"Come on," Becca says.

Glory sighs. She picks up her book and leads the way to the Humphreys' townhouse.

Matt catches up, snags her book.

"Hey!"

"I kept your page. More Steinbeck?"

"He's a good writer."

"You know there were books written after the sixties, right?"

"Of course I know that!" Glory snaps. "But I have been reading a lot of Steinbeck lately," she says, voice conciliatory. "He talks so much about life. It's hard not to read your life into his words."

He unlocks the door, holds it open for the girls and Ben to go ahead. He stands in the doorway, pretends to read the back cover. He needs to gather his thoughts, buck himself up. He is going to do this. He strides down the hallway. He has hidden the bookmark carefully on a wooden slat under his mattress next to the Dempster's bag of money. He retrieves the slender piece of paper, holds it gingerly between his thumb and forefinger. His stomach heaves, but he strolls easier by the time he reaches the living room. He smiles widely and presses the paper into Glory's hand.

"What's this?"

"Arts and crafts from Humphreys Hobby Shop," he says, surprised he can maintain the lightness in his voice. "You never have a bookmark. You always walk around with your finger on your page. So, I thought, you know, it would be good if one day you can actually use both hands."

Glory says nothing.

His calms slips. Terrified. He is so terrified. He has read this wrong. He has read her wrong.

Becca and Ben press up against her. Becca lifts the paper from her fingers, shows it to Ben.

"Huh. That's cool, Matt," Ben says. Matt has taped school photos of them on a piece of construction paper, printed neatly on top, Glory's Book. "Those pictures are from a couple of schools back."

Glory remains motionless, mute. Becca presses the slender paper into her hand. She slips the bookmark into the pages of *The Chyrsanthemums*.

"Where's your bathroom?" she asks.

"Our townhouse is exactly like yours," Ben says, eyebrows shooting up.

She slaps her book into Ben's stomach. She walks to the bathroom, head high, closes the door softly.

Matt blanks his face, blanks his mind. This is what he does when things get too much with Dad. Ben and Becca trail him into the kitchen. He takes down three bowls and a coffee cup. He grabs the vanilla ice cream from the freezer. He runs the metal spoon under hot water, scoops ice cream into each dish. Ben stands so close to him that their arms brush. He is grateful for the kid's presence, the calm of his touch.

"She really likes the bookmark, Matt," Becca says.

Yeah, what-the-fuck-ever.

"Needed to do something with those extra pictures. Only way I can get rid of Ben's ugly mug."

"It's not my mug that's ugly," Ben says.

How stupid could he be to think she actually liked him? The guy who fucks Kennedy. That's all he is. "Grab a chair, Becca. There's chocolate syrup in the top cupboard."

Ben and Becca take their bowls into the living room. He follows with the coffee cup, Glory's bowl and the chocolate syrup. He sits in the old armchair.

Ben and Becca settle on the sticky vinyl sofa, Becca's feet tucked under his legs. Ben turns on the small TV.

Matt cuts his ice cream with vicious digs of his spoon. Stupid. Stupid. How could he be so fucking stupid? She doesn't want anything from him. She is strong by herself, has always known who she is and she is not someone who needs him. He is a royal fuck-up. She won't want anything to do with him anymore. Not even to be his friend. Fuck!

Then her hand rests on his shoulder. He didn't hear the bathroom door open, didn't see her coming down the hall.

"Thanks for the bookmark," she says. She is smiling.

34

ALLIE STANDS IN THE DOORWAY of the girls' bedroom. It is Sunday morning and the ringing of the bells at the Evangelical Pentecostal Assembly woke her. The bells usually do.

"Hey, Mama," Becca says. "Whatcha up to?"

Ben snickers.

"What?" Becca says.

"'Watcha up to?'"

"What's wrong with that?" Becca sits up straight.

"You shouldn't be on Lyne's bed," Allie says.

They are playing Uno. Ben is still sprawled out on his stomach. Bedrooms aren't good places for boys and girls to be alone. There will come a time when Uno won't be the game they want to play in the bedroom. She has to make sure that doesn't happen.

"It's bigger than Glory's bed," Becca says.

"You should be playing in the living room," she says. Yes, the living room is safer, a good habit to get into.

"Glory said we were too noisy. She kicked us out," Ben says, slightly petulant.

"Maybe Glory should have come in here instead."

"She said *we* had to leave," Becca says.

Allie sighs. "Maybe we should start going back to church." Now where did *that* come from?

Becca turns around fully. "Church?"

Now she remembers why they stopped. She would dress the girls pretty, even curled their hair, put in bright coloured ribbons. What Mother used to do to her and her two sisters. But after years of sitting two or three pews behind Mother, she decided that was enough. She and the girls stopped going to church.

"You went to church?" Ben asks. The boy props himself up on his elbows.

"Yes," Becca says. "I used to sit with Grandma."

That's right. She'd forgotten. Only Becca would sit with her grandmother. The girl was too young to be repelled by Mother's lack of warmth.

"How come we stopped going, Mama?" Becca asks.

Why in the world did she blurt it out? She hasn't thought about going to church for years. "I don't remember. Just go back to playing cards."

"Uno, Mama," Becca says.

"My dad said he'll bring me real cards. Then we can play real card games." Ben says softly, "He'll probably forget."

"We have cards," Allie says brightly. Too brightly.

"Whatever," Becca says. Then she and Ben are sprawled again, flipping cards down as fast as they can. So easy with each other. That will change. Sexual tension does that.

35

JACK SETS THE TOOLBOX DOWN on the kitchen table along with the radio. It's not even a clock radio. But it does have FM. He pinched it from the back of a shelf at Rath's Garage. He plugged it in but of course the damned thing didn't work. In the gloom and the grime of the back room, he was confident he could fix it. But now, in the quiet of the kitchen and the sunlight streaking in through the window, he isn't as sure.

Where the hell are the boys? They are never around. It's ten in the morning, for Chrissake. They should still be in bed. That's what weekends are for. But Matt has probably dragged Benny off somewhere cutting lawns.

Just the thought of Matt's industriousness zaps his energy. He hangs his head, rams his knuckles into the table to support his sudden weight. He was once like that. So much energy to spare. Now, he has to dig deep to find just enough to get through the day. He could use some of Matt's energy. He could use some of his company. But that's not what's going to fill the kitchen right now.

So radio it is.

But first, he needs to fortify himself with coffee. A beer would be good, too. What the hell. A beer is ready now. He pushes himself off the table and takes a Blue from the bottom of the fridge. He'll have to pick up another six-pack today. He unscrews the cap, flips it into the sink and takes a long swallow. Yeah. Beer beats coffee on a hot day.

He pulls out a chair, falls heavily into it. Another swig from the bottle and he's ready to tackle the Sony AM/FM radio. He undoes the back, places the tiny screws carefully next to his bottle. If one rolls on to the floor, it'll be hell to find in the godawful pattern of the yellowed lino.

"Jesus. That's it?" The wires are corroded and one lead has fallen from the contact. Finally something easy to fix.

He dissolves baking soda in a bowl of warm water and returns to the table. Ten minutes of scrubbing with the dish cloth and the wires are gleaming. He uses a tiny Philips-head screwdriver to connect the lead to the battery. He screws the cover back onto the radio. "Let's give this a try." He rubs his hands together, carries the radio to the counter. He unplugs the coffee maker and plugs in the radio. A quick twist of the on button and static fills the air. "Ha!" He beams, wishes Matt were here to see the magic he has worked. He wants his boy to remember a time when his old man was more than . . . the beer sitting on the table. "Christ." He flips the switch to FM and slides the dial. There's a surprising number of FM stations in the Edson area. He stops on a rock station playing Nickelback. He knows this song. He sets the radio on the top of the fridge, the cord stretched to its limit.

36

THE FIRST TIME LYNE PUT makeup on Becca, the girl was eight and wearing Mom's wedding dress. She remembers that day clearly. Becca was so excited because it was real makeup. She catches her little sister's face in the mirror for a second before Becca turns away, pretending to do a find-a-word.

"Get down here and I'll put some of this new sparkling eye shadow on you," Lyne says, surprised at her own harshness.

Becca is surprised, too. She drops her find-a-word book.

"I see you watching me," she says, voice softer now. "Come down. Let's give this a try."

"Really?" Becca crawls to the end of her bunk, hangs over to better see the array of makeup spread across the top of the scarred dresser. Bottles and tubes and jars have been pulled out of the neat rows. "Grandma says Mom used to pretty herself in front of this mirror."

Lyne hears the air quotes Becca uses when she says "pretty herself." Grandma has some odd phrases, odd words. Hell, Grandma is just odd.

"I know. I've heard the stories, too. Like a million times."

Grandma gave them the old dresser and mirror set with matching bench when she turned twelve. The set would be pretty if it were buffed and lacquered. Or handsome, as Grandma called it, blond wood inlaid in the chestnut. The last time she was here she tutted her disapproval at how worn the dresser had become. Lyne felt for Mom, understood why she had wanted to get away from Grandma, from that knowing look, those judging eyes, the obvious distaste.

"Are you coming down or not? I don't have all day." Try to do something nice and what does she get? "Well?"

"How about you make up Glory?" Becca says.

Lyne shifts her gaze from the top bunk to the bottom. Glory is sitting cross-legged, her book resting on her bare calves. She is reading a paperback copy of *The Pearl*. Lyne read that book in English this year. She nudges the mattress. "Well?"

Glory looks up. "What?"

She taps her fingernails on the dresser, recognizes this state her sister is in. Glory and her books. It is all about getting lost in somebody else's story. The girl knows nothing about the life that goes on around her.

"You want me to?" She waves her eyeliner pencil.

Glory sits up as straight as she can without bouncing her head off the bottom of the top bunk. She carefully lays a bookmark on her page. "What?"

"God, Glory! Give you a makeover!"

"Why would I want a makeover? I don't even wear makeup!"

"Well, you are going out tonight," Becca says sing-song.

"Going out?" Lyne looks from Becca to Glory.

"We're going to the movie with the boys," Becca says.

"No big," Glory says. Her eyes drop to her book.

Lyne speaks slowly. "You're going to a movie with Matt?"

"And Becca and Ben," Glory adds quickly. She juts out her chin.

"I think you would look pretty with some makeup," Becca says, hangs over the end of the bed.

"You're going to a movie with Matt. Jesus, Glory!" Lyne shoves Becca back up on the bunk. "What is wrong with you?"

"There's nothing wrong with her," Becca says. She monkeys down, stands next to Glory.

"We're all going," Glory says. "All four of us. The four of us do things together all the time."

Her poor, stupid sister. She *really* doesn't know anything about the real world. She probably sees Matt as her pearl, all shiny and smooth. But he is flawed. He has way too many blemishes.

"He's a good guy," Glory says softly. "I know you don't like him, but you don't know him. He works hard to take care of things when his dad's not around."

"He's banging Kennedy!" she spits out. "Guys like Matt only want one thing."

149

"That's not true. He's a good guy." Glory's voice is tight.

"Jesus." It hits her that Glory is not reading to escape the humdrum of the real world anymore but to escape the confusion she feels about Matt. The real world is overwhelming. But everything is already decided in the pages of a book. Poor, poor Glory. This will not end well.

"Well, are you going to give her a makeover or not?" Becca says.

"Come here, Glory." She gets up from the small bench and looks at her sister. Really looks at her. Glory is pretty, borders on beautiful. She doesn't need makeup. But just the right touches, some effort to her hair, a step up in the clothes she wears, and it would push her over that edge, would put her solidly into beautiful.

She sighs. "I can see why Matt would be attracted to you."

Glory slides in, looks at her through the mirror. "He's not. We're just friends."

"I still think you're making a mistake. He's not a genuine pearl." She chooses a translucent shade of pink lipstick and pulls out the brush.

"You understand how warped that is, right? That Delwood is only showing *The Force Awakens* now?" Matt crosses his ankles on the coffee table, slouches down on the fugly couch.

"Well, you see, Matt, that's what's so good about Delwood Theatre," Becca says.

"Come again?"

"We're a retro theatre! They pay big bucks for this in the city. We get it here for half price!" Becca beams.

"You're so full of shit!" He speaks through a wide smile. "Whatever. Where's Glory? We need to get going."

"We'll be right back," Ben says and trots after Becca.

Matt turns on the TV, flicks through the five meager channels. He couldn't believe his luck that they got TSN. He stops on an Edmonton Eskimos and Winnipeg Blue Bombers game. Maybe watching guys pound the crap out of each other will calm him the fuck down. All day he has thought about going to the movie with Glory. Fuck, he even changed his shirt three times after supper! What is with that? What the fuck is wrong with him?

Then he hears her. He turns off the TV, worries about his shirt. He starts for the bathroom to check himself out in the mirror one last time but his world starts spinning. He drops to the couch, lowers his head between his knees. Fucking breathe! He doesn't know what this feeling is, doesn't know what Glory is doing to him. But she is doing something. He can't deny it. And it feels so damned good. And so, so different. And so fucking scary.

Ben flies through the door. "Come on, Matt. Becca's parents gave us money for popcorn. Let's go."

"Chill, bro." He scrubs a hand down his face.

"You okay?" says Ben.

"What? This body's better than okay. It's fucking hot. You said 'her parents?' The old man's home tonight?"

"Uh huh." Ben scuffs his toe into the carpet. "I think we interrupted something."

"Get a lesson in life, did you?"

"No. Ugh. No. But it was close."

"Okay, Princess Leia, let's haul ass."

Ben shoots him his version of a dirty look then bounds out the door.

He worries about *their* dad coming home tonight. Dad is due and he doesn't want to have to face his old man in whatever mood he will be in.

He slips on his running shoes, makes sure the door is locked, joins Ben on the front stoop. And stops. Just behind Becca is Glory and she looks gorgeous in an orange sundress with spaghetti straps and slightly dipping neckline. Her skin is already bronzed from her study sessions on her front stoop. Her cheeks have a touch of colour that goes beyond the sun. Her hair is twisted in a fancy do.

"Hey, Matt," she says. She speaks softly. So soft.

He swallows. "You're coming with us?"

Her smile drops.

He stares at her perfect pink lips, now puckered with worry.

"Matt!" Ben yells. "Stop ogling and let's go!"

"Jesus! I'm not ogling, dumbass." He moves to slap Ben across the back of his head. The kid ducks and laughs and takes off with Becca.

Glory fists her long flowing skirt.

"C'mon," he says. They fall into step behind Ben and Becca. She smells like lilacs. He itches to hold her hand. He shoves his hands deep into his pockets.

The cinema is a short walk and he fights to find words to add to the conversation. Ben and Becca speak freely and Glory joins in. She can't feel the same way about him. She isn't having trouble talking. But he catches her eye almost everytime he glances at her.

When they arrive at the cinema, she moves forward, pays for her and Becca. He antes up for him and Ben.

"Look, there's seats up front," Ben says.

"No way," he says. "You sit in the front and I'll sit on you. Gotta hit the can. Get drinks and find some place to sit — in the middle." He spots Ben ten dollars and makes a quick escape. In the bathroom, he splashes cold water on his face, looks in the warped mirror. What the fuck is he doing? He has never felt like this before. All twisted up. Fuck. Fuck. Fuck!

When he returns, Ben has plunked himself down almost in the middle of the theatre, almost in the centre of the row. Smart ass. Becca sits next to Ben and they have a tub of popcorn between them. Glory has a drink in her hand, a tub of popcorn in her lap. There arc empty seats on either side of Ben and Glory. He hesitates. The second drink — it must be for him — is in Glory's cupholder. She smiles at him and he slides in next to her, shifts in the red seat, puts a little distance between them. He has only been to movies with girls to sit in the back row and make out. He wants so badly to touch her. This, whatever the fuck it is, is getting out of control. He holds tightly to his Coke, stuffs popcorn in his mouth with his other hand, keeps his eyes on the screen. But then Glory gasps when Han Solo falls to his death and slides into him. He watches the freckles on her face dance in the flash of the dueling lightsabers. He leans into her, puts his arm around the back of her seat, his fingertips brush her bare shoulder. He is sure she shivers. She fits perfectly next to him. He never wants the movie to end.

Matt jumps when someone touches his shoulder. The sparkly tips of Kennedy's fingernails glisten as the credits roll.

He drops his hand behind the seat, brushes her exposed knee. He pulls back quickly. But it is not as if he doesn't know her body. Intimately.

"There's a party at Tony's," she says. "Want to go?" She tries for easy, but the lines at the corners of her mouth give away her stress. He knows her face like he knows her body.

Ben stands. He crosses his arms, leans against the row of seats behind him. He looks at Kennedy then back to Matt.

"Good times." Kennedy licks her lips and what Matt used to think was a come-on he now understands to be nerves.

He takes in Glory. She is rigid in her seat, eyes studying her hands. Her nails are naked.

"No. I don't do parties."

"C'mon, Matt. You know you want to."

"No, Kennedy." He forces a wide smile. "Gotta make sure Ben stays out of trouble tonight. He's got himself a girl."

"Hey," Ben starts and Becca kicks him.

Kennedy glares. She stands up, puts both hands on her hips, says with as much disdain as she can work up, "Your loss."

He studies the floor, listens to the hard click of her heels. Fuck. "Come on. Let's head."

Ben latches on to him while Glory and Becca walk on. The kid says nothing.

He yanks his arm free. "I know, Ben. It just came out."

"Why don't you just tell her it's an at-school-only thing?"

"What?"

"Tell her she's only your noon hour hookup." There is no disgust or judgment in Ben's voice. "I'm not stupid, you know."

"Never said you were. But it's over. No more noon hours."

"I'm not stupid," Ben says slowly.

The brothers lock eyes. Matt drops his head, says, "Let's go."

He hates that the kid thinks he is lying. But there is no reason for Ben to think otherwise. He has always needed girls and sex to escape his fucked-up life, to allow him to breathe. But now. Now he wants something different. Maybe *he* is being stupid. To think that he can go for something different, something pure.

It is still bright outside, still warm. Glory hikes the skirt up on her dress so it rides just above her knees, swishes it from side to side. The light breeze is welcome in the stillness of the evening. Kennedy's invitation hangs like a shroud over their walk home. He doesn't want to tell Glory it is over with Kennedy. He doesn't want to bring those distinct parts of himself together. Not with her. Not in front of her. He hates that they have collided so often. But who is he kidding? It isn't as if she doesn't know about Kennedy. All he would have to say are three words: It is over. Just three words. But what if she doesn't believe him? What if she looks at him the same way Ben did? So he walks in silence, a step behind her.

"Want to come in and watch music videos?" Ben asks when they arrive home. "MTV is actually coming through okay on our crap TV."

Matt scans the curb, scans down the street. Dad's BMW is nowhere in sight.

"I should go home first, let Mom and Dad know we're back," Glory says. She looks at him then looks away. "Why don't you head on in? I'll be right there."

He unlocks the door, lets Ben and Becca slip by. He stays on the stoop, watches Glory walk to the blue door. The sun, low in the sky, gently bathes her. Her body is trim with soft curves. Sometime before he joined her outside the cinema, she must have rearranged her hair, pulled it back into the loose ponytail with the low elastic. She is perfect and he wants to be with her. He is scared shitless that it is all slipping away.

She leans against the closed door, pushes down tears. She doesn't understand what is happening. She lives for these moments with Matt. But what are these moments? What do they add up to? Are they a whole? Or are they simply bits and pieces that will never come together?

"Oh!" She grinds the heels of her hands into her eyes.

What is this thing with Matt and Kennedy? She cannot give him what Kennedy gives him. She can't be that girl. Lyne is right even though she didn't say it. She didn't have to. Lyne's face clearly said that she was stupid for thinking she could have something real and good and wonderful with Matt. But Lyne doesn't know Matt the way she does. He is smart and brave and loving and, and beautiful. But he is with Kennedy. But not tonight. Not tonight. He turned Kennedy down to be with her. He turned Kennedy down twice.

When he brushed his fingers across her bare shoulder then rested his hand there so softly, she thought she would melt under his touch. She wished the movie would never end.

She toes off her sandals, listens for her mother and father and their nighttime activity. It is quiet. Maybe they have fallen asleep. If they have, she will leave a note on the table, let them know she and Becca are at the Humphreys'. She takes a deep breath and smiles. At Matt's.

She flicks the light on in the living room and startles.

Dad is sitting on the couch, dressed in boxers and a wifebeater, nursing a beer. "How was the movie?"

"It was good." She shifts her weight, leans against the wall.

"Come over here," Dad says kindly.

She sinks down on the couch, tucks one foot under her flowing skirt. "What's up?"

"I heard you and Becca and the boys across the way." He takes a drink of Kokanee, runs his fingers up and down the sweating bottle. "Listen, Glory, I'm not very good at these things, but . . . "

"What?" She shifts on the couch, moves away from him. Her stomach tightens and her throat is dry. She imagines pulling the bottle from his hand, downing all of what is left. Panic gurgles inside her, comes out in a harsh bark.

"What are you doing with this boy?"

"What do you mean?"

"You're too good for him, Glory."

"What do you mean?"

"He's a boy who gets around. He only wants one thing."

"How can you say that?" She focuses on the beer bottle, thinks about the cool amber liquid. Bitter. Is that what Matt is? Cool but he'll leave her bitter? She pushes farther away when Dad reaches out. "You don't know him."

"What about the Larson girl?"

Kennedy. She wants to yell, I don't know. I don't know.

"All I'm saying, Glory, is Matt is the kind of boy who only wants one thing. That's what he's getting with Kennedy. That's what he's going to want from you."

"You don't know him. You know nothing about him." She burrows into the corner of the couch, whispers, "I don't know what to do."

Summer Holidays

37

MATT STANDS ON THE STOOP outside the Rutgers' door. Blue. No girls in the window.

How did it get to this point? There are four people in there who have a hate-on for him. Well, maybe three. Mrs. R. probably *dislikes* him. Becca is the only person for sure who doesn't hate him. He hasn't knocked. He can still escape home, forget about his plan. It seemed like a good idea ten minutes ago when he was lying in bed. But now, he is not so sure. And anyway it doesn't sound as if anybody is up. No way Mrs. R. will say yes if he wakes the entire household.

"Fuck!" He runs his fingers through his hair. It is a Dad-gesture that he is doing more and more these days. Which is all fucked up because Dad is home less and less.

"Why are you here?"

"Jesus!" He almost pitches down the steps.

"Why are you here?" Lyne's voice is a fierce whisper. "Come down now."

Matt hesitates before doing what she says. "Where did you come from?"

"Coming home." She smells of campfire and beer. She has on Jeffries' T-shirt. It hangs low, covers either the shorts or skirt she is wearing.

He looks around as he follows her a few paces from the house. He didn't hear the Camaro. "Where's Jeffries?"

"It's late. He dropped me off down the street so Mom and Dad wouldn't hear his car."

Lyne's makeup is smudged, her eyes a little red and . . . are those bruises just above her elbows? They could be fingers that tightly gripped her, wouldn't let her go. He has seen Dad-sized fingerprints on Ben's arms. Jesus.

"It's uh, it's early," he says.

"What?"

"You said it was late. But it's early. It's like 8:30." He fights to keep his eyes from returning to the bruises.

"What are you? My Hello Kitty alarm clock?"

He hunches his shoulders. "What-the-fuck-ever."

"Wild grad party," she laughs bitterly. She sinks down on the bottom step. "What are you doing here?"

There is no challenge in the question this time. He sits down next to her. "I wanted to ask your mom a favour."

Lyne keeps her gaze on her hands, loosely linked, hanging between her knees. He pictures a cigarette dangling from her fingers.

"I wanted to see if Ben could hang out this morning. I have some running around to do."

"Ben is always here. It's no big."

161

He speaks to his feet. "I usually do a little something for him at the beginning of the holidays. After he wins an award. And I need to do some shopping."

"Becca said he won an academic award. How? You've only been here like a month and a half."

"Kid's scary smart." He feels Lyne's eyes digging in. "I collect his work from the schools we go to in a year so they can figure out his real marks. Kid works fucking hard. He shouldn't be screwed over because Dad moves all the time."

"How many schools this year?"

"Delwood's our third," he says. "And this was a good year."

"Huh."

He waits for the usual that-must-suck comment.

Lyne wraps her arms around her body, rests her hands below the darkening fingerprints. "My sister is worth a Harlequin romance. She *deserves* a Harlequin romance."

Matt tugs at the loose threads of his cut-offs. He looks at Lyne, nods.

"Don't you prove to her that life isn't a Harlequin romance," she says. "You fuck with her and I will crush your balls."

He squirms but he squares his shoulders and replies in the same serious tone. "I like your sister."

"You fuck with my sister and I will crush your balls, do you understand me?" Her voice is harsh now and he can't help but look at the deep red bruises on her arms.

"I understand you," he says.

She rests her elbows on her knees, her chin in her hands, looks down the street. "This doesn't mean I like you. I like my sister. This is a truce."

He fights to hold in the questions that want to tumble out. "I can deal with that."

Lyne stands stiffly. "I'll let Mom know. Bring Ben by in an hour."

"Okay." He stands up, takes a step away then stops. "Lyne . . ."

"That's it."

She sounds stretched tight and he doesn't push. He waits for her to disappear into the townhouse before he heads back to his. A rap on the window stops him. He turns around and there is Glory. Her long white pajama shirt is cluttered with pink rosebuds. She offers him a half smile, half wave. He wonders how much she heard. All the windows are open.

They haven't spoken since after the movie. Since he turned Kennedy down. Since she collected Becca from the Humphreys' townhouse and didn't say a word to him.

He smiles broadly and relief washes through him.

Glory spies on Matt from behind the canned tomatoes in Delwood Grocers. He is shifting his attention between the pack of hamburger buns in his hand and the whole-wheat buns on the shelf. The store's two large picture windows are newly cleaned. The sun shines in brightly. Matt's face is creased in concentration, his eyes dark.

Stalker isn't doing it for her, so she clutches her shopping basket, sneaks up behind him. She touches his elbow and he bobbles the hamburger buns.

Up close, the sun on his face softens his worry lines. He smiles. "What are you doing here?"

"Picking up a few things for Mom."

"Well, I'm getting my Gordon Ramsay on," he says.

"What?"

"I'm planning a surprise barbecue for Ben. Congratulate him for his award. Kid worked his ass off."

"That's really sweet." She keeps her eyes on the hamburger buns. "Was that what you were talking to Lyne about this morning?"

"Yeah, sort of."

"You and Lyne were talking about Harlequin romances."

"Yeah, because that's what she and Jeffries have," Matt says tightly.

The air around him has gone heavy, the ease sucked out. She has said the wrong thing. "What can I do to help?"

"Do you know how to make hamburger patties? It's cheaper than buying the ready-made stuff." Matt lets loose a short nervous bark. The handful of shoppers in the store glance their way.

She can pretend nothing is happening, too. "Mom will have a recipe. I mean, it can't be that hard, right? All you're doing is slapping together meat and eggs and breadcrumbs."

"So you'll help?" His tone is a combination of hopeful and teasing — and relief.

"It's not rocket science or anything. Just, you know, disgusting." She snorts, covers her face. "I can't believe I keep doing that around you."

"It's kinda hot," he says.

She turns away. She feels like a yo-yo. Up and down and around and twisted. Everything about him twists her up. She doesn't know what to do about him. Dad is wrong. Matt is good. And he makes her feel good. He won't break her heart. He won't.

"Fuck," he mutters. He moves away, hamburger buns clasped in his hand.

She follows, still firmly attached to his middle finger, still firmly yanked along behind him. Up and down and around and twisted. So twisted. She puts what she needs into her wire basket. Matt awkwardly juggles buns and hamburger meat and eggs.

"Do you maybe want to put your eggs in here?" she asks.

He avoids her eyes, places the eggs in the basket.

She desperately wants to rewind. Go back to how it was before. To when he turned Kennedy down and before Dad condemned him. She had felt chosen.

Matt stops in front of the vegetable bins, picks through the tomatoes. He plucks one from the bottom row, starts an avalanche.

"Fuck!" He grabs tomatoes and she joins in. They manage to keep most of them from hitting the scarred wooden floor. She looks at the tomatoes in her hands, in Matt's hands, the few on the floor and snorts again. This time she doesn't turn away.

They leave the store with Matt carrying two bags and Glory one. Their arms brush and they do not move apart.

Allie stands at the front window, wipes her hands on a too-damp dish towel, watches as Doug and Matt maneuver the Humphreys' kitchen table out the door. If she had known he was going to need a table, she would have offered theirs. But the boy has probably hit his quota on asking for favours.

He seems like a self-reliant young man. Born of necessity or pride, she is not sure.

There is nothing easy about the smile on his face. She suspected he felt awkward around Doug. Now she knows. Ben is the same way. The younger boy is rarely here when Doug is home.

"You know, we could've used our table. Not so far to move," Doug says, stumbles over a hose thrown in the yard between the two houses.

His rough voice carries through the open windows. They were up late last night, drinking beer, watching TV. It surprised her that he didn't seem too put out this morning about the celebration for Ben. Maybe he wants to get to know the boys better. Lord, all Becca does is talk about Ben. And all Glory does is never talk about Matt.

Matt easily sidesteps the hose. "Next time."

"You plan on making it a habit to use our barbecue?" Doug almost yanks the table from the boy's grip.

"Uh, no." Matt lurches forward. "No. I didn't mean it that way. I . . . No."

"Take it easy, Matt. I was joking." Doug smiles.

That smile is all too familiar. It is his don't-fuck-with-me smile. The smile he always uses on Rick. That may be why the boy has started honking, waiting out in the car for Lyne. She twists the dish towel, wonders what she has missed. Did Doug have words with Matt in the house? Did he catch Matt and Glory *doing something*? Lord, she hopes not. It is enough that she has to worry about Lyne with Rick. But Glory. That girl doesn't know enough. She would think Matt's smile, his charm were all for real, actually meant something.

She slaps the towel onto the couch, slips her feet into Lyne's Flojos, hustles out the door. "Hey. How's it going?"

Matt looks up, relief plain on his face. "Mrs. R."

Doug turns, tips his chin at her. "Where should we put this?"

She raises an eyebrow and he shakes his head slightly. "Put it behind the house so Ben won't see it when he comes back with Becca."

"Hey, Mom," Glory yells from the Humphreys' doorway, bowls stuck in the crook of each arm. "We have a tablecloth we can use?"

"We do," she says.

Matt kinks his neck to look back at the girl and Doug gives the table a tug. That sudden head movement did not go unnoticed.

She leads them to the backyard. "Put it here."

Matt drops his end of the table and trots back to help Glory with her load.

"What's going on?" she asks, voice low. When Doug doesn't answer, she backhands him across his arm.

"Ow! What?"

"You're giving that boy your death glare. What's going on?" She twists two fingers into the empty belt loop on his jeans, pulls him into the house. "What happened?"

He goes to the fridge, pulls out two bottles of Kokanee. He screws the top off of one, passes it to her. He opens his own and drains half in one long pull.

"Did something happen in the house?"

"In the house?" He stares at her.

"Good Lord, Doug! Did Matt do something to Glory at his house!" She slams her bottle on the table.

"Do something to Glory?" Doug speaks slowly. "Jesus! No."

"Then what's wrong? You practically cut off his balls with that look."

"Huh." He smiles so briefly she isn't sure she caught the upturn of his lips. "Is there something going on between them?"

She pulls out a chair, slides into it. She claims her beer from the table. "I don't know. I expect so."

He collapses into the chair across from her. "She's too good for him, Allie."

It has been a long time since they have spoken about the girls, an even longer time since they have parented together. Matt's laugh engulfing Glory's giggle stirs her from her thoughts.

"I know," she says. "But what are we going to do about it?"

38

JACK STOPS SHORT WHEN HE sees Matt in the neighbour's yard. The boy has his shirt off, sweat glistening on developed muscles. The gold ring hangs from his neck, the small diamonds reflecting the sun. He hates that goddamned ring. Every time he sees it, he wants to rip it off.

Matt is pushing a lawn mower, neither focused on what he is doing nor aware of his surroundings. He could easily slip away without Matt seeing him. But there is a tug in his gut that he learned long ago meant need. It is usually the need for a drink or for a woman. But right now it is the need to be with his boy. It is so much easier with Matt when they are alone. Maybe that was what Miriam was thinking when she said they only needed one child. Her pregnancy had not been easy.

He waits until Matt is pushing the mower in his direction then he waves. The shock on the boy's face is quickly replaced by unbridled joy. It is an openness he has not seen in a very long time. Then the shutters fall into place. And he struggles to breathe. Christ, that hurts. But what else can he expect? He hasn't been father of the year for a long, long time.

Matt turns off the lawn mower, but doesn't close the distance. "Dad."

"Matt."

"Hey." Matt stares at the neighbouring house. "So, uh, how've you been?"

Jack slams his fists in his pockets, fights the desire to follow Matt's gaze. But, hell, *he* knows where he was. He motions to the end of the two yards. There is a three-foot high wooden picket fence separating them. Matt hesitates before pulling his T-shirt from the handle of the lawn mower, swipes his face and chest then slips it on. They meet in the back alley.

"Fine," he says. "You?"

"Good. Whose place is that?"

He sighs. "You don't need to know that."

"How hard do you think it'll be for me to figure it out?"

Christ. He runs his fingers through his hair. "Rathenburgs'."

Matt nods. "You're still there?"

"At the garage? Yeah."

Matt taps his fingers on his thighs. When the silence stretches, he says, "Didn't see your car up front."

169

"It's in the garage." He nods toward the building in the neighbour's backyard.

"You coming home?"

"No, I got to get going here. Due back at the station in about half an hour."

Matt looks at his watch.

Jack waits for — dreads — a smart-ass comment about an afternoon quickie. "How're you set for money?"

"I'll take some if you can spare it."

He works his wallet out of his hip pocket. "I'm getting paid today, so here." He turns over a few bills.

"Thanks." Matt doesn't count the money, tucks it into the front pocket of his cut-offs.

"So, this is one of your yards, huh?" Christ. When did it become so hard to talk to his boy?

"Yeah. This hot, dry weather isn't helping any. We have about a dozen yards but not working much because there's been no rain."

"I guess."

"By the way, Ben's up front, you know, now that you've asked. He's weed-eating." Matt's anger is sudden. But it is gone as quickly and the boy studies the gravel beneath his feet.

Jack reaches out, hesitates a moment before lowering his cool hand to the back of his son's damp neck, squeezes. The tension eases out of the boy's shoulders. "You okay, Matty?"

The boy nods once.

He releases his hold. "Got to get going or I'm going to be late, son."

"I suppose," Matt says, but doesn't move.

The boy sounds strung out, faded. But he can't stay. He has to work. He turns away, feels Matt's eyes on his back. Maybe tonight, after his shift, he will sleep at home. Get up early, make the boys breakfast. Miriam once said that "maybe" was the ugliest word in the English language.

39

ALLIE STEPS INTO THE GIRLS' room. The only time they are all quiet is when they are sleeping. Her eyes travel to the window without the screen. She has been on Doug's back to talk to the landlord about fixing that. The window is small, but she is certain Lyne uses it for quick exits and entrances. Hell, that is what she did back in the day. Most of the time to hook up with Doug. Or to make him jealous.

She is wearing one of his T-shirts. After all these years, she should be used to him not being in bed with her every night, but she misses him. His shirt smells of Musk and Irish Spring soap. His single claim to manhood in the bathroom.

Lyne moves restlessly in her sleep, moans. But her eyes remain closed. She doesn't wonder what her eldest daughter dreams about. She was that way at this age, same needs, same desires, same drive.

She scans the rest of the room. It is a tight fit for three girls. They have talked about getting a larger place, but they can't afford to move on Doug's salary.

The pink pink walls need repainting. It is hard to believe the girls chose this colour. None of her girls are girly that way. Lyne is all girl, but never frilly. When Doug gets around to repainting the walls they won't be pink any longer. She has no idea what colour the girls will agree on. There will be bloodshed though, that is certain. Hm. Maybe this shade of pink isn't so bad.

Becca shifts in her bed. Allie crosses the room quickly, makes sure her youngest doesn't roll off. Becca made a fuss last year about the guardrail and Doug, like he always does, gave in to her, removed it. Becca ended up on the floor once.

She stretches up on her toes, covers Becca's forehead with her hand to settle her down.

"Mom," Lyne whispers.

"Hey, baby." She tiptoes back to Lyne's bed. She brushes her fingers through the girl's hair. A drowsy Lyne is so much easier to show love to. "What's wrong?"

"Not feeling so good. My stomach hurts and so does my back."

Allie pulls down the bright yellow sheet, pulls up Lyne's night shirt, rubs the girl's flat belly. "Oh God. You're not pregnant, are you?"

"Mom." Lyne says sharp. "I'd have to have sex for that to happen."

"You and Rick don't have sex?" She has prayed for that. She doesn't pray often.

"No," Lyne says. But the earlier strength in which she spoke is no longer there.

Allie's eyes flit to the purpling bruises on Lyne's arms. She hasn't asked about them. "You need to be careful. Make sure you don't wind him up too much." She remembers pushing and pulling at Doug, fighting and making up. She is certain it is some of that makeup sex that led to Lyne. Yes, it was a hell of a fight and now she can't even remember what it was about. Does Doug remember? What she does remember is getting wasted and being desperate for him to forgive her, letting him fuck her right there with his friends egging him on. What will Lyne do to keep Rick? Because Rick is Lyne's way out. But she needs to play it right. Trapping him won't get her a ring. Probably not even child support.

"He knows what I'll let him do. He knows."

"Still. Knowing and then the heat of the moment, well, those are two different things."

"Jesus, Mom, I'm not you!"

"You keep saying that, Lyne, but I don't see a whole lot of difference." She retreats to the edge of the bed. "All I'm saying is that if there's a chance of you and Rick having sex, you need to let me know. We'll go to Edson, see a doctor there, get you on the pill."

"He knows what I want and he knows I don't want that," Lyne says harshly.

Allie always regretted not being able to talk to her mother about sex. She doesn't want to push Lyne away now when talking is more important than ever. She accepts that Glory would sooner turn to a book than confide in her and there are no sexual thoughts in Becca's head whatsoever. But Lyne. She is at a crossroads.

"All I'm saying is that if you think it will go that way, let me know. We'll put you on the pill." She settles her hand gently on Lyne's forehead. When the girl doesn't pull away, she runs the back of her fingers down Lyne's cheek. "All I'm saying is that I don't want you to end up here."

"I know that, Mom. I know that." Lyne rolls away.

173

Glory hears Lyne's shallow breathing. She pushes up on her elbow, whispers, "Are you okay?"

"I'm good," Lyne says into her pillow.

"She doesn't mean that, you know?"

"Mean what?"

"That we were a mistake."

"She never says you and Becca were a mistake. She always says I was a mistake."

"Mom loves you, Lyne." She has never seen Mom look at Lyne with regret. "You and Mom only fight because you are so much alike."

"I know." Lyne turns toward her. "But she wishes she never got pregnant with me. Face it. She never would have married Dad if she hadn't been pregnant."

"You don't know that!"

"Oh no? You see how different her life is from Auntie Marcie's or Auntie Tracy's? It's only because of Dad."

"You don't know that."

"Grandpa would have paid for Dad to become a plumber," Lyne says. "But Dad turned him down. If Dad was a plumber, do you think we'd be living here? Do you think we'd be trailer trash?"

"We're not trailer trash," Glory says fiercely.

"What are we then?"

"We live here, but this isn't us."

"What's the difference?"

"We're more than this," she says. "We're more than what's in our house, what's in our shed. We're more than Delwood."

"Is that what Matt tells you?" Lyne asks.

"Matt has nothing to do with this."

"He's no better than us, Glory."

"He never said he was." She takes a deep breath. "It's Rick, you know? *He's* no better than us."

"He's got money and he buys me things," Lyne says.

"That's not what it's supposed to be about. That's not love."

She has been thinking about love — Matt? No, not Matt! — thinking about what Steinbeck had to say about love. She googled him on the computer in the school library, found a letter he had written to his son. Steinbeck told the boy that love could not be hurried. If it was right, it would happen.

"If Rick has to buy you all these things then it isn't right. He should be able to show you he cares without having to spend money."

"We live in the real world, and you need money in the real world," Lyne says.

"It shouldn't be that way," Glory says. "It shouldn't be like that."

The early morning light is stark.

40

MATT KEEPS HIS BACK TURNED. Ben stands in the hallway, rubbing his bare feet against the low pile carpet. Little shit. He asked the kid to do one thing. One fucking thing. But, oh no, the great and mighty Ben couldn't be bothered to even do that much. Fine. He will continue to ignore the little shit.

"C'mon, Matt. I'm sorry, okay?"

There is a distinct lack of whine in the kid's voice. He knows he has screwed up big time. In a moment or two he will be offering to help. Well, too fucking late for that.

Ben continues to scrape his feet. The noise is grating. "What can I do?"

Grow up? Help out once in a while? Suck it up and know this is their fucking life?

"Nothing." Matt wipes the sweat from his face on the shoulder of his shirt. He continues to scrub the tub. Anger does a hell of a job on old chipped enamel.

"Matt." Ben takes a step forward.

"Go 'way."

"No. I'm not going away."

He knows the kid has his feet planted, arms crossed at chest level: Ben's warrior stance.

"Fine. Stand there then. I don't give a fuck. Enjoy the show."

"You *asked* for my help!"

"Yeah, and I'm pretty sure you said, 'No.'" He stops scrubbing, looks over his shoulder. "Or was that my other brother? Oh, no, wait. I only have one brother. So I guess that means you, Ben. You said, 'No.'"

Ben drops his arms, takes one more step into the small bathroom. "Can't I change my mind?"

"You a girl, Benny?"

"No!" Ben shrills.

"Only girls change their minds. You sure you're not a girl, Benny?" He sits on the edge of the tub. His knees are killing him from pushing down so hard. "Am I going to have to buy you a bra?"

"Not a girl," Ben says.

"Then stop acting like one!" He slaps his open palm against the side of the tub.

Ben jumps back.

Matt will blame his pissy attitude on the five-minute run-in with Dad yesterday. It was unexpected, caught him off-guard, caught him hoping when Dad's voice was gentle that he would come home. But it never works that way. And, Jesus fucking Christ, he just finished grade ten, how fucking stupid can he be to still believe things can be different? All that happens is he comes home and feels like shit.

He straightens out, goes to run his hand through his hair, stops before he gives himself a Scrub Free treatment. He takes the small step to the sink, runs the water cold, shoves his hands into the stream. When his fingers feel as if they will fall off, he adds hot water, generously lathers up with the bar of Ivory, rinses. He runs his hands wet over his face, through his hair. He closes his eyes so he doesn't have to see his reflection, doesn't have to see his brother either.

"I wanted you to do one thing, Ben. One thing. That's all."

"I'm sorry, Matt." Ben sounds as if he is six years old.

"One fucking thing." He feels as if he is sixty. He holds tightly to the sink.

"I'll do it now, Matt. I'll take the garbage out now."

"Sure, you do that."

Ben hovers, shifts from foot to foot. He waits for the kid to say more. When Ben leaves, he sinks down on the ledge of the tub again. It doesn't matter how much scrubbing he does the enamel will never shine, the grout between the tiles will remain mouldy, and the sink will still be rusted. He hates being a have-not. Just because they live on this side of town, does that mean he can't want more for Ben and him?

41

IT IS EXPENSIVE. SHE DOESN'T have to be a jeweller to know that. The pendant is solid gold and the five little stones outlining one side of the heart are diamonds.

"Lean forward," Rick says. She does, sweeps her hair up with one hand. He struggles with the clasp. "There. Show me."

She turns around to face him.

"Looks good." He reaches to touch the pendant that hangs in the valley of her breasts, but draws back. His voice is rough when he asks, "Do you like it?"

"It's beautiful." She rubs her thumb over the row of small diamonds, but doesn't close the space between them.

"Lyne," he pleads.

"What?" she snaps. Mom once told her that Dad beat the crap out of his own father for pounding on Grandma one too many times. And then he kicked Grandpa out of the house. But Grandma took him back. Did she get a fancy necklace? Not that Grandpa could afford diamonds and gold. It must have been the poor man's version of the makeup gift.

She has spent the entire week ignoring Rick's phone calls. He came to the house and she refused to answer the door. Mom has been looking at her strangely. And Glory seems to know something. But Glory can't know. If anyone knows, it is Mom. But Mom hasn't told her to dump Rick. And that has to mean something.

Because here he is with this expensive gift, still wanting her.

"Look, I'm sorry about what happened grad night, okay?" His eyes are focused on the pendant, his voice hard-done-by. "Things just got carried away, okay?"

"No, it's not okay." But, God, he bought her diamonds! She is dying to see the pendant in the visor mirror, to see how it looks on her. The girls at the next party will be talking about it. "I told you no."

"You did, babe, but you looked so fucking hot in that short skirt and tight little top. You turned me on and I'd been drinking and I couldn't hold back." He rests his fingers on her bare thigh, leans in. His voice is husky. "C'mon. Can you blame me? You were the hottest chick there. Fucking hot."

"I told you no, Rick." She is sick with herself that she wants to pull him in, to feel him against her, to have his tongue follow the path of the chain and the pendant. She wants him. But he held her down, tried to force her to do it. He was so drunk. And she was so scared. She kneed him in the balls and he rolled off. And now, now this exquisite necklace! This is how much she means to him?

"I know you did," he says, backs away. "And I promise I'll never do that again."

"You damn well better not," she says. But she cannot hold on to the anger. The longing in his grey eyes convinces her.

"I've been missing you so much, babe," he says.

She leans in, kisses him. She is hungry for him. He breaks off the kiss and his tongue starts to follow the chain of the pendant.

42

IF BECCA DUNKS THAT FRY in the blob of ketchup one more time, she is going to get it shoved up her nose. Luckily for Becca, she doesn't.

"What is your problem?" Becca asks after chomping down her fry. She picks up another and begins her ketchup-dipping ritual again.

If Ruby's weren't half full and if Kennedy weren't seated two booths down, she would walk out. When did Becca become so annoying?

"And I'm not annoying." Becca paints ketchup around her plate. "You're just tense."

Glory's mouth drops. Did she say that out loud? No way. No way did she say that out loud, which means she must be telegraphing her annoyance. Becca is right. She is tense. But why wouldn't she be? There is Matt's squeeze. Ex. Maybe.

If she had any kind of aim, she would load a fry with ketchup, throw it, and hit Kennedy right between her professionally plucked eyebrows.

She shifts her gaze back to Becca, shrugs. "You are a little annoying."

Becca harrumphs, pushes her almost empty plate across the table. Glory helps herself to a fry, keeps it far away from the ketchup. She likes gravy.

"Well, what is it?" Becca asks. She is a pitbull. Once she has something on her mind, she keeps at it. If Glory doesn't answer now, she will answer in half an hour, because Becca won't let it go. It will be ripped, shredded, bloodied, but Becca will have her answer.

She closes her eyes, stalls for time, gets lost in the cacophony of sounds, the smorgasbord of smells. They don't come to Ruby's often. It is the hangout for kids on the other side of town. But Dad slipped her a ten today, and she had the urge to come here. Becca wanted to invite Ben and Matt, but the boys couldn't make it. They needed to cut some old lady's lawn, Becca said. But Glory still flashed on Matt with Kennedy. Which was foolish, because where would Ben be? And Ben wouldn't lie.

And here is Kennedy at Ruby's, too. Looking cool and pretty. And probably thinking about Matt. Probably thinking about the last time she had sex with Matt.

Glory huffs. How stupid could she be to picture herself here, Matt sitting next to her?

"What?" Becca asks, her voice urgent.

"Kennedy is over there," she says. Becca twists around. "Don't look!"

"Oops!" Becca turns back quickly. She shoves down the bench, presses her back against the window, inches over slightly to see Kennedy.

Glory pushes into the corner of the booth, too.

"I bet Kennedy comes here a lot," Becca says.

"I guess."

"What's the big deal anyway?" Becca asks. "He didn't go with her after the movie. He came with us."

Glory flinches, feels naked. Becca can read her so easily. But does Becca know that she doesn't want to be an "us?" At least not an "us" that includes Becca and Ben. The few french fries she helped herself to sit heavy in her stomach. She is jealous. There sits the girl Matt does it with, and she is jealous.

"He likes spending time with you, Glory," Becca says.

"And he likes spending time with Kennedy, too."

"Oh." Becca squirms in her seat and her cheeks turn red. "Is that what you want?"

"No!" No, that is not what she wants — but to hold hands and to have him kiss her? She would die for that. "I don't understand why he was with her so much." Except Kennedy is pretty and older and rich.

"Lyne says it's what all guys want. And he's a guy, Glory, and Lyne says Kennedy does it with any guy, so why wouldn't Matt do it with her?" Becca pulls in the plate, starts dipping a cold fry in ketchup. "That's what Lyne says."

"When did Lyne say that?"

"All the time. She says guys only want one thing." Becca drops her fry, pushes the plate away again.

"I don't think that's true," she says.

"You think Matt's in love with Kennedy?" Becca whispers.

"No! Not that. I think it is all about, you know, sex with them. I think Lyne's right. Sort of. Guys will take it if it's offered. But I don't think it has to be all about that with every girl. I think a guy can like a girl and it's not about, you know." Now she whispers, "I don't want him to be with her."

And as if cued, Kennedy is right there. But even with her entourage of three, she looks uneasy. She is being protected, not leading a small army.

"Glory."

"Kennedy."

Kennedy plays with the strap of her Swatch. "I don't usually see you here," she says.

"We don't come much."

Kennedy eyes the nearly empty plate. "They have good fries here. Good onion rings, too."

"Yeah, yeah they do." Glory congratulates herself for not visibly shaking like the small earthquake she has become. Why is Kennedy speaking to her? The other girl always ignored her at school.

Kennedy licks her Dragon Red lips. "Did you like *The Force Awakens*?"

"It was good."

"Yeah, the sequel should be good, too," Kennedy says.

Becca slides to the end of the booth. "We should get going, Glory. Ben said they'd be home by three and it's just about three."

Kennedy looks sharply at Becca. She steps back from the table. Her eyes narrow and Glory can read her. She is putting it together. She knows that Ben is never far from Matt. Her smile falters and then it disappears.

Glory wants to gloat. But Kennedy looks devastated and even if Matt only wants one thing from her — and please, God, let it be only about that — Kennedy cares about Matt. Maybe she has even fallen in love with him. But that doesn't matter. It means nothing. Because she will be with Matt this afternoon. Kennedy is history. Isn't she?

43

JACK WAS HOPING ONLY FOR Matt, but Benny tags along. Of course. Me and my shadow.

"So, you got my message." He wipes his hands on a grease-stained cloth. He is in the back of Rath's Garage. His shift has finished but the BMW is in desperate need of some TLC.

"You've been busy, huh," Matt says.

There is a Rav 4 and a Focus already on the elevated track. The Beemer is only jacked up. The bay door is open. The sunlight shows the grimy walls, the gritty floor.

"Has been a busy few days." He leans on the back passenger door of his car, motions to the wall behind the boys. "Pull on one of those overalls. Might as well keep your clothes clean. Oil's a bitch to get out. Benny, go to the cooler in the front and grab us some drinks."

Matt nods at Benny, who takes off for the front of the garage.

Do the boys not think he sees their silent language? That every time he tells Benny to do something, that Benny seeks permission from Matt? Each little interaction has him alternately grieving and pissed off. Today, it is too hot to accept it for anything other than it is: his fuck up.

Matt pulls on blue coveralls, fights with the inside-out sleeve. "I thought it was time Ben learned a thing or two about keeping a car running. Wouldn't hurt."

"Nope, wouldn't hurt." He unlatches the hood of the car, loosens the oil filter cap.

"So an oil change, huh?" Matt's shoulder brushes his.

"Yup. You've helped me with a couple before, but it's been a while."

They need to take care of the Beemer. It is their home. Ever since he ran away from his parents, Miriam's parents, too, just before Benny turned three. The BMW has been their only constant. It carries everything they own within its metal frame. Benny knows no other life. Jack wishes *he* knew no other life. That he didn't know this life. Christ. He could make himself sick going around and around.

He braces himself, clasps tightly to the opened hood. He has got to get his shit together, focus on his boys. Matt likes working on the car and is good at it. And the boy is right. Benny is old enough to start learning the inner-workings.

"Got Cokes," Benny says. He passes them out then stations himself on the far side of Matt. "Cal said to help myself to a snack, but I told him maybe later. Is that okay, Dad?"

He glances at the kid. "Yeah, later sounds good, Benny. An oil change can be a mess."

He recaps his bottle and Matt follows suit. Soon they are under the hood and then under the car.

After a while, he stands up, stretches his back, checks out Benny. The kid has been sitting quietly, nursing his Coke. But the amount of silent looks that have passed between Benny and Matt in the past hour and a half could fill a manual. A How-to-Understand-Fucked-Up-Kids manual. No, a How-to-Understand-the-Kids-You-Fucked-Up manual. Let's call it what it is.

"You need something, Dad?" Matt asks.

Need a fucking do-over. "Yeah, Matty, pass me that cloth, would you?"

The boy startles and then slips into pleased. He replays his words. Oh, yes, the nickname.

And Matt takes it as an opening. "You've had this car a long time."

Hell. A trip down memory lane. A long and not so winding road. Rath must have a bottle of whisky hidden among his order books. "Bought it in grade eleven."

"Thing's a relic." Matt grins, runs his hand along the front of the black car.

It is the only thing he has left of high school. That and memories. "They made things strong back in the day. Even teaching you how to drive stick didn't hurt it."

"Hey! I wasn't that bad."

"Yeah. All I needed. Alex Tagliani sitting next to me."

Benny cackles.

Matt wags a finger at the kid. "Wait until it's your turn. We'll be humping our way down the back roads!"

"I got a few more years to go, Matt," Benny says and another unspoken look passes between the two boys and he gets it: Matt will be teaching Benny.

"Why didn't you get an automatic? They had automatics back in the day, didn't they?" Matt smirks.

"Ha ha." He flicks a cloth at the boy's head. "Your grandma and I got into a fight and I was too stubborn to back down."

"Grandma?"

"You want to hear the story?"

"Sure." Matt makes himself comfortable at the counter where his little brother is sitting. Benny's feet are perched on a lower shelf, his leg jumping up and down. Matt rests his elbow on the kid's knee.

"Your grandma considered a stick to be a poor man's car. But it was cheaper than an automatic and, hell, I really wanted this car. As it was, I still didn't have enough money and she said too bad." He swigs his Coke, wishes for rye to add to it.

"How'd you get the money then?" Matt says. "Knock off a bank?"

Benny snickers.

"Smart ass. Your grandpa. He floated me the cash. I paid him back in the summer, caddying at a private golf course."

"Why would Grandpa give you the money if Grandma didn't want you to have the car?" Matt says.

"Because Grandpa hated Grandma's airs and graces and having to put on a face. He used to say it was all bullshit." An unexpected melancholy hits. "He loaned me just enough for a stick."

"Huh." Matt scuffs his toe into a spot of grease. Benny's face is wide open. That same wonderment Miriam had when he talked about growing up with no money. Miriam's parents had old money. Lots of it.

"Enough," he says gruffly. "Let's get this done."

Matt drains his Coke.

"Benny, there's a couple of litres of oil on the counter beside you. Crack them open, would you?"

"Sure, Dad." Benny makes quick eye contact with Matt then jumps off the counter. He opens the first jug and Matt takes it from him. "You're a mess, Matt."

"Still look better than you," Matt says.

"Only in the dark," Benny shoots back.

Jack grunts. Matt has a streak of grease across his forehead, another on his cheek.

"Come add the oil," Matt says.

"Really?" Benny squeaks.

"Come over here," Jack says. "Bring the second litre."

Benny hesitates. Jack's gut churns. Matt's eyes flick at him.

"Matt, that tub over there? That should be wide enough for Benny to stand on."

Matt empties the meager contents from the metal tub. He positions it at the front of the car. When Benny steps up, gets ready to pour, Jack stops him, his hand on Benny's arm. Benny stiffens and Matt moves in.

He wants to throw the jug of oil through a wall. He pulls his hand away, motions for the container. "If you turn it around, so the spout is at the top like this, it'll pour better, less air bubbles," he says.

"Oh, okay." Benny sucks in his bottom lip and begins to pour. His hand shakes.

He wants to steady the kid's grip.

But it is Matt who wraps his hand around Benny's. "Good work, bro."

The kid sloughs off the praise with a twitch of his lips.

"Doing good there, Benny," he says. And when the boy turns around, that slight twitch of his lip is full-blown. His face is brighter than the high beams on the BMW.

44

THE MOMENT HER MOTHER'S WHITE Camry comes into view, Allie crushes her cigarette on the step below her. She doesn't even take a last drag. Or pinch off the end for later use.

"Damn." She will always be her mother's daughter, always seek her mother's approval. Lord, she hopes her girls never get this way.

Mother pulls up to the curb. She is a careful driver. She doesn't get out right away, though. Her attention is drawn by the kids in the front yard of the Humphreys' townhouse. Becca is showing Ben how to do cartwheels and Matt is alternating between goading his brother and encouraging Glory to join in. But cartwheels have never been Glory's thing. Although her middle child could easily talk Ben through the steps.

Glory's laughter is free and easy, something that has come more and more since the end of school. She is leaning into Matt. Are they holding hands? She doesn't shift to get a better view.

The slamming car door brings Allison's attention back to her mother's unannounced visit. And that is more than a little nerve-wracking. Mother is wearing a light pink pantsuit. In this heat. Lord, she has got to be hot. Her hair is ash blonde. Dyed.

"Allison." The greeting is cool. Mother's eyes drop to the crushed cigarette. "Really."

Allison tucks her wayward strands behind her ears. She hasn't run a brush through her hair yet this morning. "Mother." She tries not to respond in the same brisk manner.

"Who are those boys the girls are with?"

"Those are the Humphreys brothers. They moved in there a couple of months ago." She doesn't bother to shove over. Mother will not sit on the concrete stoop.

"They moved in just before the end of the school year?" Mother's shoulders are stiff. She works the strap of her handbag, a slightly darker shade of pink than her suit, as she stares at the activity in the other yard.

"Yes."

"Who would move so late into the school year?"

"Their father, I guess."

Mother's light blue eyes are judging. "They have no mother?"

"No."

"You shouldn't allow the girls to play with them then. You don't know how they will behave with no mother to guide them, teach them. Motherless boys are rudderless."

Guide them? Teach them? She shakes her head.

Mother raises her left eyebrow.

She has never seen the right eyebrow go up.

"Call the girls over to say hello," Mother says. There is still no warmth in her voice.

"Hey, girls!" she yells. "Grandma's here."

Becca is the first to start in their direction, but she stops, motions to the boys. "Come on. Come meet our grandma."

"That's okay." Matt shakes his head.

Ben hovers between following Becca and staying with Matt.

"Come on," Glory says. She stands, tugs Matt up with her.

He shakes loose and grimaces. But he follows.

Allison can't help but grin. Have to give the boy credit. Looks like he would rather face a pride of lions. Well, so would she.

"Hello, Grandma." Becca pecks her on the cheek. They are almost the same height. Glory stands back with the boys.

"Come here, Glory." Mother beckons with her hand.

Glory touches her lips to Grandma's cheek, too.

"And who are these two young gentlemen?"

Allison steps forward, settles her hand on Ben's shoulder. "Mother, these are the Humphreys. This is Ben and his brother, Matt. Boys, this is my mother, Mrs. Patterson."

"Hello, Mrs. Patterson," Ben says, flicks a smile.

Matt nods.

"Well, it's nice to see someone has manners." Mother's voice is tight. She holds her eyes on Matt.

Oh, yes, there is no way Matt will pass Mother's inspection. The boy makes no effort either. He stands taller, clear that he does not need this woman's approval. Allison wants to shake him, tell him to help himself out, help Glory out, too. But maybe he knows it will make no difference what he does or says, judgment has already come down.

"Mother, would you like to come in, have a glass of iced tea with me?"

Mother looks from Matt to Glory. "You need to be more vigilant, Allison."

"What?"

"You need to protect your children from outsiders."

"What?"

Mother purses her lips. "At least Lyne is with the Jeffries' boy."

"What?"

"Is there no other word in your vocabulary, Allison?"

"Jesus," Matt mutters.

Mother's head snaps back to Matt. "What did you say, young man?"

"Mother!" Allison steps in quickly, firmly grips the older woman above the elbow. "Come in and have some iced tea."

"Allison!" Mother shakes free. "You have to pay attention!" She pushes past, up the stairs and into the house.

"Come on, girls, come visit with your grandmother." She holds the door open for Glory and Becca to enter first. It is mean but she needs the shield. She takes a moment to watch the boys trudge back to their yard. Their voices carry on the air.

"I think Dad's mom was like that," Ben says.

"Yeah?"

"I think she must have been like Becca's grandma."

"Yeah?" Matt says.

"That's why Dad is mean," Ben says.

45

"HERE, RICK." LYNE HOOKS HER thumb at Delwood Grocers. She can barely breathe through her anger.

"Here? I'm taking you home," he says.

"I need to get some groceries."

"I'll wait. Give you a ride."

"No!"

"Jesus, Lyne. What-the-fuck-ever." Rick shoves the car into second gear, pulls the Camaro around sharply, stops in a hail of gravel and dust. "Don't know what the fuck your problem is. I said I was sorry. I gave you the fucking necklace."

"And you said you would listen!"

"I did listen!"

"You weren't listening to me! You were listening to Tony!" She pushes away from Rick, her back pressed against the passenger door. "I had to yell before you stopped."

"At least you didn't have to knee me in the balls!"

"And that's supposed to make things better?" she says. "You promised me."

Rick smashes his hand against the steering wheel. "They expect things, Lyne. You know that."

"And I expect things, too!" She gets out of the Camaro, slams the heavy door.

"Yeah and I give you things. Necklaces and fancy handbags and a cellphone. I give you things," Rick yells through the open window. "I fucking expect things, too."

She stalks back to the car. "And I give you those!"

"Not everything, you don't." He takes a deep breath. "Jesus. Just get back in the fucking car."

"No." Her heart is beating up in her throat and she can't force any more words out. Rick yells after her but she keeps walking, ducks into the store. She hides behind the cans of tomatoes until he pulls away, spitting more gravel. She throws her head back, straightens her shoulders and leaves. But her knees are wobbly and she sinks down on the peeling bench in front of the grocery store. Deep breaths. She needs to take deep breaths. Or cry. Or laugh hysterically. She fingers the pendant. Glory's words play through her head, Rick's parting words a soundtrack over her sister's. And then there are her own words. This is the real world. She wants the nice things Rick buys her. She wants Rick. But not this part of him. She closes her eyes, takes a slow, deep breath. When she is ready to return to the world, she opens her eyes, sees Becca and Ben on the rusting swing set. When she used to go to the playground that set had three swings. The chains for the third swing are now twisted unevenly around the top bar, the seat hanging by a single bolt.

Becca and Ben are deep in conversation even as they fly up into the cobalt blue sky.

Lyne remembers pumping hard, hard, hard trying to get lost in the clouds. There are no clouds this afternoon. What do the Olsen Twins have to be so serious about?

She crosses the street, keeps out of sight. She leans against the metal slide, savours the heat that warms her body. It is only now she realizes that her fight with Rick has left her cold.

"What's it like to move all the time?" Becca asks, holding firmly to the chain of the swing.

"I hate it." Ben pumps his legs harder.

"I would think it would be kind of romantic, being able to start all over again. Fresh. A new you," Becca says.

A new you. That does sound romantic. And so, so appealing. There are so many things she would change about her life.

"What's romantic about packing all your stuff into one box, one suitcase and one backpack?" Ben says. "Having to say goodbye to all your friends? Having to start a new school every few months? It sucks!" He stops kicking, parachutes from the cracked wooden seat.

Lyne tucks behind the slide, not ready to be seen. Ben stalks to the bench, throws himself down, clenches his arms tightly across his chest. She has never seen Ben angry before. Even in the kitchen, when he was baking cookies, he was upset, not angry. He looks as if the wrong word will make him throw a punch. Or dissolve into tears. She knows that feeling well. She aches for him and that surprises her.

Becca stops pumping, skips her feet gingerly along the ground to slow her momentum. She drags her toes as she makes her way toward the bench. She pauses in front of Ben. He looks up, offers a weak smile. She sits down next to him, nudges his knee with hers.

"I never thought about it that way. Mama and Daddy were born here. They're going to die here. I don't want to die here," Becca says.

Ben's eyes grow wide. "There's a lot of time before you die. You'll go to university, get a job somewhere. Once you leave here, you never have to come back."

"It must be awful not to have a home."

The shock on Ben's face makes Lyne's stomach drop.

"I have a home," he says. "I have Matt."

God. What a sad, sad life.

Becca blinks rapidly and when she speaks, her voice is thick, "Have you ever lived in any place nicer than this?"

"No. Dad can't afford anything better." Ben runs his nails over the bench, peels off a fleck of paint. "I used to make Matt wash everything when we moved. Wash all the dishes and all the towels and all the sheets. And scrub the floors and the bathtub and the counters. And he would. He would do it all for me. But we've moved so much now that I tell him he doesn't have to do it anymore."

"Oh," Becca says.

"And anyway, it doesn't matter where we move to. Dad doesn't change. He's always the same."

"What do you mean?"

"You must have heard?" Ben's voice is hard.

"I've heard some stuff."

"Well, whatever you've heard, it's true." Ben kicks his feet. "That's my dad. Fucks the married women."

"Ben!" Becca, perched on the edge of the bench, shrinks back.

"Well, it's true," he says, but his face flushes a deep red.

"So it's a good thing you move?"

Ben doesn't say anything. He leans forward, scrunches his big toe into the pebbles. His canvas sneakers are still at the swing set along with Becca's Crocs. He squints into the sun through his long bangs says, "Not this time. I've never had a friend like you."

Becca's smile is bright.

Lyne slinks away. Every place is Delwood for the Humphreys. There is no romance in that.

Glory closes the cover on *The Litte Mermaid* and a tiny girl with red pigtails asks, "Is he your prince?"

"Pardon me?"

"Over there. That boy. He's been listening to you the whole time. He has got to be a prince." The girl points a pudgy finger. "He has to be your prince because he's been watching you."

Glory twists. Matt is leaning against a rack of paperbacks, thumbs hooked in his belt loops. He raises two fingers from his waist, doesn't look the least bit repentant at being caught.

Oh, how she wants him to be her prince! She would drink a magic elixir and walk on feet shot through with sharp pain to be with him. She looks away. She needs to catch her breath. Why is he sneaking up on her at the library?

"Okay, girls," she says, "story time is over. See you again next Wednesday."

The girls wave goodbye and Matt saunters over.

"Hey," he says, grin wide.

"Hey," she says, tries not to get lost in the brightness that follows him.

"Ah, the Disney version of *The Little Mermaid*. Every little girls' favourite." He takes in the books spread out on the table next to her. He reaches for the Hans Christian Anderson version. "He didn't write a happy ending for it."

"It's still a good ending," she says. "Ariel becomes a spirit and ascends."

"Not originally." He turns the book over in his hands. "The prince rejects her and she becomes sea foam. Story over."

"Well," she says and starts piling the books. "Are you taking that out?"

"No." He scrunches the book before he adds it to the pile, flattens it out. "I don't know why I said that. I'm sorry."

"All of today's fairytales have been made happy. Happier yet by Disney," she says. She brushes past Matt with her books.

He follows a step behind. "You need help shelving those?"

She doesn't know how this boy can turn her inside out. From the high of catching him watching her to the low of him saying happily-ever-after is an add-on. She nods. She doesn't trust her voice. Matt takes half the books from her. They move silently among the children's book section. The bright red and yellow shelves cannot disperse the gloom. She finishes first, settles on a plush stool to watch him. He moves sluggishly. Gone is the light step he had earlier. He puts the last book on the shelf and then sinks down next to her, close but not touching. His hands clasp the denim at his knees.

"I'm sorry," he says.

"It's not a big deal, Matt," she says. But it is. It is.

"I have a hard time with happily-ever-after," he says.

"You know," she says, "happily-ever-after is the modern version. Today's version."

Only moments ago the room was bright, the colours warm, the children's laughter lingering in the air. She wants that feeling back. She wants the boy who makes her smile. She wants to make him believe in happily-ever-after.

Matt puts his hand on the bench next to her knee, palm turned up. She laces her fingers through his. Her prince.

46

DOUG COMES HOME A DAY later than expected. There was a time when Allie lived by his schedule. But she has out grown that, thank God.

When he strolls into the kitchen, no, *struts* into the kitchen, heading for the fridge, she has this dreadful moment when she cannot breathe. But then it is gone along with the thoughts she doesn't want to give words to.

"Hi."

His face is lit by the opened fridge door. "Thought you'd be in bed."

"Thought you'd be home yesterday."

He pulls out a beer, tilts the bottle. She nods and he grabs a second Kokanee. He twists the lid off of one, sets the bottle in front of her. He opens his, drinks deeply, then sinks into the chair across from her.

"Yeah, about that." He starts peeling the label from the bottle. "Job went longer than we expected."

"Uh huh." She is not going to do this. She is not. "I just thought you'd be home yesterday."

"It was the plan, Allison. Just didn't work out that way."

He rarely calls her by her full name. Her heart beats faster, harder. Is it possible to have a stroke at thirty-five? Is this what a stroke feels like? God. Settle down, settle down.

"You okay?" Doug reaches across the table, brushes his fingertips across her knuckles, a hesitant touch.

"You didn't call," she says. When did she become this simpering woman?

"Yeah." He lifts his hand. "I thought I'd still manage to leave yesterday, but that didn't work out. Then it got too late to call."

"That's it?"

He stops halfway through raising the bottle to his mouth. "What else would it be, Allie?"

"What else could it be, Doug?"

"What do you mean?"

The dusky light makes it harder for her to read his face, but he is grizzled, his brow creased, his blue eyes flat. His aura is heavy. Whoa. She needs to stay away from Lyne's New Age magazines.

"I don't know what I mean. Tired, I guess." She finally takes a drink, lets the wetness sooth her parched throat. "Mother was here. She always drives me a little crazy."

"I know she does. What did she want?"

"To tell me I'm a bad mother."

"Huh?"

"I don't know. She saw Becca and Glory together with Ben and Matt and she told me I shouldn't let the girls be friendly with the wrong kind of boys."

"'Be friendly?'"

"Her words." She takes another drink, tugs at the collar of her T-shirt. It is Doug's shirt.

Doug shifts in his chair. When his socked feet brush against hers he pulls back. "What is happening with Glory and that boy?"

"I think they're going out."

"Think?"

"I'm pretty sure they were holding hands."

"Jesus, Allie!"

"Don't you bitch at me, Doug! If you're not around to tell her no, it's not all on me. They're your kids, too!" She slams her bottle on the table. It doesn't shatter. It should. Because she doesn't want to shatter alone.

"I'm tired," Doug says. "Let's go to bed."

"Yeah, okay."

He stands, waits. When she remains a statue, he walks away. In his wake, he leaves a light flowery scent. Roses, maybe. He hasn't brought her flowers in a long time. After a few minutes, she goes to the fridge, takes out the last two bottles of Kokanee, opens one. She needs to sleep.

47

MATT CAN STILL DRIBBLE CIRCLES around Ben. Hell, he can be blindfolded and still dribble circles around the kid. Ben's recent growth spurt has left him clumsy. But next summer he will have grown into his coltish limbs and then Matt will have to work at it. But even if the kid is nowhere near the challenge Dad can be on a good day, Ben keeps trying. Kid is stubborn. Maybe Mom was stubborn.

He bites his cheek to keep from smiling. Ben won't appreciate his efforts being made light of. He tucks the ball under his arm. "Hey, Steve Nash, want to do that drill again?"

"Yes! I've got to keep my head up." Ben flicks his bangs, sends beads of sweat flying.

"It's coming along, bro. But, hey, water break."

Their water bottles are sitting in the shade of the bleachers. The asphalt at the school court is hot, the heat coming off of it in waves. The markings are faded, the three point line almost non-existent. The court is supposed to be resurfaced sometime this summer.

"That's a good basketball, huh?" Ben asks. He throws more water down his neck than he does down his throat.

"Awesome basketball. It pumped up no problem." Matt shoves the ball in between the bleacher rungs. He never told Ben about scrimmaging with Dad.

"Think you could play college ball?" Ben asks.

He chokes on his water. "What?"

"I think you could play college ball. You're really good. Maybe you can go to university on a basketball scholarship."

He takes another drink, swishes the tepid water around in his mouth before swallowing. "Ben, I'd have to play high school ball to have any college or university even look at me."

"Maybe next year."

"I don't know. Dad would have to stay in a place long enough for me to make the tryouts and be around for the season. Basketball is a fucking long season."

"It could happen," Ben says softly.

The idea is exciting. But he quickly stomps down the feeling. He has learned to depend only on what he can control. Dad moving isn't one of those things. That's why he turns to girls. He can control who he bangs. He can control letting go, feeling high with them. But there are no more girls now. Only Glory. Only one girl. And where she is taking him, he has no control over. And letting go like that? It's incredible.

"Dad played ball at the U of A," he says.

"Really?" Ben's voice cracks. He takes a drink. "Really? I didn't know that."

Dad only talks to him and he has never been able to figure out what triggers those moments. Dad offers his memories in bits and pieces and Matt holds them close. But there is nothing Dad can reveal about himself that makes what he does to Ben all right. Moving all the time hasn't helped Dad. It has tired him out. Made him desperate. Definitely has left him mean. And that screws with Matt's heart because he remembers a time when Dad was caring. Ben has never had those first-hand memories. So secondhand memories? They aren't worth fuck-all.

He bounces the ball on the bleacher step. "Yeah, he was a Golden Bear. I'm not sure how many years he played, but I do know he got a basketball scholarship."

"See? Maybe you can do that, too. Maybe if you remind him, he'll be willing to hang around some place long enough for you to get the chance." Ben puts the cap back on his bottle and holds his hands out for the ball. The kid takes off, does a perfect lay-up. Then he dribbles to the free throw line, puts the ball up. It rims the basket and shoots out. Matt catches it, and in a single motion sends the ball through the air, swishing through the hoop.

"Holy!" Ben looks from the basket to him.

He shrugs but the obvious worship in Ben's voice makes him feel damned good. He would love to play on a basketball team. It would be incredible to have Ben in the stands yelling his name. Glory, too. His girl and his brother. To be about more than keeping his head above water, more than watching his little brother's back, more than fucking girls to forget about the shit that was — is — their life.

Ben dribbles the rebound back to the free throw line.

Matt steps in front of him. "Okay, bro, move your feet, keep your head up, keep the ball low."

Ben follows every one of his instructions.

48

LYNE YANKS OPEN THE FRONT door of the townhouse but stops when she hears squealing. She waits and it comes again. Not from inside. The backyard. Great. That probably means

Matt's in the backyard not doing something with Glory. She snickers. He must have taken her threat to cut off his balls seriously. She's got to hand it to him — he's got great self-discipline. To go from getting it fifty times a week — to listen to Kennedy talk about it — to celibacy. Rick's balls would shrivel up and he would die.

Because it will brighten her day to see Matt squirm, even in this new relationship they are grudgingly forging, she skips down the stairs and heads for the backyard.

What the hell? Something reeks!

"We're going to have to use the whole bottle of bleach on this!" Becca says.

"Which will make Mom real happy when she needs to wash Dad's work shirts," Glory says. But she doesn't stop Becca from splashing the bleach on something striped on the ground. The hose is going, too, gripped in Glory's hand.

"What the hell are you two doing?"

Glory swings around and Lyne steps back quickly. The water cuts a path just shy of her.

"What are you doing?"

"Washing this stinky hammock," Becca says and she splashes more bleach on it.

"That's what that is?" She steps closer. "God, that stinks. And I don't mean the bleach."

"Cat piss," Becca says.

"Where did you get that?"

"Ben found it," Becca says.

"Where?"

"He found it in a back alley," Glory says. She swings the hose the length of the blue and white striped fabric.

204

"There was a reason why it was in the back alley," she says.

"But it's not broken or ripped or anything!" Becca says and she splashes more bleach.

"Give me that." She grabs the bottle of Javex from Becca. "It smells of cat piss and . . . and . . . weed!"

"I know! So give me back the bleach!" Becca holds out her hand.

"Not happening," she says. She backs away and the heel of her sandal snags in the divot created from the long-since-gone Humphreys' kitchen table. "Becca, go get the heavy broom from the shed. And Glory, just keep spraying it."

Becca throws her a nasty look but trots off to the shed.

Glory glances backwards at her, but keeps spraying.

"What are you going to do with it?"

"Matt says he'll work something out in their backyard. They have a post from an old laundry line and he said he'd attach something to the back of the house," Glory says.

"Yeah, okay."

Becca returns with the broom and puts all her energy into scrubbing the fabric. Glory keeps swinging the hose back and forth, comfortable, confident.

It has been a long time since she has felt like Glory looks. She doesn't have that sort of comfort with Rick. It has been all push and pull. Has she ever felt the confidence that Glory is telegraphing? No. She fought to get Rick and now it's all about keeping him. All her moves are carefully planned. Until they're not and he's trying to push his dick into her. But even then she has to calculate the Kennedy-factor. Being angry at Rick too long will open the door for the bitch.

49

ALLIE TRIES NOT TO FLINCH when Marge tugs hard on her hair. Natural blonde, thank you very much. She never liked Marge in high school and every time she comes to Marge's Miracle Makeovers she likes her even less. The salon is bright and airy and fake, fake, fake. It is all about the gossip. Nobody cares about the truth. But Marge's is the only salon in town and she can't be bothered to drive the thirty minutes south to Edson. She'll do that for a belly ring, but not for a haircut. That's the problem with living in rural Alberta, there is never much to choose from. In anything.

"Oh, sorry," Marge says.

Another tug from Marge's comb and that is it! Allie knocks the tray of hair clips from the arm of the chair. "Oh, sorry." Her voice is saccharine, too. "My hand slipped."

Sandra Marples, sitting next to her, looks up from her *People* magazine. If the town gossip isn't enough, celebrity gossip will fill the need.

Allie resettles in the chair. In the mirror, she sees Marge's pinched mouth, but now her comb is tamer, the snips of her small silver scissors smoother. Snip, snip, smooth, smooth. Like all the lies Doug has been telling. When had she become so blind? Willing to believe whatever he said because it couldn't be about . . . that. But all the lies are adding up to only one thing.

"Bruce got a new job," Sandra says, putting down her magazine. "He's driving truck now. For Bison's."

Working on the road. Allie wants to tell Sandra to get ready to kiss her marriage goodbye. Not that Bruce is such a catch but he pays the bills.

Just like Doug. She has never worked. If she were to ask her parents to support her and the girls, they would. But she can't go back. Her mother's righteous attitude would be too much. But maybe she could help out in the back office of Patterson's Hardware. She could track the work done by Daddy's off-site contractors. Glory is decent on the computer. Maybe the girl could teach her how to do an easy spreadsheet.

"Bison pays good," Marge says, "and it'll keep Bruce away from you, hon, his hands off of you."

"Things are getting better," Sandra says. She holds out her wrist, tries to jangle the cubic zirconia bracelet, but the chain is too tight. "He got me this, you know."

It's goddamned fake diamonds, Allie wants to yell. She keeps quiet, weighed down by the hot air. Marge's air conditioner is broken and the glass door is propped open. It does little to get the air flowing through the shop. She flicks a clump of hair off the arm of the chair, watches it drift to the ground, break into single strands, four or five touching down, disappearing into the pattern on the vinyl floor. Is that her life? Disappearing? No, her life disappeared years ago, when she was in high school, when she set her sights on Doug. When she told Daddy that Doug would take care of her and the unborn baby. When she told Daddy that she loved Doug. What else could she say? That she had screwed up? Huh. No, she screwed him. And she got pregnant. And her mother took it as a personal sin. So she stuck her chin out, threw her shoulders back, walked away from the easy money and the easy life for the boy who was supposed to be no more than her bad-boy phase. And now, now he is some other woman's bad-boy phase. No. That can't be. He wouldn't do that to her. She gave it all up for him. She squeezes her eyes tightly, squeezes back the tears that threaten to fall. She must be wrong.

"Did I get hair in your eyes, hon?" Marge asks, fluffs the pink towel across her hot face.

"Don't drop anything, Ben," Matt gets out between clenched teeth. "We're being watched."

"What? Where?" Ben makes like a bobble-head doll. Patterson's Hardware is almost empty.

"The old guy up front." Matt wants to be pissed about being pegged as a potential shoplifter. But truth is, he's shoplifted enough to be a pro. The couple of times he got caught with a jar of peanut butter or a package of ham slices stuck in his coat, he was able to string together a good enough sob story to be let off with a warning. He tried not to think too hard on how most of his story was an accurate depiction of his fucked-up life.

"I just want to look at that iPod." Ben stretches but still can't reach the top of the rack.

"Why?"

"Why?" Ben says.

"Not as if you can buy it. Fuck. You can't even reach it."

Ben blows his bangs out of his eyes with a long, deep breath. His put-upon face slides into place. "I know I can't buy it. But I still want to look at it."

If he tries dragging Ben out now, the kid will throw a fit. The old man at the front of the store has already rubbed the skin off his hands, looking all kinds of antsy. And a bitch-fit from Ben now will trigger the alarm bells in place for the next time they are in Patterson's. And there are only so many stores that sell duct tape. It is his turn to blow out a long, deep breath. He reaches down the iPod.

Ben turns the package over, reads the back. "Huh, it's not the newest iPod Touch. I didn't think it was. And it's not even marked down."

What the fuck? Which part of they can't afford it does Ben not get?

Ben rights the package, looks at the blank screen. The kid isn't into music so why the fuck is he so interested? And even if they did get an iPod Touch, they can't afford iTunes cards on a regular basis. Not as if they have a computer to download songs from.

"Finished getting your music-geek on, Miley Cyrus?" He holds out his hand and Ben reluctantly places the small package in his palm.

"Can I help you young gentlemen with anything?" The voice booms behind.

"Fuck," Matt says and the iPod slips from his grasp.

Ben's hand shoots out and he rescues the device from shattering on the floor. "No, sir," he says. "We were just looking. I thought it was the newest iPod Touch, but it isn't."

The man looks wary, but Ben's instant dimples reel him in. "No, we're even out of the iPod Nanos. We'll be getting a new shipment shortly. You can check back then."

"Sure, we'll do that," Matt says, voice tight.

Ben's eyes gleam. Matt's stomach churns, but the kid should know by now when he is trying to blow someone off.

"Here you are, Roland."

Great. A fucking staff meeting.

"Oh, hello, Mrs. Patterson," Ben says. His head swivels between the woman and the man.

Mrs. Patterson studies Ben then turns back to the man. "Roland, these are the two boys who live near our grand-daughters." Her voice is chilly like her ice-blue pantsuit.

Ben's smile drops.

"That's us," Matt says, shoves his hands in his pockets. He has the urge to grab Ben and run the fuck away. He doesn't like Mrs. Patterson any more now than he did when he met her on the front lawn of the Rutgers' townhouse.

Roland Patterson nods his head, sticks his hand out to Ben. "I am Mr. Patterson. The grandfather."

Ben grins and shakes Mr. Patterson's hand.

"Tell him your name, bro," Matt says.

"Oh. I'm Ben. And this is my brother Matt."

Mr. Patterson offers his hand. The handshake is firm. Dad says a man can be judged by his handshake. According to Dad's criteria, Mr. Patterson is a fair man. And he caved at Ben's dimples.

Unlike Mrs. Patterson. "What do you have there, Ben?"

"Oh. It's an iPod. We were just putting it back," he says.

Mrs. Patterson holds out her hand and Ben passes the merchandise over.

What-the-fuck-ever. Does she think they're going to pocket the fucking thing with her and her husband standing right the fuck there?

"Roland, this is an older model. And it looks slightly scratched. Why don't we just give it to the boys?" Mrs.

Patterson says, one eye on Ben, one eye on Mr. Patterson. Mr. Patterson stands mute. Ben looks as if Christmas has come early.

No fucking way is he taking anything from this stuck-up bitch.

He hooks his elbow around Ben's neck. "We'll hang on for the new shipment."

"We throw out the old stock. Or donate it to charity," Mrs. Patterson says. Her voice has not thawed.

Matt opens his mouth, but it is Ben's voice that comes out.

"Thank you, Mrs. Patterson. We'll come back. Let's go, Matt." Ben drags him to the door then he turns around and says, "I'll tell Becca I met you, Mr. Patterson."

They are half a block away from Patterson's Hardware before Matt braces his feet on the sidewalk, pulls Ben to a halt.

"What the fuck!" he yells to the empty sidewalk. He turns to Ben and his voice is lower, harder. "What the fuck?"

Ben shrugs. "I know. Weird, huh?"

"Weird? Weird?! Not the fucking word I would use!" He turns around, paces two steps back to Patterson's Hardware.

"Matt," Ben says.

"I can't fucking believe that bitch!"

"Matt," Ben says. "Let it go."

The boy's words are soft, but they hit hard. He hangs his head. Let it go. He lets too many things go. Way too many. But this he will do for Ben.

Jack hates working at Rath's Garage. Check that. He loathes working at Rath's Garage. The only perk is Tanya Rathenburg. That woman is sex on two legs. Oozes the scent. He has long suspected that Rath knows his wife gets it on with other guys. And he figures Rath knows about him and Tanya. There's the sideways glances the old man throws his way, along with the occasional shitty shift. He has accepted those minor fuck-yous as Rath's way of maintaining his manhood. Maybe if Rath lost some weight, shaved a little more often, showered once in a while, Tanya wouldn't be looking elsewhere. But as long as he isn't fired and he can keep boning Tanya, who is he to complain? Especially when he can deliver his own fuck-yous to Rath by doing Tanya in the old man's bed.

The door scrapes open up front and he puts down the fuel pump he is cleaning, wipes grease from his fingers with a shop cloth. He makes his way from the cluttered work station in the back to the doorway leading to the sales counter. Cal, that little bugger, is supposed to be manning the front. The boy is nowhere in sight. As usual. He should drag Matt in, introduce him to Rath, get the boss to give his boy a job. Matt can do better than mowing lawns. He can make good money at the garage, pick up a skill or two. Boy is already good with his hands, good with mechanics. That would prove to Benny that his old man has some pull. The kid needs a bit of humility knocked into him. Benny still believes in rainbows. It is Matt's fault. He does whatever the kid wants, lets the kid think life isn't full of shit. Well it is. It is full of shit and the sooner Benny realizes that the better. Nobody ever gets what they want. There is no pot of gold at the end of the rainbow. There is no goddamned rainbow.

"Hell, Cal," he mutters. He throws the cloth on the counter, gives the guy in front of him a quick look. He's a regular. "What can I do you for?"

"Just put twenty in my tank," the man says, pulls out his wallet.

"Need to top up on oil? Windshield wiper fluid?" He looks over the guy's shoulder, out the streaked window. "It's going to rain one of these days."

"Nah." The man takes out a couple of tens. His driver's license falls to the counter and Jack catches the name: Doug Rutger.

Rutger must be a travelling tradesman, something like that. That would be a shitty job to have, always on the road. But on the upside, lonely housewives up and down the highway. Maybe not so shitty after all.

Rutger ignores his fallen license, instead focuses on the shelves behind the cash register. "But, you know what? I'll take a couple packs of Export A."

Jack unlocks the cabinet, slides out two packs of cigarettes, puts them on the counter next to the license. The photo is old, should be retaken.

"Don't smoke that much, but I'm always out of cigarettes. Beginning to think my oldest girl is helping herself," Rutger says. He stuffs his ten-dollar bills back into his wallet, pulls out a fifty. He slides his license back in, too.

"I never really got into that habit," Jack says, rings up the sale.

"Stealing or smoking?" Rutger asks around a lop-sided smile.

He stops with his fingers poised over the button of the register. "Neither, I guess. Well, no pilfering cigarettes. I did snag a bottle or two from my old man when I was a kid."

"Only a bottle or two?" Rutger pulls the cellophane off one of the cigarette packs. "I knew guys who were taking one or two bottles a week as soon as they hit twelve or thirteen."

"Party a lot, did you?" He leans back, watches Rutger crinkle the cellophane, leave it on a corner of the counter.

"Oh, yeah. Nothing like those who-gives-a-shit high school days. Especially in a town like this. Nothing else to do." Rutger puts all his attention into tapping out a cigarette.

"Yeah, them good old days. Before the kids came around and the responsibilities piled on," Jack says.

"You can say that again. Now it's the kids and the . . . old lady . . . and all those goddamned bills."

"Yeah, life just keeps on giving."

"Don't it?" Rutger sticks a cigarette in the corner of his mouth. Jack taps the countertop. "I won't light up in here." The cigarette bobs as Rutger speaks. "Although last time I checked, Rath smoked like a fucking chimney."

"Nicorette now. Tanya's on his case to quit."

"Guess that's a start. Guy's a fucking slob."

"Regular Jabba the Hut."

"Ain't he?" Rutger's grin is sly.

Christ. He shouldn't have said that last thing about Rath. Everybody knows he's boning Tanya, but putting it out there is just plain stupid. But Rutger started it.

"You're my neighbour," Rutger says.

"That so?"

"Yeah, we live a couple door down from you."

What the hell? They're supposed to be instant buddies now? Complicit in crime? No. No way. Rutger wants something. Well, fuck him.

"That's it?" he asks sharply.

"Yeah, ah, that's good." Rutger fumbles with the other pack of Export A. His feet drag on the tar as he crosses to the pumps. He stands by his Ford Supercab, hesitates at the driver's door. A moment later he is gone.

50

GLORY SITS WITH MATT IN the shade cast by his front stoop. Despite the heat, she wants to be close to him, can't get enough. His arm is wrapped around her shoulder and she is tucked into him. She wants more than these stolen moments, yearns to make memories that aren't cloak and dagger.

Becca and Ben are inside. Becca's shrill voice carries. "You can't write 'fuck!' You can't swear in Scrabble!"

Matt chokes on the Freezie he is sucking on. "Go, Ben!"

Glory giggles, licks her lips to clear off the raspberry from her Freezie, wants desperately to help Matt with the ice blue on his lips. Their eyes meet and she is certain he knows exactly what she is thinking, exactly what she wants. The Freezie turns to fire in the pit of her stomach. She waits, waits.

Another screech from inside and Matt ducks his head, scrubs his fingers through his hair.

She drops her eyes, needs to reorder her thoughts. "There's something off about my mom and dad." She speaks slowly. "They have a pattern and their pattern is off right now. Well, it's been off for a while. It's sort of like a mating pattern, I guess. They follow certain rules, do certain things. It's always been that way. Dad gets back from a custom job and, you know, they end up in the bedroom. It's kind of disgusting but, well, that's them. But now, things are different. Their pattern is off."

"Huh." Matt's face is split in two by his blue-Freezied lips. "Your mom and dad have a *mating pattern*?"

"Okay, I know that sounds weird." She twines her fingers with the hand Matt has over her shoulder. "Makes them sound like penguins or something."

"Penguins?"

"Okay! It was the first thing I thought about. You know, we are eating frozen ice!"

He erupts in laughter. "Oh yeah. A Discovery Channel wildlife special. The mating ritual of the emperor penguin a.k.a. the Rutgers."

"You're such a, such a . . . ooh!" She pushes against him, pushes away the urge to kiss him senseless, to have him kiss her senseless. God, she wants this boy's lips on hers.

"Not sure what special would be on the Discovery Channel on the 'ooh,'" Matt says. He is laughing so hard, he is crying, struggling to sit up.

She turns her back to him, folds her arms across her chest. "C'mon, Glory. I'm sorry."

"You're not sorry." She turns to give him a fierce look but cannot deliver when she sees the tears streaming down his face. She wipes his cheeks with her thumbs.

Matt stops her hands, brings them one at a time to his lips and kisses her wrists. He lowers them to his chest, rests them over the ring that dangles from his neck. They stare at each other, barely breathe.

"You're cheating!" Ben's voice sweeps out through the window, hot and heavy.

They break apart and Matt drops her hands. They lean back against the stoop. She is grateful the cement is cool.

"Did you know that emperor penguins mate for life?" Matt asks after a moment.

"What?"

"Emperor penguins? They mate for life. I helped Ben with a school report once."

"Okay?"

"You said your parents had the mating pattern of a penguin." He waggles his eyebrows at her. "You know, emperor penguins mate for life but they fool around."

"What?"

"They're social animals. They have life mates, but they get a little on the side, too. Everybody does."

Glory draws away.

"Everybody screws around," Matt says harshly.

"Are you saying my mom or dad is cheating?" She stares at his fingers looped around her wrist. She tugs and he lets go.

"No. No. I'm not saying that. Not about your parents." Matt's voice is hoarse. "Jesus, Glory. I didn't mean that."

She is cold, moves into the sunshine. But the sudden heat isn't enough to warm her. Because she knows, just knows, it is true.

51

"DAMN IT!" ALLIE KICKS THE flat front tire on the piece-of-shit car she has been driving forever. Now what? She has bags full of milk and meat. No way she can haul these groceries home on foot. And she is not going back in there to tell Sandra Marples, with her new dangling cubic zirconia earrings and fading black eye, that she has to put her groceries back because her POS car has a flat. "Damn it!"

"Hey, hey," a soothing voice with a hint of humour breaks into her cursing.

She whirls around, ready to bite off the head that belongs to that voice. It is Jack Humphreys. He has that look men wear when they think a woman is going to burst into tears. She is pissed off right now, not ready to collapse into a puddle of weeping goo. She can handle the damn situation! She just needs a minute or two.

"I'm fine," she grinds out.

"Yes, you definitely are fine," Jack says, "but your car doesn't look so fine."

Lord, that smirk is sexy. It has been a long time since a man has come on to her.

"And kicking the tire isn't going to make it any better."

"But it sure as hell makes me feel better." She glowers at him, kicks the tire one more time.

Jack holds his hands up in surrender, makes his way to the driver's side of the Chevy Malibu. He opens the passenger door. "Well, when you're done feeling a little better, why don't you put those groceries in the back seat?"

Damn man and his damn calming voice. And damn sexy smirk. She moves around him, places the groceries on the Hudson's Bay blanket thrown across the bench seat.

He closes the door, steps back. "If you have a spare and a jack, I can easily switch it out for you. Even if it's not full-sized, it'll be enough to get you to Rath's."

She moves to the trunk. "I should have both."

"No husband to help you out here?"

"No." She twists the key in the lock, pops the trunk. "He's on the road right now."

Jack nods. He stands so close, she can smell him. Lord. Old Spice. She pushes aside plastic bags and empty pop bottles, lifts the carpeting from the floor.

"Well, you're in luck. Full tire here. You don't even have to go to the garage."

He pulls out the tire and the jack, leaves the trunk open. He motions to her to head to the front of the car. "Well, then, let me show you how it's done."

Allie hears much more in those words than a lesson in changing tires. This is the man who has a reputation after being in Delwood barely any time at all. She feels like a school girl. She runs her hand through her hair, smooths her crumpled shirt, pulls down on the waistband of her short denim skirt, makes sure her belly button ring is exposed. She studies Jack's face. She has only seen him from a distance. He is an aged version of Matt. He is worn, eyes red-rimmed, lines pronounced. He is not much older than she is, but he has been living hard, drinking harder. She tracks his hands. They are strong, move without hesitation, make quick work of changing out the tire. What else could those hands show her? Lord. What is she thinking? She is a married woman!

When he is finished, he rubs his hands down the front of his jeans, grabs the flat and the jack, throws them in the trunk. He shuts the lid gently, removes the keys.

"If you're planning on doing any highway driving you should bring your car in, get the tires balanced." He jangles the keys. "And get yourself another spare. We have a few worn tires lying around. I can swing you a deal."

"Okay. Thank you," she answers coolly, holds out her hand.

He places the keys in her palm, squeezes her fingers over them, rubs his thumb gently across her knuckles. "No problem."

Holy shit. Her fingers tingle.

Matt approaches Glory like she is a skittish colt. Or maybe he is. "Hey."

"Hey," she says and there is no trace of anger in her voice or in her eyes. "What are you doing here?"

"Amazing thing. Windows. I was walking by. Saw you." He motions to the dusty pane of glass that takes up the entire front wall of Delwood's post office. He stuffs his hands in his pockets. If he doesn't have them tucked away he is going to touch her. And the fat old biddy with the white hair and little curls standing in front of them is doing a fucking poor job of minding her own business.

"I'm buying stamps," Glory says, nods to the front where one of the two wickets is closed. "This line is moving slower than molasses in January."

"Slower than a one-legged dog on tranquilizers," he says.

"What?"

"Slower than a herd of snails travelling through peanut butter." He works hard not to crack a smile.

"What is wrong with you?"

"Are you impressed yet with all my idioms?" He steps in close to her, loses his battle, loops one finger around her pinky. "I'm sure I know more idioms than anybody else in this stupid Podunk town."

Glory's smile is full now. "I'm sure you do."

"Hell, you and I are probably the only ones who know what an idiom *is*."

"Young man," says the fat old biddy. "That is not a nice thing to say about the town in which you live."

"Uh," he says.

"Mrs. Bailey." Glory untangles her finger from his.

"And you, young lady, should pay attention to whose company you are keeping. What would your grandmother say?" Mrs. Bailey's face is pinched, her voice frosty.

"Don't need air conditioning in here. It's already frigid," he mutters.

"Matt!" Glory says.

"What was that, young man?"

"I said the air conditioning was nice and strong in here and thank goodness." He smiles, hopes it is disarming. No point in giving Grandma Patterson another reason to hate him. Stupid fucking cow. This one, too. Fuck, he hates small towns. "It is hot out there, isn't it?"

Mrs. Bailey defrosts a little. "It is."

"Mrs. Bailey, this is Matt Humphreys. He lives near us. And Matt, Mrs. Bailey goes to Grandma's church."

221

He steps it up a notch, pulls out the smile he saves for old ladies when he is without Ben and trying to get hired to mow a lawn. "Nice to meet you, Mrs. Bailey."

"Hmph." Mrs. Bailey looks at Glory with something close to warmth. "So, you have found a boy who likes to read as much as you. Children don't read at all these days."

Glory looks as if she wants to abracadabra herself out of the small post office and he digs his fingers into his palm to keep from laughing.

"The reading habits of children are such a shame," he says seriously. "Oh, look, Mrs. Bailey, it's your turn now."

"So it is." Mrs. Bailey hustles ahead as much as her girth will allow.

When the old lady is out of hearing range, he says, "I forgot to tell you me and Ben met your grandpa."

"Where?"

"At the hardware store. I didn't clue in that your grandparents were the Pattersons of Patterson's Hardware."

"Now you know," Glory says on a sigh. "How did it go?"

"Well, uh, your grandpa seems all right."

"And?" Glory asks.

He flushes.

"Didn't go so well with Grandma, did it?"

"Let's just say it's a good thing I'm not a home owner because I wouldn't be a home owner being helped."

They stand quietly for a moment. He runs his fingers across the back of her hand. Nobody is watching them now. "Look, I'm sorry about what I said about the penguins. I wasn't talking about your parents. I wouldn't do that."

"I know," she says. "And I'm sorry I got upset."

"So we're okay?"

"We're okay," she says.

52

WHEN SHE TURNS THE CORNER, Lyne cannot believe what she sees. The Camaro is parked on her street. What is he doing here? There is a reason she has not been returning his phone calls! And now here he is. Her stomach flutters but she won't admit that it is more anticipation than anger.

She pushes open the front door. The rumble of Rick's voice punctuated by her mother's laughter stops her cold. Her mother is talking easily to the boy she has been avoiding.

She stalks in. "What are you doing here?"

"Lyne!" Mom's voice is sharp.

She speaks quieter, but the edge is still there. "Why are you here, Rick?"

"I wanted to make sure your phone was working," he says around a mouthful of pumpkin pie. There is an open tub of Cool Whip in front of him, a spoon slouching off to the side.

"You call my cell, not the house," she says.

"Thought maybe you'd lost the charger, you know?" He sounds unsure of himself and that little-boy look makes her stomach fluttery again. This is how he sounds when he tells her about fights with his father. This is how he sounds when he needs her.

"Whatever," she says. She plays with the dangling heart pendant.

"Yeah, your mom said your phone was alright, too. Your house phone." Rick sits up a little straighter, splays his hand on the table top.

She misses those hands all over her. She doesn't object to those hands when they are soft. "Rick . . . "

"I know." He darts a quick look at Mom. "I know, okay?"

She sinks into the chair next to him. He touches his knee to hers. He must have been desperate to come here, to sit in the kitchen with her mother. God. This has to mean something.

"This is really good pumpkin pie, Mrs. Rutger."

"Thank you, Rick. Would you like a slice, Lyne?"

"No, Mom."

"I'm sorry, okay?" Rick says quickly, quietly. He clasps her hand and she can't believe how having him touch her like this makes everything she wants to say fly out of her head. How is she going to make him understand that she doesn't want to do that with him? How can she make him understand she doesn't want to get pregnant?

"Rick."

Then Mom speaks. "Whatever it is, I'm sure you kids can work it out. Why don't you take a drive, find some place quiet to talk?"

No! Panic rises in her. She cannot be her mother. Her fingers trail along her necklace. But why should she be? Rick is not like her father. Rick has so much more. The way he is looking at her right now, those grey eyes begging for forgiveness, clouding over with need, telling her she is important. And that fluttery feeling is back again. She nods at him. "Okay."

Rick grins widely. "Thanks for the pie, Mrs. Rutger." Then he turns to her.

With his hand on the curve of her ass, he is immediately back to the boy with the cocky attitude that drives her wild, who makes all the girls at school want him. And he is choosing her.

53

JACK IS SURPRISED TO SEE a house on the far side of Rath's Garage. He never drives in this direction and even though the house is in easy walking distance from the garage it's hidden deep in a stand of poplars. If it weren't for the black and orange garage sale sign sticking out at the end of the lane, he is sure he would have walked by.

Another shit show of a day does that to him. The next time Cal does his Major Tom impersonation, he's going to help himself to some of the boy's stash. God knows only toking up will get him through days like these.

But weed, any drug for that matter, has never been his choice of poison.

But if Tanya doesn't start reeling it in, he will toke up. He's got no issue with quick feels in the back room or taking his lunch break to screw her in her house. But this game she's playing with him and Rath? It's not going to end well. She's becoming more and more obvious in the garage. Doesn't matter that he stays in the shop at the back when he knows his boss is at work, Tanya still seeks him out, sticks her tits in his face, rubs him hard with her eager hands.

"Christ. Stupid woman."

So he's stretching his legs. Needs to get away from Tanya before one too many come-ons leads to him pushing her into the back seat of the Lincoln in the shop and screwing her brains out. He's not ready to walk away from this job.

This garage sale is an easy distraction.

The house is old. Weathered black trim around the doors and windows, white paint peeling from the wood. It's one of those add-on jobs, lean-tos and rooms tacked on as the family grew. Even the run-down dog house has an addition. The garage is a double-wide, same wooden job. In the gravel driveway five tables are piled high. Peering around the tired-looking woman in the ankle-length peasant dress, he sees even more crap lined up against the walls in the garage. There's probably some golden finds in there if he had the energy to pick through it all. And if he really cared.

The first table is covered with books. Mostly paperback, romances with the stud guy and beautiful woman on the cover, westerns with the gun-slinging hero striking a deathly pose. But there are some hardcovers.

He lifts a handful of paperbacks, comes across a Steinbeck. *The Grapes of Wrath*. Matt read an ungodly thick Steinbeck a year ago. He can't recall the name of the book. The boy got assigned the extra reading for a special class project. Matt doesn't know, but the language arts teacher phoned and talked to him. The overwhelming pride he felt was extinguished quickly by the accompanying anguish. But he gave the teacher permission to push the boy.

He drops the book, buries it among the trash novels. He pushes on through to the last of the tables, layered deep with board games. Might as well start a fire with those and roast marshmallows. Kids don't do anything but PlayStation or Xbox these days.

"Huh." He spots three decks of cards. Two are wrapped in elastic, but one is in its box. And the box is marked Bicycle. Jesus. He should get these for Benny. He opens the pack. They're a mixture of blue and red Bicycle cards. Hell. He'll have to sort them into suits, make sure all the cards are there. He counts them quickly, chuckles when he hits fifty-three. Sure didn't take the kid long to figure out that riddle.

"Jack."

He jerks around, knocks down the taped-up boxes of Monopoly and Risk and the Game of Life.

"Tanya."

She looks inviting, shirt unbuttoned, tied just below her breasts. Ample breasts. Her stomach is flat and tanned, makes her legs look even longer. Christ.

"Hey," she says.

He works the cards back into the box. "Gotta get these first."

"Cards?" Tanya moves closer.

"A loony," the woman in the faded dress says. Her face is harsh, as if she expects him to walk away with the cards. "A loony. For the deck." She holds out her hand. Her dull eyes dart between him and Tanya.

He digs into his front pocket, pulls out a handful of change, drops a large coin in the woman's hand.

"Done, Jack?" Tanya says. "Got the car."

Done? So, so far from done. A deck of cards can't begin to make up for everything the boys don't have. He pockets the pack, follows Tanya's swaying hips. Maybe she can screw his brains out. He doesn't want to think about his boys.

54

MATT IS GRATEFUL THERE WAS duct tape in the toolbox. He is in no rush to return to Patterson's Hardware. He patches the garden hose, steps back, appreciates his handiwork. It is the first week in August and the weather still hasn't broken. He took a few dollars from the Dempster's bread bag and bought the slightly used slip and slide, hose and sprinkler from a garage sale. He didn't feel too guilty about digging into their stash. Mrs. B. has lined them up with a number of new customers, including the Ukrainian Orthodox Church. She sits on the maintenance committee. He imagined her pleading their case, two wayward boys in desperate need of spiritual guidance — and let's not forget the money — and how such charity from the church could make the difference, save their souls. Under any other circumstance, he would take pleasure in being a heretic, but the dry weather means work is sporadic. There is always something to do around the church. Maybe Mrs. B. has friends in other churches because there are a fuckton of churches in Delwood. Ha. Maybe Grandma Patterson. Yeah. He has a better chance of seeing the Second Coming than expecting compassion from that uptight bitch.

Still, even with the church and the lawns, he needs to depend on Dad coming home on a regular basis to help out with the bills.

"I think this should work now," he says.

Glory comes up behind and rubs his shoulder. He wishes he were brave enough to take off his shirt, imagines the feel of her hand on his bare skin, wonders if her touch could sear any more than it already does.

She leans forward to examine his work. "You think?"

He breathes in her light lilac scent. He wants so badly to turn around and kiss her. "Put the hose on. Let's see if this holds and if the sprinkler's in the right place." He flinches at his shaking voice. He dares to look at her and her smile is a supernova.

She skips to the tap, twists it on full. The water shoots out, cold as ice, blasts him. He yells, jumps back. His bare feet hit the slip and slide and he goes down hard on his back.

"Fuck!" The air rushes out of his lungs. He tries to scramble up, can't get his footing. He bats the water away from his face. "Turn it off! Turn it off!"

At the tap, Glory shrieks high-pitched laughter. Then she ends the spray of water with a few twists of her wrist.

Matt is soaked. His wet T-shirt clings to his shoulders. Glory, her face flushed, bends over him. Her eyes sparkle.

He can no longer hold back. He reaches out, snags her wrist, brings her down in the water beside him. She squeals, rolls over by his side, face up to the sky.

Her halter top is soaked, accentuates her curves. Her face is lit, her hair splayed behind her like a halo. He holds his body up with his hands braced on either side of her halo, waits for her to say something, to tell him to stop. But her eyes slide shut. And she is beautiful. His angel. He lowers himself, kisses her. It is a soft kiss. The type of kiss he has never given before. Her lips taste like cherry gloss. All Glory. He wants another taste of that cherry, all wonderful and sweet and tart and daring. He ducks down, brushes his lips to hers, holds on a moment longer. Then she reaches up, holds on, too.

The screen door slams behind them and he breaks the kiss, pulls away. Glory's eyes are still shut, her face still soft. He flips on to his back, appreciates the cold water. After a moment, he stands, wills himself to be calm. He reaches down and she grasps his hand. He pulls her up and they stand, hands still clasped, bodies almost flush, not looking at each other. He hears his heartbeat, Glory's heartbeat, too.

"What happened?" Ben's eyes flash from the water on the slide to him and Glory holding hands.

"Yeah, what happened to you?" Becca asks.

He drops Glory's hand. He rests his palm on the water that prickles her bare back, gently rubs his thumb through the dots of water, joins them. Ben can't see that.

Glory says, "I turned on the sprinkler and Matt slid on the slip and slide. It was pretty funny."

He wants to kiss her again. Desperately. But Ben is here. Don't kiss her. Don't kiss her. But, God, he wants to kiss her.

Becca's eyes have not left Glory, and he sees something soft, an understanding in her face. And Glory is glowing. He loses himself in the deep richness of her blue eyes. She is everything he could love. He ducks his head. When he looks up, her eyes are still on him. Jesus fucking Christ. What is he thinking? Good girls don't happen to boys like him.

"You came out to laugh at me?" he taunts Ben. The kid licks his lips again and again, wants to say something. He is terrified of the words that will come out of his little brother's mouth. "Go fool around with the sprinkler. It's stuck. See if you can MacGyver it."

Ben stares a moment longer, then stomps to the sprinkler, fiddles with it. "Got it," he says, peels off his shirt.

Matt tugs off his shirt, too, feels the ring tap against his chest. He twists his shirt, delivers a stinging slap to Ben's legs. Then he takes off after Becca.

Glory's fog is broken by Lyne's question: "What's up?" How much did her sister see?

She keeps her eyes on Matt chasing Ben and Becca. "Oh, we're just getting the slip and slide working. It's so hot."

She gives her sister the once over. Lyne is wearing a revealing bikini top, the same low riding cutoffs she wore when she let everybody know that Matt was . . . with Kennedy. Matt will take one look at Lyne and be reminded of the other girl. Reminded of what he is no longer getting. She does not have Kennedy's body. She can't offer him that.

"Hey, Lyne," Becca yells, takes refuge in the shade of the overhang on the townhouse. "Going to join us?"

"I can stick around for a bit," Lyne says.

Matt nods in Lyne's direction. "Hey."

Glory doesn't know why it happened. She only knows that in the beginning of summer Matt and Lyne put aside their mutual hatred for each other. That bitterness that was between them has disappeared.

"Rick will be here soon and we're going to a pool party."

"Rick's coming?" Her perfect afternoon is fading. Rick and Matt are like wild dogs with each other.

"Don't worry," Lyne says, "I'll get him out of here before they start their pissing contest."

"Thanks," she says, warmed by Lyne's approval, warmed by the afternoon heat, warmed by the boy who is here with her now. She runs her finger along her lip, thinks of the second kiss, the way her brain no longer worked, the way her stomach twisted, the way she wanted to lose herself. She has a boyfriend!

Can Lyne tell that she is so in love with Matt that it hurts? Does Lyne know what this feels like?

Matt shoves Ben lightly. "Go on. Turn on the tap."

At the rumble of the Camaro Lyne twists the water out of her hair, runs her index finger under each eye to catch streaking mascara. Rick pulls up to the curb. The passenger door opens and Kennedy steps out. What the hell? The little slut is wearing hardly anything. A bikini top that is barely there and low, low riding shorts that show the strap of her thong bikini.

A fierce hatred surges through her.

She stays where she is, hands on her hips. Rick slides out of the Camaro, a grin covering his face. She wants to wipe it off. How dare he come to pick her up with his ex-squeeze. Matt's ex-squeeze, too. Maybe a beat-down wouldn't be such a bad thing. With Glory and Becca and Ben watching, Matt would be plenty motivated to teach him a lesson.

"Hey, babe." Rick's grin slips a little. "What's going on?"

"I was wondering the same thing," she says.

"Kennedy wants to ask the asshole to come to the party." He covers Lyne's hands with his on her hips, tries to pull her in.

She leans away. "Matt's with Glory."

"He never broke up with me," Kennedy says.

"Grab a brain, Kennedy. He's with my sister."

"Jesus, Lyne," Rick says.

"Hey, Matt," Kennedy calls out, swings her hips as she walks to him.

Matt rubs his hands on his wet swim trunks. "Hey."

Kennedy hooks a finger into the strap of her bikini. "You gonna stick around with these kids or come play with me?" She fuses her body to Matt's, slides her hand down between them, cups his balls.

Matt backs away. "Not interested."

"Fuck you, Matt Humphreys," Kennedy spits out.

Ben steps up beside Matt, his shoulder grazing against the older boy. "That's the problem, isn't it? He's not going to fuck you."

Matt ogles Ben then his attention shifts back to Kennedy. "I told you there was no commitment," he says.

"I got my clit pierced for you," Kennedy says.

"And I came back. That was the only thing I promised."

"You came back three times!" Kennedy holds up three fingers, shakes them in Matt's face. He doesn't look away.

Rick turns to Lyne. "She really fucking did that for him?"

Lyne doesn't answer. She can't take her eyes off the scene that is unfolding. Kennedy is near tears, her desperation clear. Glory has taken a step back from Matt, looks stricken. Becca is standing next to Glory, silent support. Ben is still pasted to Matt, a solid shield.

"I never meant to hurt you," Matt says. "I told you from the beginning it was nothing more than fun. No commitment. I told you that. You said you were fine with it."

Kennedy walks back to the car. Halfway there, she turns, face contorted. "And I lied. You're not better than Rick."

Rick grunts, follows. He calls over his shoulder, "Y'all have fun now."

"Come on, Becca," Glory says. "We're out of here." She pulls the younger girl away with her.

"Glory," Lyne says.

"I have to go, Lyne." Glory is blinking furiously. Gone is the confidence of only minutes earlier.

"C'mon, Lyne." Rick leans against the open door. Kennedy is at his side and his hand is low on her bare back.

Lyne wants to explain it all to Glory. Why can't she see that Matt has eyes only for her? But if she stays, Rick will use it as a reason to screw Kennedy. He is already halfway there. She can't have that. She turns away.

55

ALLIE KICKS AT A PINK sandal. She will stumble on it again if she doesn't put it away because Lord knows, Becca won't stop long enough to make room for it on the shelf. Not that her other two girls would stoop to clean up after themselves either. No. That's her job, cleaning up after the girls and Doug. And never a thanks. And who was she kidding that putting off laundry would mean Lyne or Glory might do it? Oh no. Now she has four loads to wash. There are three piles lined up against the living room wall waiting for her. This damned townhouse is so small the only place the washer and dryer fit is in the mudroom. She will be stuck in there all afternoon, the heat rolling in from outside, the dryer spewing lint.

If she had a laundry room like Marcie, she would do laundry every day.

"Who needs to do laundry every day?" she mumbles as she goes through the pockets of Doug's jeans. She hates doing laundry. The washer and dryer are ancient, ugly and avocado green. Lord! Avocado green! With shoes for three girls and almost as many coats, the mudroom is full, barely enough space to breathe much less move around.

She slams the fourth pair of jeans into the washing machine. God. How many jeans can one guy go through in a week and a half? She brushes away her damp hair with the back of her hand. Her hair is just starting to grow back after the hack job Marge did. Marge's Miracle Makeovers, yeah, right. It would take much, much more than a miracle makeover to improve Marge. Nothing short of an act of God. Does God do acts like that? She will have to ask Mother. After all, Mother has a direct line to God. She titters. Then she looks around to make sure none of the girls have snuck up on her. They would think she was losing it.

"Oh, God. I need a vacation." She steadies herself on the edge of the washing machine. Maybe . . . The girls should be old enough. Lyne would whine about it, but she could take care of Glory and Becca. Or she can foist her girls on Marcie, add some colour to her sister's perfect world of red and stainless steel. Then she and Doug can take off somewhere. They haven't been anywhere together. Ever. She could go with

235

him on a contract run, see what he does, eat in the diners he always stops at, stay in hotels with him. It wouldn't cost any extra. A business expense Daddy would pick up. It would give them a chance to find that spark again, away from tedious chores and prying eyes and constant questions. The idea of her and Doug again, like old times, is daisy fresh.

She almost forgets to check the pockets of the last pair of jeans, too caught up on planning her romantic trip, how surprised and pleased Doug will be. She digs them out of the washer, pulls out two crumpled slips of paper from a front pocket. She smooths them with her hand, lays them in the shoebox on the dryer where she collects all the expense receipts. She spins the dial to heavy, lingers a moment, her fingers running in the cold stream of water. The top receipt catches her eye. La Senza. What?

She wipes her fingers on her cut-offs. Her hand shakes when she pulls the receipt from the box. La Senza. Dated three weeks ago. *Lace babydoll. $32.50.* She gently places the paper back into the box, flattens it, and walks away. She sinks down onto the couch. The water rushing into the washing machine fills her ears. Cold, cold water. If that lace babydoll is red, the cold water would keep the colour sharp. But she doesn't have to worry about washing that lace babydoll because it is not in her drawers, not in her closet. That lace babydoll is not for her.

She can't leave that receipt in the box. What would Daddy say? Mother? She rushes back to the mudroom, takes the receipt gingerly between her index finger and thumb. Then she crushes it. But she can't throw it away. This is it. This is everything she thought, everything she feared. She stumbles to her bedroom, stands still in front of the closet. Purse. She needs a purse. One she doesn't use often. She pulls the gold evening bag from the shelf, marvels over how steady her hands are, throws the crumpled piece of paper into the purse. She pinches her finger as she snaps the clasp shut. She slides the evening bag back onto the shelf. She sucks on her puckered finger. Then she runs to the bathroom and throws up.

56

IT IS STRANGE TO BE hanging with Glory, but this strange is good. She has noticed a change in her sister since Glory and Matt started spending time together. But she isn't sure if they are still going out. Glory hasn't said anything and she hasn't had the time to ask. She's been with Rick at one party after another. One party after another where Kennedy keeps coming on to him. So he keeps pushing her to do more and more. There really isn't much left except *that*. She is tired of this constant battle. But she can't tell him out right that she doesn't want to do it. No, that she is scared to do it.

"I don't know why we have to take these stupid pies," she says. At least she isn't the one lugging the Tupperware container.

"We're doing Mom a favour," Glory says.

"And what's with that? She's been in bed more than she's been out of bed. Jesus, you don't think she's pregnant, do you?"

Glory snorts. "Get real, Lyne. They've been doing it forever. They know about birth control. And anyway, she hasn't been throwing up or anything."

"Yeah, I guess. I remember when she was pregnant with Becca, she spent half the time in the bathroom. So why do we have to take these to the stupid bake sale at the church? Not as if we even go there."

"You know how Mom gets after Grandma visits. All repentant-like."

The Evangelical Pentecostal Assembly looms ahead. When Lyne was little she thought the church was huge. Now the building isn't large but the judgement is. "Grandma can be a bitch," she says. "What I don't get is how Grandma ended up with Grandpa. I mean, he never goes to church."

"I guess she prays hard enough for both of them," Glory says.

"No, seriously."

"Maybe Mom wasn't the only one with bad-boy infatuation."

"Huh."

"Or maybe Grandma had the saviour-complex."

"What? That she needed to save Grandpa's soul?"

Glory shrugs. "It's possible."

"Lyne, wait up." It is Rick.

Now the church looks inviting and she quickens her pace.

"What's going on?" Glory whispers fiercely, walks faster to keep up.

"Nothing." But she doesn't slow down.

"Jesus, Lyne, wait." Rick catches up, latches on to her arm. "Didn't you hear me calling?"

"I didn't hear anything. Did you hear anything, Glory?"

"No, I didn't hear a thing."

"Ha fucking ha." Rick loosens his grip. "Where're you going?"

She looks at the church.

"Oh, right, bake sale. My mom's going to be there. I'll come with you." He slides his hand into the back pocket of her tight shorts.

She hates how he goes from pissed to accommodating in thirty seconds flat. He is like this with everything. Especially the other way around. And that way frightens her, keeps her off-balance.

"We don't need an escort, Rick. Streets aren't that scary," Glory says.

"Not talking to you," he says.

"In case you haven't noticed, Lyne and I are going together."

"When did your sister become such a bitch, Lyne?" Rick snarls. "Oh yeah, probably around the same time she started doing Humphreys."

"I'm not doing Matt!" Glory says.

"Come on, Lyne." Rick pulls her in tight. "Let's skip this lame-ass bake sale and head out. I'm going to be gone soon and I'll only be able to see you on weekends." He rubs his thumb along the waistband of her shorts. It sends a shiver through her body.

"You'll only be able to see me on weekends?"

"Yeah, and even then, babe, I won't be able to come back every weekend. This course I'm taking is supposed to be fucking hard."

"You're not going to break up with me at the end of summer?" She can't believe what she is hearing. It is what she has been worried about, that he will dump her, find a willing girl in Edmonton.

"Course not, babe. Why would I?"

She tugs him in for a long, hard kiss.

"On the streets now? Where's the red shining fuck-mobile?"

"Matt!" Glory says.

Lyne breaks off. Rick tries to pull her in again, but she keeps him away, hand pressed to his chest. She wants to see whatever this is between her sister and Matt. Glory's face is bright but Matt looks uncertain.

"Humphreys," Rick says coolly.

"Jeffries." Matt's tone matches.

"Or should I say asshole?" Rick says.

She tugs at Rick. "Leave them alone."

"What?"

"Let's just get out of here." She runs her index finger along the chain of her necklace. "C'mon, boo."

"You keep doing this. Sticking up for this asshole."

"I'm not sticking up for him. He's going out with my sister."

Rick tightens his grip, pulls her into the alley.

"Let her go," Matt says.

"What was that, asshole?"

"You're hurting her, you prick. Let her go."

"I'm okay, Matt," she says quickly. But Rick's fingertips brand her.

"You're still fucking talking to this jerkoff?" Rick digs his fingers in more.

"Rick!" Glory steps toward her, but Matt slides in first.

"She going to get a clit stud for you too, asshole?" Rick says.

"Shut the fuck up, Jeffries."

"That's how you like 'em? With all those holes?"

"Shut the fuck up."

"Rick, let's go. Come on." Lyne pulls at him. The glint in Matt's eyes, Rick's rigid jaw line — there is only one way this can end. It has been building since the slip and slide. Even before then. Rick swings her out of the way, tightens his grip on her arm. He shoves one-handed at Matt. She fights back the panic.

"Something going on here, kids?"

Rick lets her go. The boys step apart.

Lyne works up a smile, faces the RCMP officer. "Nothing is going on."

"Rick? Rick Jeffries. Haven't seen you since the end of the season, kid."

"Hey, Constable McDermott. Yeah, how's Keith doing?" Rick plasters on his suck-up smile. She has seen him use it with teachers when he's spinning an excuse for missed homework.

"He's holding down a summer job, making some money before he heads off to MacEwan University in the city." Cst. McDermott does a quick survey of the group. "How about you, Rick? What are your plans for the fall?"

"I'm off to Edmonton, too. Doing power engineering at NAIT."

"Following in your old man's footsteps, eh? He must be proud."

"He's pretty happy," Rick says, the words measured.

"You going to be playing hockey there?"

"I'm not sure. Dad and I are still discussing it."

"That's right. Your old man played Junior B in the city, didn't he?"

"Yeah," Rick says, shifts from one foot to the other. "How about Keith?"

"No. He said the last three years you all played with Edson was enough for him. He took a pretty heavy check there at the end of the season, you know, separated his shoulder."

Rick nods. "I remember."

Cst. McDermott glances behind. A small crowd has gathered. "Keep moving, people." Then he switches his attention to Matt. The policeman stands tall, throws back his shoulders, makes his girth considerable. "Do I know you, son?"

"Me?" Matt says.

"Yes, son, you." Cst. McDermott shows his teeth, more a stretch of lips than a smile.

"No. No you don't."

"What's your name, son?"

"Matt Humphreys."

"Your dad works at Rath's."

"Yes, sir," Matt says and surprise colours his answer.

Cst. McDermott keeps his eyes on Matt a beat longer then shifts to the girls. "Everything okay, Rick?"

"Yeah. We were just talking," Rick says.

"Your girl?" Cst. McDermott nods at Lyne.

"My girl," Rick says, slides his hand into hers.

She forces another smile.

"Well, why don't you and your girl take off then?"

"Okay." Rick wraps his arm around her waist, pulls her in snuggly.

"Lyne," Glory says.

"I'll see you at home, Glory."

"Lyne."

"Everything's okay." She softens her rough voice with a flicker of a smile.

"Okay," Glory nods. "Okay."

Cst. McDermott stays behind with Matt and Glory.

When they reach the Camaro, she hears the policeman's deep voice. "See that I don't get to know you too well, okay, son?"

"Yes, sir," Matt says.

This time, she hears no surprise in Matt's voice. Instead, she hears conviction.

"Dad's going to fucking kill me," Matt says. Fuck. What has he done? He picks up his pace as he heads home, Glory fast on his heels, still clutching the Tupperware container.

"You didn't do anything wrong, Matt." Glory touches his elbow, tries to slow him down.

He stops abruptly, turns to her. "You don't get it!"

She startles back.

He hangs his head, runs his fingers through his hair. "I just . . . I can't . . . I'm sorry. Jesus, Glory, I'm sorry. Fuck."

"It's alright," Glory says.

"No, it's not alright." He looks around. They are near the United Church and he weaves his fingers in hers, guides her to the back of the building. He pulls her down on the warm wooden steps.

She squeezes his hand. "Talk to me."

He swallows down his panic. "Number one rule for how we live is to keep off the radar."

"Number one rule? For how you live? What do you mean?"

Nobody knows this about them. Nobody. Dad would be so pissed to find out he was spilling his guts to Glory. But all he has done since he has come to Delwood is bare his soul to this girl. He clings to her hand. "Have you met my dad?"

"You know I haven't."

"You know where he works, right?"

"Yes, Rath's. Everyone knows that."

"You know he's not on call, right? Doesn't work twenty-four-hour shifts?"

"I know that," Glory says. "I don't understand. What are you getting at?"

"Dad takes off for days, weeks, Glory. He leaves us on our own. Sometimes I barely have enough money to buy milk."

"Oh."

"It's how we live."

"Matt . . . "

Now that he has found the words, he can't stop. "If I get us on the cops' radar, it could cause trouble. If they get what's going on, that I'm taking care of Ben, that Dad's hardly ever around, they'll call Children's Services. I have to tell my dad."

"Matt . . . "

"If Children's Services gets a hold of us, I'll end up in a group home and Ben'll be in foster care. We won't be together."

"You've thought about this before, haven't you?" Glory's voice breaks.

"All the fucking time," Matt says.

"Matt . . . "

"Don't. I don't want your pity." He can't take that from this girl. He drops her hand. "I'm just telling you how it is. I'm just telling you I fucked up."

Glory reclaims his hand, holds so tightly his fingers cramp. "I'm not giving you pity. You haven't screwed up. Nothing happened. You don't have to tell your dad."

"No?"

"I don't see why. The cop isn't making a report or anything. And the RCMP station isn't in Delwood. This will all blow over. Your dad will never know. You'll see."

"What if you're wrong? I've got to tell him." He is almost hyperventilating. "I can't have Children's Services coming and taking Ben away from me."

"I'm not wrong. Children's Services will never know anything about this. Please, Matt, don't tell your dad," Glory says. "There's no reason for him to be mad at you."

He stares at her. "Okay." He can breathe. Ben will be safe. "We won't have to leave town then."

"Leave town?"

"Welcome to our life. It's one big road trip. When we get noticed, we move," he says. "That's why we settle in small towns. They don't have a lot of government services. And when people do figure something's wrong, well, they usually ignore it. It's too much work for them to do anything official. It's just social workers and cops and teachers we have to worry about."

He taps the Tupperware on Glory's lap and she stares at at it. "The people whose yards we cut? Well, they just bake us cookies when they find out something isn't quite right." He laughs bitterly.

"Matt," Glory says. She looks at him so earnestly, compassionately, it takes him back to their first meeting at the playground, when even then she saw beyond his bullshit to the boy who was smart enough to have read *The Grapes of Wrath*. He slides his hand under her hair, cups her neck, draws her closer.

"We're like the Joad family," he says. "Ma Joad worked so hard to keep the family together. That's what I do. I keep us together."

Glory closes the distance between them, kisses him, long and soft and wanting and full of promise. He can stay with this girl. He will stay with this girl. Everything will be fine.

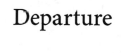

Departure

57

JACK IS SITTING AT THE kitchen table, feet up on one of the psychedelic chairs, when the door flies open. Matt tumbles in with a giggling girl and whispers, "Shh."

He doesn't recognize her. Not that he would know any of Matt's girls in this town. But this girl is not typical. She is fresh-faced. Her eyes are wide, her lips curled up in a full smile. She shines. She is wholesome. Just like Miriam. This girl has the same look Miriam had when he caught her unaware looking at him. This girl has the same look Miriam did when he first told her that he loved her.

Christ. He runs his hand roughly over his face, palm scraping coarse stubble.

Matt is still trying to get the girl to stop laughing. The glow in his eyes, the way he holds himself, the way he moves. Jesus fucking Christ. This is not the same boy he caught a couple years back getting a hand job in their apartment, not the same boy he threw condoms to and told to be careful. This is not the same boy who hooks up with girls for fun. This is not the same boy who is all about sex.

The girl's back is against the open yellow door. Matt runs his fingertips down her arms. She grips him tightly, and he bends down, kisses her forehead then her nose. The girl's eyes slide shut.

"Who's your friend, Matt?"

Matt jumps back and the girl screams. Then Benny bursts in laughing, followed by a girl about his age. She ploughs into his back, laughs along with him. Christ. Girls everywhere. Benny yells, "What the hell, Matt? Take off like that on us?"

"Watch your language, Benny."

"Dad." The word comes out short, shock on Benny's face.

Matt's girl straightens up, slips her hand into his.

Matt says roughly, "Dad. We weren't expecting you home." His shoulders are tense, his eyes hooded, his mouth tight.

"Obviously." Jack keeps his tone soft, playful.

"Hey," Benny's friend says, offers a small wave.

Jack nods at her. "Who are your friends, Matt?"

Matt's girl is bold. She is studying him, doesn't flinch when he studies her back.

"Uh, they live at the end of the street," Matt says. He shakes his hand loose. "This is Glory and that's," he indicates with a jerk of his head, "Becca. Rutger."

"Uh huh." Jack turns the name Rutger over in his mind. It is familiar. The gas station. The cigarettes. Tanya. He takes a long pull from his bottle of Blue. There are three empties lined up on the table.

"How long you been home?" Matt asks.

"A while. Wondered where you boys had gotten to."

249

"Just around." The kids are clustered in the doorway. Only Matt is firmly inside.

"You staying or going?"

Matt doesn't answer but his girl speaks up. "Becca and I need to get home. Nice meeting you, Mr. Humphreys."

"Not going to kiss your girl goodbye, Matt?"

Benny's head jerks up and he looks pissed. At Matt. Jack takes comfort at not being on the receiving end of that face.

"We have to go," the girl says. "C'mon, Becca."

Matt stands silent and the girl wraps her hand tightly around her sister's arm.

"Becca," Benny says.

She offers a shrug, allows her big sister to drag her out.

"Benny, go to your room," Jack says, voice still level.

The kid takes a deep breath, doesn't move.

"Now."

Benny looks at Matt. The older boy tips his head.

"Benny, look at me." He tightens his hand around his bottle. "*I* told you something. You do what I tell you. You don't look at Matt for permission."

"Okay."

There is nothing contrite about Benny's behaviour and that lights the fire. He snags the boy as he walks by, twists the skin on his wrist.

"Dad!" Matt yells.

He holds fast to Benny. "You listen to me next time, you hear?"

Benny nods, bites hard on his bottom lip. Jack lets him go and he takes off down the hall.

"Stupid little shit."

"Jesus, Dad."

Jack closes his eyes tightly, waits for his breathing to calm, his heart to stop racing, his head to stop thrumming. How can Matt not be disappointed in Benny? He drops his foot from the second chair, kicks it out. "Sit."

Matt hesitates, attention focused down the hall.

"Kid's useless. He's got to learn to do what he's told. Don't need you pushing your nose in all the damned time." He takes a pull from his bottle. "He's too damned soft."

"Jesus, Dad," Matt says, this time harsher. He falls into the chair. He stares at Jack for a heartbeat or two then drops his gaze to the table. He fingers the circles of condensation.

"What are you doing with this girl?"

Matt looks up sharply, eyes darkening with defiance. "Nothing."

Matt is only like this when he is standing up for Benny. What is going on?

"What are you doing with this girl, Matty?"

"We're just hanging out. Just having fun."

It is written all over his face how he feels about this girl. Jack remembers seeing this same look in the mirror when he started falling in love with Miriam. But that was a different time, a time long, long ago. It will never be that time again. There is no going back.

Matt leans forward, drops his hands between his knees. His eyes are soft and he takes a breath but Jack doesn't want to answer any of the questions he is about to ask. He isn't ready to share the secrets of love with his boy, isn't ready to tell him that love can be taken away too quickly.

"You're supposed to be having fun, Matt, not getting tied down. That's not fun. You're too young for that kind of shit. She looks like a good girl, the kind who's going to want you to promise her the moon. She's not your kind of girl. We're going to leave. You know that. You don't need the headache this kind of shit brings with it."

Matt ducks his head, grips hard to the seat of the chair, rocks forward. When he looks up, his eyes are dull. "Yeah, okay, Dad."

"Good boy."

"So we're leaving soon?"

The boy's easy switch in focus is a relief. Matt is always eager to accommodate. On all things but Benny. Yet this acquiescence seems too quick. But he will take whatever gifts he can get. "Not sure. I've got a thing or two going. I'm looking at something just outside of town."

"Really?"

"What? You don't think your old man can get a new job?"

"No. That's not it. I thought you were, you know, okay at Rath's." Matt grabs a beer bottle, scrapes his nails along the label.

"It's the same old same old. I'm thinking about trying something else. I'll see what happens." Matt's fingers work steadily on the blue label. He stopped surgarcoating things for the boy a long time ago, but that doesn't mean he likes to see the worry. He finishes his beer, lines it up with the two bottles still on the table. "I'm looking at construction work on a barn. It's a little far to be driving in every day, so if I get it, I'll bunk out there for a bit."

"Yeah, okay."

Christ. The boy sounds so defeated. "How're you doing for grocery money?"

"We could use some."

Defeated and well trained. A not-so-subtle reminder that he is an inadequate provider, an inadequate father. He sits up in his chair, lifts his hip, pulls the weathered wallet from his back pocket. He hands over a ten and a twenty. "This'll do?"

"That's great. Thanks." Matt drops the money on the table, turns back to the empty bottle.

Jack needs more beer. He needs to reach that point between the comfortable numbness liquor offers and the zing the alcohol pushes through his blood. He doesn't need to dwell on his inability to deliver. He tries not to get caught in this place. Today, Matt and this girl, it is unexpected. Three more Blues will take him out of the in-between space, will push him past caring about his inadequacies, push him past missing Miriam with every breath in his body, push him into prowling the bar, into letting go with a hookup.

"Matty," he says, "you need a girl who can make you feel good, that's it. Guys like you and me, that's what it's about. Nothing more."

More than that and your heart gets broken.

It is a sullen Ben that Matt finds lying on his back, eyes fixed on the water stains on the stippled ceiling. He sits down on the corner of the kid's bed. "Come on, bro."

"What are you doing?"

He is drained. So tired. Dad. And Ben. And Glory. And the cop. The fucking cop. He should have said something to Dad. But he is not ready to move on. Fuck, he hopes he hasn't made a mistake by keeping quiet. The bile rises in his throat and he swallows hard.

"You won't understand. I don't know if I even understand." He had wanted to ask Dad about Mom, what it felt like. But Dad wouldn't let him. Dad shut him down.

"Understand what? That you're messing around with Glory? That's what you do."

"I'm not messing around with Glory."

"That's what you *do*, Matt."

"This is different." Ben doesn't know what he is talking about. Because this thing with Glory feels so right. Pure. It *is* different.

"You've only ever been one way with girls." Ben rolls so his back is to his brother.

Matt drops his head. "That's not fair, Ben."

"When is anything ever fair?" Ben asks, his voice low.

It kills him that the kid knows this is their life. It kills him that this is their life.

"Never," he whispers.

Glory tucks herself into the corner of the couch, stares out the picture window. It is a disgusting mess. Has a million streaks. Mom should clean it. She read somewhere that the best way to clean a window is to put vinegar in water, use newspaper to smush the mixture on the glass. They have vinegar but definitely no newspaper. Maybe flyers. But all that colour would bleed onto the window. Doesn't matter. She has Windex and paper towel. She will use what she has. She starts in the centre of the picture window, squirts Windex, rubs circles through the drips. It is difficult to see any improvement. Matt was about to kiss her. Oh God. Matt was about to kiss her! But his father ruined it all.

"Hey," Becca says. "Why hasn't Mom cleaned this window?"

"Who knows?"

Becca sinks down on the couch. "Do you think they were scared?"

"Scared?"

"They almost never talk about their dad and Ben got all tense. It was like he was scared," Becca says.

"Scared? No. Matt didn't look scared. Just, maybe, cautious? Maybe a little more than cautious. But not scared."

"I suppose," Becca says. "But Ben's eyes, Glory. No, he was afraid of something."

Maybe about moving? Maybe about Children's Services separating them? But would Matt have said anything to Ben about Cst. McDermott? No, she is sure he wouldn't have. But will he say something to his dad today? He can't! She is not ready to lose him. She is not ready for this to be over. It hasn't even started!

"Ben had bruises on his wrist after his dad came and went last time," Becca says softly.

She turns to stare at Becca.

"Maybe his dad hurts him?" Becca whispers.

"Did you ask him?"

"He said he was fooling around with Matt and they got carried away."

"Well, it's possible." But she can't imagine Matt being that rough with Ben. Never. Her mind flashes to the afternoon they met McDermott. Matt was so angry about how rough Rick was with Lyne. And then on the church steps he told her everything about his family. He would have said something if his father was hurting Ben!

"Look." Becca points. "He's leaving. He just got home and he's leaving again."

Mr. Humphreys pauses on the doorstep, arms loose at his side, fingers flexing. Glory worries he is going to look their way, but he doesn't. Instead, he strides to the BMW, folds into the car and pulls out without shoulder checking.

"Come on. Let's go," Becca says and she is already half way to the door.

"Let's give them a minute." She sprays the window and slowly wipes it. Nothing is clearer.

58

ALLIE CRAVES CAFFEINE. SHE MECHANICALLY goes through the motions of filling the pot then leans against the counter, closes her eyes, loses herself in the sound of dripping water, the pungent smell of coffee. She has always liked that smell. She wishes she didn't have to wait until the coffee maker completed its magic. Doug is good at switching pot out for mug, never getting burned. She has never had that talent. Obviously she doesn't have a lot of talents. Because Doug is good at switching her out, too, and not getting burned there either. All she knows is to wait. When the water stops dripping, she grabs the mug emblazoned with "World's Best Mom" from the draining rack and fills it. She wraps both hands around the faded writing and raises the mug slowly to her lips, allows the scent to fill her. Then she sips.

"Burn your tongue?"

Allie opens her eyes to see a smiling Lyne. "No. I have *this* down to a science."

"I see that." Lyne pours more apple juice into her glass.

"What happened to your grapefruit?"

"This is supposed to be better."

"This?"

"A glass of apple juice in the morning, fruit salad at lunch and an apple at supper."

"Uh huh."

"I can still have grapefruit as part of my fruit salad."

"Yum."

"Mom!"

Allie savours her coffee. It has been a while since Lyne has sounded, looked so carefree. Maybe she and Rick have worked out their differences. Maybe that is what the diamond pendant hanging around her neck is all about. Maybe it is a commitment from Rick. "Hey, have there been some B and Es around here that I don't know about?"

"B and Es?"

"Or maybe someone selling drugs?"

"What are you talking about?"

"There's been a cop car around a lot lately. Either driving the streets or parked outside."

"Parked where?"

"Hm. Across from the Humphreys."

"The Humphreys?" Lyne pales. She spins her half-full glass on the table.

Allie says slowly, "Is it drugs?"

"God, Mom! Can you see Matt selling drugs with Ben in the house?"

"So what *is* going on? Something to do with their father?" She can believe that. Maybe the man hit on the wrong wife.

Lyne finishes her apple juice in two quick gulps. She speaks into the fridge as she puts the juice back on the shelf. "I haven't a clue."

"Are you sure?"

"Course, I'm sure. I'm hardly ever home. If anybody knows what's happening, it'll be Glory. Matt's her boyfriend."

"Okay." She raises her empty hand, backs down. Somehow she has managed to kill Lyne's carefree mood.

59

GLORY HAS BEEN HUNTING THE smoky grey kitten for days. The little thing with the short fur has been stalking the streets for months. She told Matt that the kitten had different coloured eyes but he only humoured her. She needs to catch the kitten, prove to him she wasn't seeing things.

She has followed the kitten a block now from her townhouse. The furball shoots out from behind the wheel of a parked Honda, races down the street then attacks a tire on a rusted Ford truck. It climbs the tire, an impressive feat as the treads are worn smooth. It seeks shelter from the heat — and possibly her — in the wheel well.

"Oh, come on, kitty kitty," she croons, tries to entice the cat to abandon its hiding spot. It is little and it shouldn't be out on its own. She leans her knees against the tire. The black rubber sizzles her bare skin and she falls. Then there are hands on her shoulders, steadying her.

"Hey," she says.

"What are you doing?" Matt asks.

She hooks her hands around his wrists and the sizzle that passes through her body now is stronger than the sting of her knees striking the black tire. She lets him pull her up. She turns around and he kisses her.

Then he starts to play with her low ponytail. "What are you doing here?"

"You remember that kitty I told you about?"

"The one with the different coloured eyes?"

When he looks at her this way all she can think about is kissing him. Lots. Lots and lots of kissing. And maybe hands. A heavy make-out session. They haven't done that yet. She drops down, leans forward to peer into the wheel well. She needs space to think. Her mind gets so muddled around this boy and those lips.

"I chased him here and he climbed up the wheel."

"Look out Man Tracker! Glory, the kitty hunter, is on the loose!" Matt laughs, crouches down to look where she is pointing. "Hey, I see it."

"Really?" Her voice squeaks. Snorting or squeaking, tongue-tied or non-stop chattering. This boy. This boy. This boy.

"Shh," he says, grins so wide Glory swears the sun has nothing on him. He rests his hand on her shoulder, reaches in for the cat.

"Be careful. The tire is hot."

"Yeah, but I'm hotter," he says.

She snorts.

"Can't believe somebody would let something so small run loose like this." He slowly, slowly reaches in. The cat hisses. "Got it!"

"Yeah?" No snorting this time, thank God. She places her hand on Matt's arm, draws the kitten out with him.

Matt nods at her. "Hey, little guy, c'mon."

When he clears the kitten from the wheel, he holds it up, stares into its eyes. "Huh. You're right. One blue, one green. I've never seen that before."

She takes the kitten, flashes an I-told-you-so.

"Go over there, under the tree." He points across the street where a small wooden bench surrounds the thick trunk of a maple. The homes along here are small, rundown, not in much better condition than where they live. She hugs the kitten to her chest, allows Matt to guide her across the road, his hand on the small of her back. They ease themselves down on to the worn bench. She leans into him and the kitten purrs loudly. She turns the kitten around so it can see him. Its small paw shoots out, bats at the gold ring hanging from his neck.

"Hey! Rocky! Don't do that!"

The kitten bats again. She laughs at Matt's indignant face. He grabs his ring and the claws of the kitten scrape lightly across his knuckles.

"Killer cat!" he says.

She places the cat on her lap, holds it lightly with one hand. She reaches out with her other hand to finger the ring that rests in his open palm. The band is scrubbed to a dull gold. She picks it up. "You used to tuck this ring inside your shirt. But you haven't done that for a while."

"Yeah."

"Where did you get it?" She holds the ring reverently.

"My mom gave it to me." He gently lifts it from her fingers, rubs the three diamonds inset in the middle. "Before Ben was born."

"You always wear it."

"I used to wear it on my hand. Mom put tape on it so it was snug on my thumb." He drops the ring to his chest. "I peeled the tape off a little at a time, but then it got too small. A few years back I put it on the leather string, started wearing it around my neck."

"Matt," she starts tentatively. She threads her fingers through his. He pulls her hand onto his chest, covers the ring. "What happened to your mother?"

He should have been expecting this question, expecting her to ask. After all, he has told her so much already. But this, this is so painful. He tightens his grip on his ring, on her fingers. She makes a small sound and he loosens his hold. He is surprised that tears sting his eyes. He has gotten used to not having his mother around. He has pushed those feeling of loss down deep. Hasn't he?

"She died when Ben was born." He hesitates. "She died having Ben. Eclampsia. Rare, but, well, yeah."

"Oh my God. I'm so sorry." Glory covers her mouth. The kitten slides off her lap, but doesn't bolt. Instead, it pushes up against Matt's jeans.

"He was a beautiful baby, you know?" Of course Glory doesn't know! He hasn't shown her the photos. Thank God Ben didn't find those pictures when he found Dad's textbook.

Dad would have gone ballistic. It has been a long, long time since those pictures were out. It has been even longer since Ben asked to look at them.

"When Ben first started school, he'd come home and talk about everybody else's mom. I'd try to tell him about our mom. He'd listen, but I knew it didn't mean anything to him. He was just letting me talk. So after a while I stopped. He's lucky, I guess. He never knew her, can't miss her. He never knew how Dad was before, how Dad was with Mom, so he can't miss that either."

"That must be really hard," Glory says.

He rubs his eyes, scolds himself for the moisture still there. "It's worse on Dad. It changed him totally. Ben looks exactly like Mom and that makes it really hard."

"You were five?" Glory asks.

"Just a little over five." The kitten keeps pushing at his leg, purring, and the sound comforts him. "I remember holding Benny. God, he was so tiny! The bluest eyes, Glory. These big, blue, blue eyes. He looked at me and . . . " He can't finish. It stirs feelings that he can't put words to, feelings that have become embedded in who he is.

Glory speaks carefully. "How long have you been taking care of him?"

"Forever. I don't know anything else."

"It's a lot for you to have to do. It's a big sacrifice."

He stares at her. "He's my little brother."

"I don't understand your dad."

He works his fingers through the kitten's fur, scratches its ear. When he finally speaks, his voice is so low. "Dad sees Ben as what took Mom away from him. I see Ben as Mom's last gift."

60

LYNE RUNS HER FINGERS ALONG her tall glass of iced tea. This is the first time she has been invited to Rick's home. It isn't often he needs to hang with his family, but Mrs. Jeffries insisted on a family barbecue since Jessie and her fiancé were in town. Rick bitched about it. But here they are. She takes a small sip, is grateful for something cold and wet. But it is bitter. She needed to add sugar. This is not iced tea from a can of crystals.

The orange and mustard striped umbrella above the picnic table provides shade but the heat is stifling. She heard Rick's parents arguing about whether to eat inside or out. Mrs. Jeffries wanted to move the party indoors, into the air conditioning. Mr. Jeffries insisted loudly that since Mrs. Jeffries wanted a barbecue they would be eating outdoors. The Jeffries' backyard is the size of all the front yards that span the townhouses and the street in-between.

She leans her elbows on the glass top because, of course, the Jeffries couldn't have an ordinary wooden picnic table. This looks like a Crate and Barrel set. A round piece of glass on top of a black aluminum frame, ropes weaved together intricately for the table's base. The chairs are a matching black weave and the cushions a muted orange. The placemats are mustard and match the umbrella.

She looks up, spots Rick across the yard. He seems young and uncertain, uncomfortable in a button-down shirt, light khaki pants. He needs a beer in his hand. And that cocksure attitude he always displays when he is at a party with their friends. She doesn't recognize this boy, standing with his hands shoved in his pockets, his head canted as Jason, the fiancé, talks. Jason motions with his bottle of Alley Kat Amber. She has never heard of that brand.

"Hi." Jessie settles in the next chair.

"Hey." She tightly clasps her iced tea, crosses her legs like Jessie.

Jessie is pretty. She has grey eyes like Rick, but her grey is steel with a glint, as if the sun is hitting the metal in just the right way. Her shoulder-length hair, a mousey brown highlighted with blonde, is pulled up sloppy in the back and clipped. Lyne has worn that sloppy look, knows how long it takes to make it just right.

"That's a pretty necklace." Jessie waves her glass of iced tea, sloshes a little over the side. Maybe she has a Long Island Iced Tea?

"Thanks." She fingers the pendant. "Rick gave it to me."

"Oh, little brother's got good taste." Jessie is four years older. She swivels in her chair to watch Rick and Jason. "Do you think Mom really believes he doesn't drink?"

"Pardon me?"

"I mean, there's Jason with a beer and I know Rick would kill for one. Even if it is a microbrew." Jessie shakes her head. "He always tries to milk this innocent thing with Mom."

She stares at the older girl.

"What?" Jessie says.

"Your mom has to have seen Rick hungover more than once."

"That's different, because then he still hasn't been drinking in front of her. Hell, Mom probably thinks someone spiked his Coke!"

"Your mom wouldn't think that!"

Jessie laughs, shrill and short.

Lyne sips her iced tea, wishes hers were a Long Island. "I just think it's hard to be grown up around our parents."

"Yeah," Jessie says, works the ring on her finger. "You're going into grade twelve?"

"Yes."

"You and Rick going to keep a long-distance relationship going?"

"He says we will." She taps the table with her sulfur-colour painted nails. Ha. She matches the placemats and the umbrella and the chair cushions. Must be kismet.

"Well, as long as *he* says."

Lyne looks up. "*We* want to." What is this girl's problem? Jessie should be happy, not getting in her face.

"It's hard." Jessie says. Then her features twist into a look this side of understanding. "Jason and I have always been in Vancouver together. Even at the same university, but we spent a lot of time apart with him playing hockey for the Thunderbirds. He had a lot of road trips."

"He seems like a nice guy."

"He has his moments. Most guys have their moments." Jessie presses her cool glass against her throat. Her voice is brittle when she speaks. "Does my brother have his moments?"

Lyne rubs at the fading bruises along her arms. "He needs me. Sometimes that need comes out a little strong. But it's me he's chosen."

Jessie twists the ring on her finger again. It is a large diamond solitaire, only slightly smaller than Mrs. Jeffries' twenty-year anniversary ring. Her eyes are focused on Jason. "Well, hockey boys can be badass more than just on the ice."

"I've never watched Rick play hockey," Lyne says. But she has watched him at parties, watched him push Matt around, watched him beat the shit out of Bishop. "I've never been a puck-bunny."

"You don't need to be a puck-bunny to see it," Jessie says. She sets her empty glass on the table. "I'm going to see if Mom needs help."

Lyne tracks the older girl's movements. She is sure Jessie has a killer figure but her clothes are loose-fitting. Is this her way of milking the innocent-thing with her mother?

Jessie heads to the ice cooler, pulls out an Alley Kat. She twists off the cap, makes her way to Rick and Jason. She pats Rick on the elbow, slides the bottle into his hand. Rick looks pissed.

61

ALLIE HAS NEVER BEEN A two-pot a day coffee drinker. But if she is going to sit here and angst she might as well be caffeinated. As much sense as that makes considering it is still so, so hot. Or she could do what Lyne's magazine called for — it was on the same page as Lyne's all-fruit diet — a soda and cigarettes diet. Obviously an American magazine. Swap her coffee for Diet Coke? No. It looks more sophisticated to sit out on the stoop with coffee and a cigarette. What do the Americans know anyway? Hell with soda.

And doesn't being the wife of a cheating husband make her sophisticated? Why, it's a New Age marriage! She should be upfront with Doug, tell him she wants a free marriage, they should go to partner swaps. What do they call those? Swinging clubs. If he can get it on with someone else, why can't she?

She takes a long drag from her Export A, lets the smoke out in narrow wisps. Doug thinks Lyne is the only one pilfering his cigarettes. She won't set him straight.

What about all those women who have the guts to kick their cheating husbands to the curb? They don't have bills to pay, three girls to feed. Or parents waiting for them to come crawling back. Lord, she is Sandra Marples.

She drains the last of her coffee. She doesn't have the energy to go back in the house for a refill and there is no girl to do it for her. Lyne and Glory and their boys. God. She should talk to Glory about Matt. But it can't be the same conversation Mother had with her because look how well that ended. And then there's Lyne who was invited to the Jeffries for a barbecue. That is not an invitation that comes easily. Janet Jeffries is a snobbish woman. Why shouldn't Lyne be more than a passing interest for a rich boy with a future? At least one Rutger girl should have life a little easier.

There is no movement at the Humphreys house. The boys are out working. She should be concerned about the reputation her girls are earning, tagging after the Humphreys when they do their yard work. Reputations are hard to shake and they mean everything in a small town. But it is too hot to worry. She will save figuring it all out for a day that is cool.

And where is Jack Humphreys? If the police are trying to hassle him for dipping in the wrong gene pool, well, they are shit out of luck. He's never home. She hasn't seen him since he changed her tire, used his well-rehearsed pickup line on her. It is not too hot for fantasies. Jack is a fine-looking man. And those hands, changing out the tire, so strong, so sure. Why should he just be a fantasy? If Doug can do it, why can't she? There would be no commitment. He is that type. Just in it for the sex. That's all she wants. After all, that would be better than pulling a Lorena Bobbitt, wouldn't it?

62

GLORY PLUNGES THE BLADE OF the table knife into the dirty water. She has been working at the clog in the kitchen sink for at least an hour.

"Ugh!" she yells, twists her long hair across her shoulder. "Stupid thing."

"What's wrong?" Becca asks.

She turns around to find Becca and Ben leaning on the kitchen table, grinning. They make a cute couple, Ben slightly taller than Becca. "Stupid sink is clogged. I've used a full bottle of Drano but it's still clogged."

"Mom has a trick with it. I know she uses Drano and something else and it takes like two minutes," Becca says.

"Thanks, Becca." She shoves the knife into the drain faster and faster. "That's really helpful considering she's not here right now."

"Don't snap at me," Becca says.

She throws the knife on the counter. It clatters into the pile of dirty dishes. She pulls out a chair and collapses into it, dries her hands roughly on the towel she discarded earlier. She slaps it back on the table.

"Couldn't you wait until your mom comes back?" Ben asks.

"She's getting her hair done and then I think she's going out for coffee with a friend. She took the car. She'll be gone for hours."

"And your dad's not around, right?"

Becca shakes her head. A strand of hair comes loose from a butterfly barrette.

"Well, I know Matt's around," Ben says.

"That's right," Becca says. "And he's real good with his hands."

Glory snorts.

Ben's face twists in annoyance. She has upset the boy. She still does not understand this quiet dance of looks and gestures between the brothers. But then he grins, dimples showing. "Want me to go get him?"

She pats the towel along her neck. "I thought I could do it, but I can't. So, yes, please, go get Matt."

Ben takes off. Becca leans against the table, smiles brightly.

"What?" Glory says.

"Don't pretend you don't want to see him."

"I don't want to be one of those girls who can't do anything and always has to ask her . . . boyfriend for help."

269

"What else are boyfriends for?" Becca asks.

"Oh, a few other things." Then she is smiling as brightly as Becca. She bats her eyelashes.

"Glory! You sound like Lyne!"

"Well, Lyne doesn't have it completely wrong."

"Lyne's not completely wrong about what?" Matt asks.

"Oh!" Glory grabs the towel, covers her face.

"I'm sure she'll tell you later, Matt. Or you know, show you," Becca says.

Matt closes the distance. Glory twists her hands tightly into the cloth. She can't be this close to him and not touch him. But Ben is here and Matt has drawn a line and she is firmly on the other side of that line.

"Okay, let's see what's happening with your sink." He picks up the knife and pokes around. "Yeah, going to have to open the pipe. Ben, run home, will you, and get the adjustable wrench? It's in the toolbox in the mudroom."

"Sure," Ben says and Becca follows him.

If Glory were brave enough, she would ask about that invisible line. But the way Matt is looking at her right now, the only brave she wants is to move closer. And she does. He pulls her in, kisses her slowly. She wraps her hands around his neck and deepens the kiss. When they come up for air, he asks, "Was this what Lyne was right about?"

"How did you know?"

"I know things," he says, grins slyly. "Can't argue with her about that."

The door bangs and he steps away. That invisible line isn't so invisible now.

"This what you needed, Matt?" Ben swings the wrench.

"You're hired." Matt draws the boy in, gives him a noogie as he wrestles the wrench away. He drops down, positions himself under the sink. Ben drops, too, rests his knees on Matt's leg, ready to help.

Allie squeezes her hands on the steering wheel, perfect positioning at ten and two o'clock. Her wedding ring grinds into her finger. She has no engagement ring. She needs to take off the narrow band of gold. She can't do this if she keeps her ring on.

She was here yesterday, parked on the far side of the bright red pumps, down the road at the thick stand of poplars. She was surprised nobody stopped to see if she had car problems. Car problems would be easy enough to deal with.

She has changed from Peeping Mom to — what? Cheated wife? And now what? Revenge-seeking wife? This is on Doug. She yanks at her ring. But it doesn't come off. She didn't remove it when she gave birth to any of her girls. Damn it. She can't think about that. She won't think about that. She won't think about vows and family and cooking supper tonight.

She should have taken her ring off at home. She could have soaked her hand in a sink full of Sunlight and water. If she had done it then she would have made the commitment to go through with this before she left home. She twists her ring, pulls at it. This is further than she got yesterday. Yesterday she sat in the car and watched Jack Humphreys fill the tank of a soccer mom's van. No cheating wife there. Then she drove away, returned home and stared at herself in her bedroom mirror. She didn't like what she saw. A woman with no nerve. A woman who couldn't even stick it to her husband when her husband was sticking it in another woman. Her cheating husband. Her bastard of a husband.

Damn it. Twist and pull. Damn it. Twist and pull. Damn it. Twist and vicious pull and the ring pops off.

"Oh!" She almost flings it over her shoulder.

She sneaked into the girls' room three nights ago when they were all out, made her way through Lyne's closet. Her hands shook as she pushed apart the hangers, removed two skirts and four shirts. Choosing clothes for a different man.

It has taken her three days to get here. And if she doesn't get her ass in gear, it will be yet one more day. But she promised the woman in the mirror yesterday that today she would do it. Today she would take control of her life. She would not be a victim.

She tilts the rear-view mirror, checks her face one last time. Her eyeliner is running. She has been crying. Just a tear or two. No more than that. No, no more than that. She runs a corner of Kleenex carefully under each eye. How will she seduce Jack if he thinks she has been crying? She doesn't want compassion. She wants passion.

She shoves the Kleenex back in the glove compartment, clicks the latch shut. She starts the engine, flips a U-turn, pulls up closer to the pumps.

She can do this. She will do this. She opens her door and steps out.

Jack doesn't look up when the door scrapes open. He likes to force his customers to wait. Not all of them are patient.

"Excuse me?" It is tentative, but familiar.

He shoves *Popular Mechanics* under the counter. It is not his first choice of magazine, but Rath's doesn't carry *GeoBase* or *The Peg* or any of the engineering journals he likes to flick through from time to time. He looks up. Hello. The blonde from in front of Delwood Grocers. Looking hot. All kinds of hot.

"How's the tire doing you?"

"Good." She smiles, inches closer to the counter. "But it seems to be, uh, shimmying?"

"You asking me or telling me?"

She pushes out a short laugh. "I'm not sure if that's the word, but it's not quite a smooth ride."

"Want a smooth ride, do you?"

And holy shit, does she turn red! He has heard Benny complaining to Matt numerous times about how hard it is for blonds not to blush.

She steps right up. "I like a smooth ride when I can get one, yes."

He walks around the counter, gives her a long once-over, makes sure they understand each other. Because this is nothing like how she acted juggling groceries on the street. She caught his eye then, but right now she is telegraphing available: short denim skirt, halter top cut deep. Christ. All she is missing are the hooker shoes. She is wearing flip flops.

"Where are you parked?"

"On the far side of the pumps."

"Bring your car around. I'll open the bay door."

"Okay." She turns to leave, hesitates just a moment, throws her shoulders back, gives the knob on the door a strong jerk.

Ass-hugging skirt, too. There is no way he is reading her wrong. Sometime between then and now she has decided to take him up on his offer. She reeks of need. It is hanging in the air, a cartoon trail of white swaying with her every step. He pulls out the clock sign, indicates back in an hour, locks the door. Cal called in sick today.

He saunters to the back. She will be there waiting, wondering. He flicks the switch for the bay door. Through the windshield of the car, he sees her paint on the face that says she is ready. The face is for her, not for him. Now it is his turn to hesitate. He doesn't need complicated. But she came to him. When the Malibu is safely in the bay, he flicks the switch again.

She stays in the car. He opens the door. Her hands are glued to the steering wheel. "We doing this or not, sweetheart?"

It's a Herculean effort for her to peel each finger from the wheel. He imagines that grip on parts of his body. He backs up. She slides out. He closes the car door and she steps in front of it. He puts his hands on her hips, drops his lips to hers and it is a searing kiss that he delivers and she takes.

"Gotta name, sweetheart?"

"No, Jack, I don't."

He chuckles into the next kiss. He can work with that. He maneuvers them to the front of the car, pushes her up on the hood.

She pulls away. "What if someone comes?"

"Door's locked."

"Rath has keys."

"He took Tanya out of town for a weekend of fucking."

"Okay, then," she says and it is her turn to deliver a searing kiss.

63

MATT DROPS THE GAS BILL on the pile that needs to be paid right-the-fuck-now. It's a growing stack. He left the bills on the table hoping Dad would see them, pay them. If not pay them, actually leave some money for them. But no such luck. On either front. Is he surprised? Fuck, no.

Thank God it's summer and it's been too fucking hot to need the furnace. And small mercies for not being tempted by the air conditioner they don't fucking have.

"Fuck!"

He's going to be nickel and diming this bill and the water bill. Maybe even digging into his Dempster's bag. If he hadn't been spending their tips on ice cream, it wouldn't be so bad. And that's been all kinds of stupid because he knows — he fucking *knows* — from past summers and from winters shovelling walks that the tip money is part of his operating budget. He's even mentally included a budget line that reads never-being-able-to-say-no-to-Ben's-puppy-dog-eyes.

But Glory. That's a whole different story. She's a whole different story. Why else hasn't he told Dad about that cop? McDermott has been cruising their street. But there's been nothing more than that. No phone calls and hang ups. No women dressed business-like stalking the sidewalk in front of their townhouse. If that happens he will have to tell Dad. Dad will be pissed, but he'll understand why he held off. Dad must have felt this way about Mom.

"Hey, Matt!" Ben charges in, face lit up like a thousand-watt light bulb. His hair is plastered to his head, hangs low into his sparkling eyes.

Matt can't help but answer with a grin. He splays his open hand across the paperwork.

Ben's eyes drop to the table. His smile disappears. "Do we have enough money?"

Jesus! Fuck! This stupid kid, with his stupid smile, and his stupid smarts. He's not supposed to be worrying about these stupid fucking bills!

"Course we got enough. These old ladies pay good money to watch my fine ass push a lawn mower!"

"Ew. That is all kinds of creepy!" Ben says.

The quiet is filled by the tinny strains of music. Ben's eyes open wide as he searches for the radio. "Where did you get that?"

"I didn't." Matt turns to stare at the old relic. "Dad must've found that piece of crap somewhere."

Yeah, Dad can't be bothered to pay the fucking bills, but he can dig out an old radio and put it on top of the fucking fridge. And the thing is fucking ancient, so Dad must have tinkered with it to get it to work.

"Huh." Ben says. Then he is bouncing on his toes. "C'mon, let's go play catch."

"Thought you were with Becca?"

"She's gone to Edson with her mom."

He almost asks about Glory, but that will only piss Ben off. Ben doesn't get it, doesn't get that everything is different with

Glory. And he doesn't know how to make Ben understand. It really twists him up. He wants to do right by Ben. He wants to do right by Glory, too.

He scrubs his hand through his hair. "Grab the ball and gloves. I'll meet you outside."

Ben freezes. His blue eyes piercing. "You okay?"

Jesus. Fuck! This kid twists him up.

"'Okay?' Are you fucking kidding me? I'm so much better than 'okay' I should be in movies!" He offers his leading actor smile, the one that has gotten him action in more backseats of cars than he can count. A smile he hasn't used in what seems like forever.

"Yeah, Quasimodo," Ben says and then runs out laughing.

It is a physical blow. He can't imagine his life without that kid. He sets aside the water bill, the gas bill and debates over the Telus bill. There's still a week until that due date but he slips it into the needs-to-be-paid-right-the-fuck-now pile. The Dempster's bag is going to be substantially lighter.

The song on the radio filters through the heavy air. He closes his eyes, hums along to "Ahead by a Century." Then the words hit him.

"This *is* no fucking dress rehearsal," he says hard. "Fuck you, Tragically Hip." Fuck this life.

64

LYNE STEPS BACK FROM THE full-length mirror to get a better look at her shoes. The mirror is five small squares, each lined up one above the other. But they start too high and make it difficult to see the floor. One more mirror on the bottom would be perfect. She has been ragging on Dad non-stop for the past year to get one more square. But he still hasn't done it. He could easily get it at a discount at the hardware store. Because it's not as if he doesn't work there. Duh. It is only a matter of time before Mom breaks down and gets the mirror. She has been spending a lot of time lately checking herself out.

One more step back and she can see her shoes perfectly. So what if she is almost pasted against the hallway wall and can't strike the right poses? Nice stiletto heel, pointed toe. They make her legs go on forever. Rick will bitch about the cost once he gets his credit card, but she will remind him how hot she looks in them. And Rick is all about the hot girlfriend. Well not *all*, but he does appreciate how she looks, appreciates that other guys appreciate how she looks.

The gold threads in her short denim skirt work perfectly with the gold shoes. All she needs is a gold purse. She should have picked up that little gold clutch when she bought the shoes. She twists and turns a little more in the mirror.

"Wow! Look at those heels!" Ben says.

"Jesus, Ben! What the hell? You guys are always here!" Lyne tugs at her skirt.

"How can you walk in those?" Becca asks undaunted.

"Talent," she says, straightens up, models her shoes.

"They're really hot," Becca says.

She feels golden like her shoes. It isn't often Becca compliments her. "Thanks. I wish I had a gold purse."

"You know, Mama has a gold purse. I was playing dress up with it not so long ago."

Ben snickers. "Dress up?"

Becca colours. "Shut it."

"I'm sure you looked lovely." Lyne wants to snicker, too, but that would be mean. Really, really mean. And Becca is helping her.

Becca leads the way to Mom and Dad's bedroom. She jumps up on the queen-sized bed and peers into the closet, scans the top shelf. Even the added height of the bed leaves her too short to easily see the purses. "Hm. Where is it?" She moves closer to the edge of the bed. "There it is, Lyne. Just behind the red purse."

Lyne stretches up, feels behind. Her fingers grasp what she hopes is the gold clutch and she tugs. Both the red and gold bags hit the ground.

Becca jumps to the floor, crowds her. "Will that work?"

Lyne models the bag next to her hip.

"It's perfect," Becca says, "isn't it, Ben?"

"Awesome," Ben's says flatly, but his eyes float from the purse down, down to Lyne's gold stiletto shoes.

She wonders if she is playing dress up.

65

JACK LEANS AGAINST THE DOORJAMB, hands stuffed in his pockets. The morning sun from the crack between the curtains bathes his sleeping boys. Matt's face is almost buried in his mattress, his pillow abandoned beside him. He rests on his stomach, on top of his sheets, dressed only in boxers. His arms are at his sides, palms facing up. He looks so uncomfortable, Jack rearranges himself in the doorway in sympathy.

Matt's head is turned toward his little brother. Benny faces Matt. They are each other's magnetic north even in sleep.

Benny is flat on his back, T-shirt rucked up under his arms, a light blue sheet draped across his waist. Matt did that, unknotted the sheet from the bottom of Benny's bed, pulled it up to cover the kid. Benny is constantly in motion, even in sleep. Matt has never been a restless sleeper, never a restless boy. He is busy all the time, especially his hands, but his movements are precise, always with purpose. Jack thinks about the basketball in the entryway, the last time he shot hoops with Matt. He has never played pickup ball with Benny. He has only watched the kid from a distance as Matt alternately teased and encouraged Benny, his movements always fluid, Benny's in stops and starts.

He runs his hand down his face, flinches at the forgotten tender spot on his cheek. The husband of his latest bar pickup. He should have known better, timed it better. But he hung around too long, got caught with his pants down. Literally. As he pulled on his clothes, made his way out the door, he heard her begging her husband to forgive her. No way the bank manager is going to want anybody to know his wife fucked the guy who does oil changes at Rath's. He and the boys won't have to get out of town yet, but he may as well lay the seeds. Benny gets bitchy when moves are sprung on him. This way, Matt has time to prepare the kid.

He envies the boys still sleeping peacefully. There has been no peace for him. Not for a very, very long time. Even the moments of fucking another man's wife don't do it for him anymore, don't provide the escape they once did. Funny how escape and peace are tangled up together. But they aren't. Not really.

He never thought Miriam's death would haunt him like this. God, he never thought Miriam would die. How was he supposed to know that wanting a second child so badly would lead to this? He closes his eyes, pictures Miriam holding Matty's hand against her large stomach, the smile on Matty's face when the baby kicked. When Benny kicked. Kicking and moving. That's what it is about now. Him getting his ass kicked, him and the boys moving.

He leans heavily against the doorjamb, tired beyond words. Thankfully the bank manager only grazed him with the cut glass vase from the coffee table. Those white-collar types don't actually throw punches. But he was tired way before then. Sleeping hasn't meant rest since Miriam's death.

"Hey, boys," he says, voice scratchy, "rise and shine. I'm thinking about pushing off soon."

Matt lifts his head, blinks at him then burrows his face farther into his mattress. Benny doesn't move. Matt blindly circles his fingers around Benny's wrist, yanks the kid's arm. Benny's eyes pop open, bright, wide, unseeing. His voice remains sleep-muffled, "Huh?"

"Dad's home. Dad's here," Matt says.

Jack steadies himself on the doorjamb. Soft voice, gentle touch, deep caring. Matt is all Miriam. Even though it is Benny who looks like her. He tries to relax, fight back the ache in his chest.

"Benny, Dad says we're going to be leaving soon," Matt says, voice soothing.

Benny shoots up, twists his wrist from Matt's grasp. "What? When?"

"Shh," Matt says, claims Benny's wrist again. He slides back in his bed, props himself against the wall.

"Not exactly sure," Jack says. "Shortly. Definitely no later than Thanksgiving. Likely before."

"Can't we stay until at least Christmas? Maybe do the whole school year here?" Benny is free from Matt's grip once more, up on his knees now.

Jack shifts on his feet, takes a step out into the hallway, wants desperately to avoid that intense gaze. Who is this kid to be pushing him like this?

"Shh," Matt says, not soft this time, edged.

"Matt's going into grade eleven, Dad. He can play basketball here. They have a good team. And maybe he can even get a scholarship. Go to university on a basketball scholarship like you did. Don't you want that for him? Please, Dad. Let's stay a while here."

How dare this kid question him? How dare this kid with his mother's face, look at him as if he has let them down!

"You little shit!"

Matt scrambles to the edge of his bed. "Dad, no, Ben didn't mean it that way."

The words form briefly in Jack's head, make no sense. He dismisses them. He crosses the room in two strides, yanks Benny out of bed.

"Dad!" Benny's and Matt's voices come out as one.

It means nothing. The ache in his heart has been replaced by rage. His rage is a dark fog, engulfs him, deafens him, drives him on. He squeezes Benny's shoulders. The high-pitched scream of pain means nothing. He slams Benny up against the wall, once, twice. He is about to do it a third time, when his hand is dislodged. He shifts his one-handed hold on Benny, presses hard on the kid's chest.

Matt's deep voice, hoarse now, rips into the rage. "Dad, stop. Stop. Dad, stop, please. Jesus." Matt yanks his arm and the pain shoots through his body, cuts through the fog in his mind, but he keeps Benny pinned. He turns to face Matt. It isn't the fear in Matt's wide eyes that stops him. It is Matt's anger that mirrors his own, the black that diffuses the deep brown, the black that isn't flashed, the black that is hard and steady. It may even be hatred. And he deserves it. If he hadn't pushed Miriam so hard to have a second child, if she hadn't done it for him, Matt would still have his mother.

He lets Benny go. The kid starts to slide down the wall.

Matt moves quickly, wraps an arm around Benny's waist, pulls the kid to the bed. "Dad." His voice is soft, anger, hatred gone, eyes full of fear.

Benny's face is painted in tears, his shoulders heaving, his body trembling.

"Don't talk to me like that again," Jack says. "Ever. Do you understand?"

Benny nods, long bangs flopping.

"When I say it's time to go, it's time to go. You don't question me. Ever!" He steps forward and Benny draws back.

Matt shuffles between them, hands up, palms ghosting Jack's shoulders. The perfect defensive basketball stance.

"Shut that fucking kid up," he says, and then he leaves.

It takes Matt ten minutes to calm Ben down, ten minutes to get Ben to breathe along with him. It has been a while since Dad has lashed out at them, at Ben, and he wasn't ready. He breathes in deeply, shudders along with Ben.

"I'm sorry, Matty, I'm sorry," Ben says softly. "I forgot."

The kid shouldn't have to remember. He pulls Ben in closer, doesn't want to let go. "It's alright, Benny."

"He's been gone so long, so much, I forgot. I forgot the right things to say."

"Me, too." He slackens his grip, threads his fingers through Ben's sweat-dampened hair. Ben never begs Dad to stay, but he is always inconsolable when they move, inconsolable for weeks. "It's not your fault," he says. Heat starts low in his stomach, works its way up, flushes his face. It is the same heat that propelled him when Dad was lashing out. Anger has been feeding his fear more and more these days. Anger and hatred. He doesn't know when these emotions started taking over, when they became such a strong part of his feelings toward Dad. And he doesn't know what to do with them. He wonders if Ben knows about the blackness that threatens to pull him under.

They sit quietly. Ben snuggles a little closer and his breathing softens.

"Listen, Ben, I think we're okay. I don't think Dad plans to move right away. If he did, he would have boxes."

But he is not so sure. Once Dad gets something in his head, he works steadily toward that goal. He becomes driven.

Ben twists around. "Yeah?"

"Yeah."

Ben's eyes are bright, full of hope. But they fuel the darkness. Hatred. Fucking hatred.

"Matt, get your ass out here," Dad yells.

Matt takes a deep breath, lets the air out slowly, lets some of the hatred out slowly, too. "I better go," he says softly. "The oracle is calling."

Ben snags his brother's wrist. "Matty, maybe you can play basketball here. Talk to him."

"Yeah, maybe." It is not going to happen, but he can't say that to Ben, his face so open. He pulls on his shirt and disappears into the hallway. "What, Dad?"

"Who is that?" Dad is tucked into the corner of the picture window, pointing.

He follows Dad's gaze. "Allie Rutger."

"That's not her red Camaro, though," Dad says.

Matt shivers. "How do you know that?"

"I helped her change her tire out in front of Delwood Grocers a while back." Dad speaks slowly.

Mrs. R. is dressed only in a long T-shirt, has both hands wrapped around her coffee mug as she sits on the front stoop. She is fully in the sun and her blonde hair shines. She looks young. It hits him that she is exactly Dad's type of woman.

The door flies open and Lyne comes out, Rick's hand tucked in the waistband of her denim shorts.

Dad grunts. He eyes Lyne, turns back to Matt. "You tapping that?"

"Jesus, Dad, she has a boyfriend. That's her boyfriend with her."

"They engaged?"

"Jesus, no. She's going into grade twelve. He just graduated."

"Well, then. Bet she'd be a good lay. But that mother. Allie? Oh yeah."

Oh, fuck. No. "Dad. We know her girls. They're our friends."

"I thought you said you weren't tapping that girl?"

"I'm not."

"Are you talking about the girl that was here with you? The one you almost kissed? The one you were hiding from Benny?"

He sucks in a breath. "No, no, it's not that. Just me and Ben are friends with Glory and Becca. And Lyne. That's all."

"So what's the big deal?"

"Just, Dad, we know the girls, okay? That's all." And when Dad turns away, fully focused on the scene out the window, he knows he has lost the battle. "Whatever, Dad. Could you just, please, not do it at their house?"

Dad nods once. "We'll be gone by Thanksgiving. Make sure Benny gets his head wrapped around that, okay, Matty?"

"Yeah."

66

RUBY'S IS BUZZING TODAY. IT is run-up-to-the-end-of-summer busy. It is the type of afternoon that Lyne would appreciate having another couple to share space with. Maybe Glory and Matt could join them. Yeah. Like that'll happen. Rick would rather slit his wrists than have Matt in the same booth as him. Actually, slit Matt's wrists.

But it's not as if she has girlfriends to choose from. That's what happens when she steals other girls' guys. Not that she sets out to take them. Not really. But what guy doesn't want the challenge of being some girl's first? And can she help it if the other girls are so quick to give it up? Everybody knows that Lyne Rutger does everything but that and there isn't a guy in school who doesn't want to be her first.

She and Rick are in a corner booth, hands joined across the table, a plate of fries and gravy between them. It will be easier to stick with her diet when school starts again.

"So, think you'll be able to come to Edmonton?" he asks, rubs his thumb across her knuckles.

"What?" She looks up from dunking a fry in gravy. Rick has puddled ketchup on his side of the plate, is a firm believer in double-dipping.

"I don't know if I'll be able to come home every weekend, but if you can come to Edmonton maybe once a month that would be fucking cool."

"You want me to come?"

"Yeah, I want you to come, babe. I told you. I want us to be together."

"You did."

"My sister likes you. Said you had 'an understanding.' Whatever the fuck that means. And even Mom said a couple of nice things about you." Rick blows out a nervous laugh.

What is with him? Ever since the barbecue he has been different. Kinder, softer.

Tony slides in, throws his arm around her shoulders, nabs a fry from the plate.

"What the fuck, bro?" Rick says.

"What?" Tony scissors the fry with quick teeth.

"Hands off my girl."

"Fuck, Rick," Tony says.

"Get out of there." Rick stands up.

"What the fuck?" Tony says.

She was about to ask the same thing. Usually she is the one telling Rick to back Tony off.

"Sit on the other side," Rick says.

"Fuck. What crawled up your ass?" Tony dives in to the other side of the booth and Rick slides in, presses himself hip to knee against her, places his arm where Tony's was a moment earlier. He slips his fingers under her bra strap. The change in him is immediate, from soft to douchebag.

"Why are you here, Tony?" he asks.

"Meeting Marly. Heading to Kennedy's." Tony talks around the two fries he has stuffed into his mouth. "Kennedy's mom is gone until tomorrow. You should come."

Rick says, "Yeah. Not so much Kennedy's."

Tony eyes Lyne. "I can go for a cat fight. Haven't seen a good one for a while."

"Why don't you let Kennedy do you in front of Marly, then you can get your cat fight," she says. "I hear she's desperate."

Rick almost chokes on his fry. "Girl's got a point."

"Ha fucking ha."

Rick turns his slate grey eyes on Tony before he tucks his hand into the neckline of her shirt, pulls her over for a lingering kiss.

"What-the-fuck-ever," Tony says. "Oh, there's Marly."

Marly and Jacey come over, all low-riding denim shorts and boob-busting mini-shirts. Lyne pulls Rick in, sticks her tongue down his throat, doesn't let up until Tony scoots out of the booth. Performances aren't for friends only.

Allie swallows, wonders if she has the nerve to go through with this. Yesterday she made a return trip to Rath's, full of anticipation and desire and, then, instant let down. Rath was there. But Jack took her to the back to show her tires, unbuttoned her shirt and used his teeth and tongue to make her body sing. He promised her more if she took off with him for a few days. How could she say no? She shakes out her shoulders, walks into the kitchen and stops in the archway.

"You lie, Ben!" Matt is laughing so hard he is choking on his words. He clasps Glory's hand under the table, resting it on her bare leg. For a boy who has been so much like his father, he seems different now. Glory is his drug the same way Matt is Glory's drug. She won't be naïve enough to presume she is Jack's drug. But right now she needs whatever he can give her.

"He's not lying, Matt!" Becca says from the other side of the table.

Matt stops laughing abruptly. "You weren't even there, little girl!"

Becca sits up straight. "Doesn't matter. Ben told me."

"As if he's going to tell you what really happened!" Matt starts laughing again, rubs at his eyes. "What did he tell you? That it was an Ent?"

"I didn't say that!" Ben yells, pushes himself up from his seat. His lips twitch as he tries to keep the serious look on his face.

"Well, yeah, trees can be pretty vicious, I'll give you that, Ben. Especially when you're weed-eating and they jump out and grab that plastic string." Matt forks some mac and cheese and offers it to Glory.

Ben scowls. It is a hard look on a face that was fighting back a smile only a moment ago.

Allie moves in quickly. "Hey, gang."

All faces turn toward her and she wonders if they can see through her, if they know what she is considering. If Matt knows what she is considering.

"Where's Lyne?"

"Lyne's with Rick," Glory says.

"Okay." She pulls out the chair at the head of the table, sits next to Matt. "I was hoping to tell you all at the same time, but I guess I'll catch Lyne later."

"What's up, Mama?" Becca squirts more ketchup into her mac and cheese.

"I got a phone call from some school friends who live in Calgary. They want me to come spend time with them. Kind of like a mini class reunion." She tries not to rush her words. She used to lie regularly to her parents when she and Doug were dating. Now she and Doug are married and she hasn't lied for a long time. She wonders how easy it would be to lie to Doug. She marvels at how easy it has been for him to lie to her. Anger surges through her.

"That sounds like fun." Becca spears her macaroni one noodle at a time. "When are you going?"

Becca's voice is light and she feels guilty again. "Tomorrow or day after."

"When is Dad back?" Glory asks.

"On the weekend. I figured you girls were old enough to stay a few days by yourselves. And Lyne will be able to help out."

Matt's plate scrapes harshly as he pushes it away.

"Is everything all right, Matt?" she asks. And wishes she could take the question back. What if he knows? Oh God, what if he says something?

Matt looks up, voice flat. "Everything's just peachy."

She reels in her discomfort, shifts her attention to Glory. "Even if Lyne isn't around much, do you think you would be able to handle things here?"

"No problem," Glory says. The answer comes easily and she breathes again. "I think it's cool that you're getting together with your old friends."

"Real cool," Matt says. He doesn't look at Glory.

Allie hears the resignation in his voice. He is the keeper of deep, dark secrets, a heavy burden for a teenage boy. She should feel sorry for him. Instead, she feels only relief.

Lyne shifts into fifth gear and cackles as her mother braces herself on the dashboard. When Fern's Flowers comes into sight, she slams on the brake and shifts down.

"When did you learn to drive a standard?" Mom's voice is tight but she isn't gasping.

"Rick taught me. I made him. We were at a party and he was smashed. Someone else had to take me home. After that I told him he needed to teach me." The way Mom's eyes linger on her a little too long pisses her off. "What? You think I should have let Rick drive?"

"No," Mom says quickly. "I learned to drive a stick for the same reason. Dad liked to feel real good at parties."

"Huh." She doesn't want to think about how much alike she and Mom are. This life isn't what she wants. She will never make a kid feel guilty because they were a fuck-child and not a love-child. Glory doesn't understand the distinction, but she sees it clearly. Mom feels trapped. She will never be in that position. Never. She shuts off the engine.

Mom stares at the keys in Lyne's hand, unbuckles her seatbelt. "I told you, Lyne, you don't have to come in with me."

Fern's Flowers doubles as the depot for the Greyhound bus.

"It's fine, Mom. I can wait until the Greyhound comes."

"You don't have to," Mom says. "It'll be here in less than fifteen minutes. I'll let Fern fill me in on the latest gossip. She always has the good stuff."

The way Mom is leaving has Lyne twisted up inside. There is something not right here. She felt it a couple of days ago, even before Mom said she was going to visit her friends, friends she hasn't spoken about for years.

Mom swings her legs out of the Camaro. The car is low and she has to push herself up.

"Mom," she begins.

"What Lyne?" Mom's voice is sharp.

"Nothing." She doesn't need this crap. She really doesn't. Mom can go and get loaded with her friends if she wants to. Maybe that will loosen her up. She has been the queen of mood swings lately.

"You look after the girls, all right?" Mom reaches into the backseat for her small green carryall.

Look after Glory and Becca? That's a joke. They take care of each other. They always have.

"Dad'll be back in a few days. He'll help you out on the weekend if I'm not back by then." Mom twists her wedding band.

Dad? Nobody listens to him. Anyway, he'll hit the bar, spend most of the weekend there, shooting shit with the guys, flirting with the waitresses, looking and not touching. What

Mom will be doing with her friends. That's Mom and Dad. As wild as they get.

"Sure, Mom," she says. Her eyes stray across the street to Delwood's only bar. There are a few cars parked in front of the decrepit grey stucco structure. It is one of the oldest buildings in town and shows it in the cracks and the rust streaks. The paint is peeling in the sign declaring Delwood Bar and Grill. There is a black BMW three spots down from the door. The car looks vaguely familiar. It doesn't belong to either of the town's doctors or the bank manager. They do have Beemers but they have newer models. This one is old — she can tell by the boxy style — but it is well taken care of.

The Greyhound rolls in with a high-pitched shriek.

"Whatever, Mom," she says, annoyed all of a sudden, eager to get on her way. "We'll deal. Now go have fun."

Mom tucks her bag under her arm, crosses to the driver side.

Lyne hangs out the window. "I can't believe that's all you're taking."

"I pack light. What can I say?" This time Mom's smile softens the creases on her face.

"Well, it'll give you an excuse to buy clothes if you don't have what you need."

"Yes, it will," and the tight lines are back at the corners of Mom's mouth. Mom ducks low, kisses her on the cheek.

That kiss ties her stomach up in knots. Something is happening. But she needs to focus on Rick and the short time they have left before he leaves for Edmonton.

"Be off, girl. I'll see you in a few days," Mom says over her shoulder as she makes her way to Fern's Flowers.

"Okay." She shoulder checks then cranks the wheel tight into a U-turn. Before she steps on the gas she glances in the rear-view mirror, expects to see the doorway empty. Instead, Mom is standing on the sidewalk, not moving, hung between the bus and the bar.

67

LIFE IS PERFECT. GLORY FEELS a little guilty about not missing Mom. But she is snuggled in the hammock with Matt, and life is perfect.

Matt chuckles.

"Hm?" she murmurs, shifts lazily into his side. The hammock doesn't leave much wiggle room.

"Huh?" he says, presses his lips against hers. They don't dare swing. Too much movement will stretch the ropes, cause the hammock to graze the gravel that generously covers Matt's back yard.

"That won't work," she says.

"What won't work?" Matt widens his eyes in feigned innocence.

"You're trying to distract me." She backhands him across his chest. "And that won't work. What were you laughing about?"

He scrunches his face. "You really want to know?"

"I do." Sometimes she feels like she can read him, like he is one of her Steinbeck novels.

His cheeks flush red. "I was just thinking that life was perfect."

"Really?"

"Really." He kisses her. The kisses grow in intensity. And then he pulls away.

"What's wrong?" she asks. She can feel her lips are swollen. She wants more.

"I've never had perfect before, Glory."

"Never?"

"Never," he says and kisses her softly.

"You don't miss Kennedy?"

"What? Why would you ask that?"

She tries to turn away, but he won't let her. "All we do is kiss, Matt. You had so much more with Kennedy."

"That's not true," he says. "I could do more with Kennedy, but I *have* more with you."

She doesn't say anything. Can he read her like a Steinbeck novel? Does he know that her fears about Kennedy keep her on a constant rollercoaster ride? Does he know that she is terrified he will come to his senses, realize what she gives him is not enough?

"You know I haven't been with Kennedy since, like, two weeks before the end of school?" he says.

She nods, her head against his chest. She is desperate to know what he will say next. She is terrified about what he will say next.

"I don't want Kennedy. I want you, Glory. I need you," he says. "I've never felt this way before. It's perfect. You're perfect."

Glory is silent a moment, then she tips her chin up and kisses him deeply. She doesn't stop. And he doesn't pull away.

Lyne and Rick have been romping on her parents' bed for over an hour. She has always wanted to do it — or some version of it — in Mom and Dad's bed.

They are keeping it 18A. Glory and Becca are over at the Humphreys but there is no telling when they will be back. And the bedroom door does not lock. Rick is in his boxers and she is wearing a leopard-spotted matching bra and thong set she found in Mom's drawer. Who knew Mom still dressed like this for Dad?

Rick is slow, attentive. She considers this the new and improved version. She has dwelt on these changes late at night, when she can't sleep. Wonders what they mean for her and Rick. For her. But even new-and-improved has its limits. Rick is hard as a rock and can't stop telling her how she looks like a fucking Victoria's Secret model dressed like that. And everyone knows that Victoria's Secret models don't stay dressed *like that* very long.

"Jesus, fuck, babe. What better time to do it than now?" His lips move under the leopard print bra and his fingers explore places even lower. She has had many boyfriends but none of them do what Rick does to her.

"We agreed, Rick. We agreed."

He keeps going and she isn't sure what they agreed to anymore. Why they agreed. Because holy, holy crap. Holy crap. Holy crap.

"Oh God, Rick."

"The real thing feels even better, babe," he says smugly.

She can't imagine that. She shudders and then she is floating away. He has never taken her this high before.

"Little bit of help here, babe," he says. His hand shifts from delivering her to working himself.

"Let me do that," she purrs. She is blissed out, a hot leopard in bed with the boy who says they have a future together. She crawls down the bed on all fours, shakes her kitty ass in the air and takes him in her mouth. He doesn't last long.

Afterward, she slinks up his side, whispers in his ear, "Does Kennedy make you feel the way I make you feel?"

"No," he mumbles, on the verge of falling asleep. "I want you, Lyne. Just you."

She lies very still, revels in the decision he has made.

68

MATT LOOKS AT THE THICK book in Glory's hand. "For Ben?"

"No, for you. It's *The Grapes of Wrath*. You said you really liked it. I found it in a garage sale and bought it for you."

He takes the book, flips through the pages. "Hey, your bookmark. Don't you want to keep this?" It seems like so long ago he gave it to her, showed her that she was the one he wanted to be with.

She snatches it back. "Yes! I was marking a quote I found, forgot to take it out."

"A quote?" Fuck. His girlfriend is as big a geek as his little brother!

"Yes and don't make fun of me! And don't read the front of the book until later, okay?"

"Why?"

"I wrote something in there and if you read it now I'll die of embarrassment."

"And I'm so not into necromancy."

She swats him with the book. He takes it from her, places it on the kitchen table. She lays the bookmark on top. He pulls her into the living room, settles her in the middle of the three-seater couch. He folds himself into the corner.

"What?" Her face is warm, her eyes bright.

He takes both her hands in his. They fit perfectly.

"What, Matt?" She squirms closer.

He doesn't want to tell her. Maybe if he doesn't say the words everything will stay the same, they will stay in this moment. But it has never worked that way before. Why should it work that way now? Because things are different now. He has never felt like this before. Whatever this is. Doesn't that change everything?

"I need to tell you something." He focuses on his thumb sliding over her knuckles, his heart still in the belief that things are different now, different all over. That moving to Delwood has made everything different. Everything better.

She loosens one of her hands, tips his chin up so their eyes meet. Then she leans in and kisses him. His hand settles on the back of her head, underneath her low-fastened ponytail. He pulls her in, deepens the kiss, drops his lips to the hollow of her neck. Her quick gasp stirs him. He stops kissing her, rests his forehead on her shoulder, closes his eyes tightly. He has to tell her before they get carried away. He has to tell her before they do this. And God, he wants this.

"What, Matt?"

"We'll be moving soon."

"When?"

"A few weeks. A couple of months at the most." He rushes the words. But he knows blurring them doesn't change a thing.

"But why? Isn't your dad working at Rath's still?"

"No. He quit his job. Said we'll be gone by Thanksgiving."

"But can't he find another job?"

"That's . . . not what he's about." He brushes his thumb across her cheek and she leans into his touch.

"What do you mean?"

"My dad, he's about moving on. It's how he deals with what happened to Mom. He fucks married women, gets drunk and moves. He can't think about losing Mom, so he needs to keep moving. That's been the pattern for half my life, almost all of Benny's. We'll be gone by mid-October. That's a given."

"Oh," Glory says.

He waits for her to draw back, for her to say that because they have no future, they have no now. But she stays where she is, her face buried in his palm, her eyes closed.

"Glory?"

She lifts her head, opens her eyes and they are damp. It hurts to look at her. The pain in her eyes hits him deep in his gut. He has only ever felt Ben's hurt like this.

"Do you love me, Matt?"

"I don't know. I know when we're not talking I'm miserable. I know I really wanted to make that bookmark for you. I know when you kissed me you blew my mind. I know I've never kissed a girl the way I kiss you. I know I want to touch you, have you close to me, talk to you, laugh with you. Is that love? I don't know, Glory."

She is silent and he shifts closer. He needs her to understand. He cups her face in both his hands, clings to her warmth, to being here with her. "I've never been in a relationship before. What happened with Kennedy? That's what it's always been about. I started having sex when I was really young and I got good at it. It's an escape for me. Time to forget everything I'm responsible for. And I never commit. I can't commit. I can never stay."

She blinks and the tears fall. "I love you, Matt Humphreys." It's all she says. She leans in, kisses him gently on his lips.

It is starbursts. Fireworks on the first of July. He is so full of her he is going to explode. If this is love, he will take it.

Allie examines herself in the bathroom mirror. Her black negligee is more string and lace than fabric. It reveals creamy white breasts and pink nipples, a stomach soft from three babies, a thatch of hair she has tweezed too many grey strands from. "Oh God," she says.

She and Jack have been about tearing each other's clothes off, tumbling into bed and having sex until they are sweaty and spent. Waking up, doing it again. He is good, very good. It is some of the best sex she has had in years. But she wants romance. She is ready for romance. Isn't that what getting away is supposed to be about? Tonight she wants a slow burn. She wants Jack to be gentle, to gradually take her higher until she spills over. She wants him to hold her after, to talk to her. Ask her if it was as good for her as it was for him. She wants him to tell her she is an incredible lover. She wants him to . . .

She wants him to be Doug. She wants to be wearing the lace babydoll Doug bought. To be having that weekend getaway she had been planning, before . . . before.

She sinks down on the toilet lid, cradles her face in her hands.

"Christ, Allie. You coming out of there anytime soon?" Jack says.

She rubs her index fingers under her eyes. But there are no tears. "Out in a minute."

She stands up, looks in the mirror again. Who is she kidding? This isn't about romance. This is about fucking. No more. Nothing else.

She watches another woman in the mirror unlace the black negligee with steady hands. It falls to the ground and she kicks it under the bathroom counter. The woman in the mirror has creamy white breasts and pink nipples, a stomach soft from three babies, a thatch of hair she has tweezed too many grey strands from. A face she does not recognize.

She pulls on the white terry-cloth robe that hangs on the back of the bathroom door. The hotel included two matching robes. She opens the door, steps out. Jack is in the bed, propped up against a pillow. His chest is bare. The sheet, draped over his hips, is already tented. Romance? It's just a fuck. She drops her robe. Jack flings the sheet off, reaches for a condom. She crawls on the bed, settles her thighs across his legs. It's just a fuck.

Glory twists her hair, tries to arrange it in a fancy 'do. She wants to look special for Matt. For tonight.

Becca is at the foot of her bunk bed, her chin on the metal railing, hovering above. "Just leave it in that low ponytail he likes so much."

"What are you talking about?"

"Matt likes your hair with that low elastic. Remember? He said that. You should leave it down."

"You don't think I should do anything special?"

"I think that is special for him."

Glory holds her sister's gaze in the mirror.

"You look different," Becca says softly.

"He can leave any day now. He says Thanksgiving but there's no way to know when his dad is going to come home and tell them to pack."

"I know. Ben said."

"I love him, Becca."

"I know."

"I *love* him."

"I know," Becca says. "Do you think Lyne loves Rick?"

She moves from the dresser bench to Lyne's bed, traces a yellow sunflower with her fingertip. "I think maybe Lyne has a different idea of what love is."

"What do you mean?"

"She likes Rick. I know she does. And he buys her expensive things, takes her places. Maybe that means love to her."

"And what about Kennedy?" Becca asks.

"Kennedy?"

"Kennedy and Matt? Was that love?"

"No," she says. "I think that's about being lonely. Kennedy needed him because she was lonely. Maybe she thought she was in love with him."

"And Matt?"

"He's had to grow up much, much too quickly," she says. "I think he's a boy who hasn't thought about what he wants for years."

"What does he want?"

"To be loved," she says. "I love him. I know he loves me. I know this is right."

"You're beautiful," Becca says and there is awe in her voice.

"You've got to do something for me." Matt leans against the wall, shoves his hands into his front pockets. He needs to get over this hurdle before tonight can happen. He hates that he will be disappointing Ben. But tonight is for Glory. And then he can spend all the days after making it up to Ben. Because the tomorrows with Glory are numbered.

"What do you want?" Ben looks up from *Jacob Two-Two*, one of his twenty-five-cent library books. He lost his original copy four or five moves ago. He is sprawled across the armchair, one leg hooked over the side.

"You need to stay late at Becca's tonight."

Ben closes his book. "Why?"

"Look, I know what you're going to say, but this is different." He crosses his arms, uncrosses his arms. He rubs his hands down the front of his jeans. He doesn't want to appear defensive, but the way Ben is looking at him . . .

"It's only different because this is Glory. Glory. She's not like any of the other girls you bang and leave behind. She's not like Kennedy. Don't make her like Kennedy."

That Ben knows is unexpected. But it shouldn't be.

303

"You don't understand." He throws Ben's leg off the armrest, sits down. "Glory and I have talked about this. We both want this. We'll be gone soon. Any day now. If we don't do it tonight, we might never be able to do it."

"Then don't ever do it! You've done it a million times with a million other girls! You don't have to do it with Glory. This is Glory!" Ben surges up, his face clouded with anger. He pummels Matt in the chest.

Matt blocks his next thrust, holds tightly to the kid's wrists. "I love her, Ben. I've never loved anybody before. I love Glory. This is the first time it's not sex. This time it's about love."

"I don't want you to do it with her." Tears stream down Ben's flushed face.

"It's not your call." Matt's voice is hard.

Ben swipes at his eyes. "Matt."

"This is what we want. We've been together since we moved to this fucked-up town. She knows me. She knows what I'm about. And she still wants to do this with me. Don't you get that, Ben? *She* loves *me*." It hits Matt like a freight train. "She loves me. I've never had that before."

Lyne is still riding the high of Rick's confession. All she can think about is being with him. Really being with him. She is feeling too good to snipe at Becca and Ben. They are sitting on the front stoop lobbing pebbles at a bucket in the street. Her words tumble out, easy. "You shouldn't be doing that."

"What?" Becca asks, turns forlorn eyes up to her sister.

"End of summer isn't that big a deal," she says. She has slipped unexpectedly but not uncomfortably into this big sister role now that mom's away.

"We're moving," Ben says.

"They're moving," Becca says.

"What? When?" Oh, God. It pushes her bliss away.

"A month or two." Ben hurls a pebble. It bounces off the yellow plastic pail.

"Why?"

"It's what my dad does," Ben says.

She sinks down on the step next to Becca. "What is Glory going to do?"

Becca opens her mouth, closes it again, turns away.

"Glory is going to be devastated," Lyne says.

"It's wrong," Ben blurts out.

"What's wrong?" Lyne asks.

"Matt being with Glory," Ben says.

"They're in love, Ben," Becca says.

"Matt doesn't do 'in love.' He's never done 'in love.'"

Lyne sees the guilt cross his face. "Ben?" she asks and can't believe that soft voice is hers. There is something about this boy that makes her want to protect him. He is vulnerable in a way Becca has never been.

He looks at her from under his long bangs, takes one deep breath. "Do you think people can change?"

"Change?"

"Yeah. Become different than what they normally are?" His eyes are a deep blue and she reads a plea in them for the right answer. She doesn't know what that answer is.

"I think people can change," she says. "Rick has changed."

"Not everybody changes," Ben says. The boy sounds too old. As if he has seen too much and no longer believes in fairy tales.

"No, not everybody," she says. But Rick *has* changed.

"I keep waiting for my dad to change, but he doesn't," Ben says. "Matt says Dad was different before I was born. Matt says Dad will change, that Dad'll come around. I keep waiting for that to happen, but it never does. Matt says I have to be patient."

He is quiet for so long Becca nudges him with her knee.

"Dad and Matt are a lot the same. Always about, you know, doing it whenever they can. It's never been about love." Ben is quiet again. "Maybe Matt can change."

"Glory loves Matt," Becca says firmly.

"Matt says he loves Glory," Ben says.

"Don't you believe him?" Becca asks.

Ben squints his eyes into the sun. "I want to believe him."

"Ben?" Lyne says.

He peers around Becca. "Do you think Glory can fix what's broken in my brother?"

"If anybody can fix what's broken in Matt, it's Glory," she says. The Rutger girls have that power. She has fixed what is broken in Rick.

Jack puffs three perfect zeroes. He doesn't smoke often but he found a few loose cigarettes in Allie's purse. Along with her wedding band. He shouldn't have been looking, but what the hell? Not as if they're going to have trust issues. This isn't a relationship.

Allie is still sleeping. Her old man must smoke after they screw.

Huh. Rutger probably doesn't know it's his wife who is pilfering his cigarettes, not his daughter. Rutger doesn't know a lot of things. But then again, maybe he doesn't care. He's off getting his own on the side.

But that is not Jack's concern. He is no marriage counsellor. Hell, no. After all, here he is in the sack with another married woman. He won't fool himself to think that he will have to convince her to go back to her husband. He doubts she ever thought about leaving Rutger. That's what makes these hookups so good. The sex is always hot. And there is never a possibility that the woman will want more than a roll.

He doesn't want more than this. He can never replace Miriam — even if the women he chooses are blonde, blue-eyed like she was. These women are the reminder he gives himself that because he wanted more, he lost Miriam. This is his punishment.

He pulls in a long drag, lets the smoke out in one unbroken stream. Miriam was everything. Allie is nothing.

This is what he has become. No going back. And no moving on. Just moving.

A light knock at the door draws Matt to the front of the house.

Glory stands on the stoop. She is stunning. Her hair is in the loose ponytail that drives him nuts. Her shirt is a brilliant blue, pulls out the blue of her eyes. It fits snugly, shows off her breasts, breasts he has only felt above her shirt this past week, breasts that fit perfectly in his hands. She wears a flowing skirt and her Tevas. He runs his hand down his dark green DKNY shirt, fingers his mother's ring. His mouth is dry and he can barely swallow. Fuck! He better not pass out.

There's a touch of colour on her lips, her soft lilac scent fills the air, travels on the waves of the heat. She is like a dream and he stares at her, doesn't want to speak, wake up, see it all fade away.

"I told Becca that Ben has to stay there until I come home." She sounds eager and scared and it pulls him out of his haze. He is eager and scared, too.

"Good," he says.

He draws her in, kisses her soft then hard. Her hands slip under his shirt and her fingers are little electric shocks. She peels off his shirt and he feels shy. She has seen him bare-chested before but she has never touched him like this. They stand in the doorway a while longer, her hands running over his chest, his back, his hands above her layer of cotton. The shirt is so hot to his touch he can only imagine the scorching marks he will leave on her bare skin. He wants to do that now, but he wants this to be perfect. He pulls away from her, takes her hand, leads her to the bedroom. He has promised himself he is going to take this slow. He has promised himself this.

Lyne peels one of Rick's hands from the steering wheel, places it high on her thigh. He is charged like always, but there is something more. On the weekend he is heading to Edmonton for orientation. He is scared, but he won't admit it.

"I don't want to be leaving Delwood with Humphreys thinking he's got a shot at you. I don't want that dickwad anywhere near you." He moves his hand up, slides his fingers under the elastic of her thong.

"Jesus, boo, we've got to slow this down a little."

"Just making my point. Want you to remember my touch." She pushes his hand lower, laces their fingers together.

"This is our last night before school starts," he says.

"It's only orientation. You're back for a few days before you have to start living in Edmonton."

Rick shakes his hand free. "What are you saying?"

"Just that we have a few nights together before we have to start thinking about weeks apart. I want to do things right."

She hasn't told him that she thinks she wants to do this with him. She has been turning it over in her head, the idea of giving it all to him tonight. She is sure he has condoms, but she took some from Dad's night table drawer — and what's with that? Mom is on the pill. And these condoms aren't the cheap kind. She stashed them in Mom's little gold purse. She is wearing the stiletto gold shoes, too. When Mom comes home, she will talk to her about going on the pill.

"I want to do things right, too, babe," Rick says and that softer side that she has begun to see more and more creeps out.

"Maybe tonight." She squeezes his thigh and thinks about what it would feel like to really have him in her. She needs him to want to come home. To her.

He wiggles his eyebrows. "Should be a bedroom free at Tony's."

"Rick!" She slaps him lightly across his chest.

He nabs her hand. "Tony's old lady is out of town all weekend. There's already an assload of people there. That's where we're heading."

The sound of the party filters into the street. The screen door is open and the windows wide. The music is driving. Rick pulls her out of the car, sets her on the hood of the Camaro, thrusts his tongue down her throat.

She wraps her legs around his waist. He pulls her up. They are still kissing when he stumbles on the curb.

"Let's go inside," she says.

He laughs, sets her feet on the ground. "Let's not hurt ourselves before we get in there, okay, babe?"

She tucks both her hands into his belt, walks backwards, keeping her eyes locked on his. She backs up to the first step of the porch and with her stilettos is the same height as he is. She kisses him until neither of them can breathe.

"Holy fuck, babe." Rick staggers into the railings. His eyes are hungry, but his tone is tender.

Allie smiles, stretches, allows the pale peach sheet to slip below her breasts. She hasn't felt this wanted since Doug chased after her in high school. She pushes Doug aside. She left him in the bathroom with the black negligee, hastily kicked away. This is about Jack. And it has been incredible.

"You wear me out," Jack says. His lip twitches. Four days of stubble on his face and he is still sexy as hell.

"That's a good thing, isn't it?" She feels wild, wants more. If she's going to be here, she needs more. If she stops, she thinks. If she thinks then it is all about Doug. He is fucking another woman.

"Yeah," Jack says, smiles fully now. He is all charm after sex. And before sex. "That is a good thing."

His eyes rest on her heaving breasts and she peels the sheet back. She runs her hand over her breast, her hip, slides her hand under the sheet, fists his dick.

"Christ," he says through a long breath.

She runs her hand along his shaft, applies more pressure. He bites his lip, his eyes roll back and she wants this power, craves this power. She hasn't had control for such a long time.

This getaway has not been about control. Jack has been a considerate lover. He has been all about pleasing her. And she should appreciate that. But it has left her with no choice but to accept what he gives. No, she wants this control, needs this control. Her life has been slipping away on her. She wants it back. Right now. She rolls on the condom. She throws her leg over his hip, slides down on him. She sets the pace, picks it up. He comes in a guttural cry. And she is left unfulfilled.

She rests her head on his chest, snuggles in, wants him to reach down, hold her. Needs to know there is more to this. Not even romance. Just something. Something, God, please. But in a minute, his breath evens out. He has fallen asleep. This isn't control. This is desperation. She rolls away, muffles her heartbreak in her pillow.

Glory can't think anymore. It is all about touch and feel. And what Matt is doing to her, there are no words. No words for the girl who is all about books.

Her back is pressed into the bed, his lips running eagerly from below her ear down her jaw, down her throat. His thumbs are tracing the wire of her bra under her shirt. She wants more. It isn't enough for her to run her hands down his back to, oh my God, feel him hard against her legs. She needs skin against skin.

"Take off my shirt."

"You sure?"

"Yes. Please." It is a pathetic whine.

His lips press a smile into her neck. How many girls have begged him? Did Kennedy beg him for more?

He pulls her up. His knees straddle her, his jeans rough on her naked legs. Her skirt is rucked up around her thighs. His eyes remain on hers and she nods, a minute tip of her chin. She has never been so — so what? — shy? scared? excited? All of those. Yes. And so turned on.

"You're beautiful," he says.

She slides her thumbs into either side of the waistband of her skirt, starts to shimmy.

"Let me," he says, and he pulls her off the bed. They face each other and she focuses on the ring that hangs on his chest as he gently eases her skirt over her hips and it drops to the floor. She stands there, skirt puddled at her feet, in her matching blue cotton bra and panty set. Move back or move forward? She steps closer to him. His eyes leave hers, slowly, slowly trail the length of her body. His breath hitches and he returns his gaze to her face.

She wants to reach out, to undo his belt, take off his jeans. She wants to see how she has excited him. But she doesn't know how to move.

His chocolate eyes darken. He keeps his eyes on her face, but she is drawn to the sudden movement of his hands. He releases his belt buckle, pops the button on his jeans, carefully unzips his fly. He works his jeans off. Her eyes settle on the bulge in the front of his boxer briefs. She wants to touch it. Him. Oh God. Her cheeks burn.

"Come here," he says and draws her down onto the bed. He covers her body with his and his ring presses between the valley of her breasts and it is all about touch and feel and it goes deeper than this and it sears her to her core. And she wants it all.

Lyne is drunk with kisses, with this feeling that must be love. "Say it!"

"You're going to be mine," he says.

"I'm already yours, Rick. I don't need to have sex with you to be yours."

"Sex is a good thing, babe." He nips her lip, licks the sharpness away. "And it's not sex with us. Not just sex."

Now he is slow and soft and tender and this, this is what love is. Is she in love? Yes, she is in love with Rick.

"I want to be with you. All the way," she says.

The smile that crosses his face is like none that she has seen before. He must feel the same about her. He must love her.

"Yeah?" he says. "Tonight?"

She nods, reaches up to take his lips again.

It is the absence of touch he first notices. Allie is hugging the side of the bed. A little nudge and she would be over the edge.

After all these years, he should be used to that lack of warmth. But he still hates waking up alone. Right after Miriam died, five-year-old Matt would pull a crying baby Benny from his crib and they would come into bed with him. Even then, even back then Matt was doing it. The boy would crawl into bed, tuck up into him, place Benny on the other side. Matt still comes between him and Benny. He wishes he could view the kid the same way Matt does. Benny is no blessing. But the boys are all he has left of Miriam. Stolen moments, fucks with women who look like Miriam, don't come close to filling the void.

Allie stirs. Jack closes his eyes. He heard her crying. There was a time when he was a better man, when he would have reached out to her, comforted her. But when he was a better man it was because of Miriam. And if Miriam were still alive, he would not be seeking escape in another woman's arms. He would not be that kind of husband.

He was in love. He was loved. He had it all.

It hits Matt. He loves Glory. He *loves* Glory. He rolls over onto his back, breathes deeply, splays his hand across the ring that rests on his chest, closes his eyes.

"What's wrong?"

"We can't do this." His answer comes out in a strained whisper.

"Why? You don't have condoms?"

He laughs harshly. "I have a box full of condoms. I always have condoms."

Glory sits ups, pulls her legs tight to her chin.

He looks her over. Her hair has fallen out of her ponytail, her lips are swollen, her eyes dark. She wants him. He closes his eyes and when he opens them again he sees Glory's perfect body, her perfect face, this perfect girl. "I'll be gone soon. I can't do this to you. You'll find another boy you'll fall in love with, make love to, have him stick around and love you. That's what you deserve. I can't stay, Glory. And I love you too much to do this to you."

"But we both want this," she says. "I want this."

"We can't do this, Glory," he says. "We can't. I'm sorry."

Tears roll down her face. He reaches out and she pulls away. She slips on her clothes. She looks at him, her blue eyes dull and watery, her face red. She leaves without saying goodbye.

"After tonight, Humphreys is going to know you're mine."

"What is it with you and Matt?" Lyne huffs. "He's moving anyway."

Rick draws back. "What?"

"Matt's moving. In the next couple of months."

"Next couple of months? Who told you that?"

"Ben told Becca there was no way they would last 'til Thanksgiving. It's their dad." Lyne snags Rick's belt, pulls him in. "So, see? Nothing to worry about. Matt won't even be here. And, anyway, I keep telling you, it's you I want."

"Fuck!" Rick says.

"I thought you'd be happy."

"Yeah, I'm glad the jerkoff will be gone, but I was wanting McDermott to bust his ass."

She pushes him back. "McDermott?"

"You don't think it's weird Humphreys' old man is never around? That Humphreys always has that kid brother with him?"

"Matt takes care of Ben."

"Yeah, but why?"

"I don't know. What difference does it make?"

"There's something hinkey about it." Rick smirks. "I told McDermott. He said he'd check it out."

Lyne is suddenly cold. Yes, there is something wrong about the Humphreys. Matt's old man is definitely suspect. Maybe even some kind of criminal. But Matt doesn't deserve this.

What if McDermott calls Children's Services? What would happen then? She shoves Rick and he stumbles back. "What have you done?"

"What the fuck, Lyne? Who gives a shit?" His voice rises again and he presses her hard against the wall, grinds his pelvis against hers.

She tries to squirm away. "That's my sister's boyfriend. She'll give a shit. I have to phone her, warn her."

"What the fuck?" Rick steps back, face red, breath coming in hard and ragged.

"I give a shit." She pulls her cell from her purse.

He snatches the phone, shoves it in his back pocket. "Fuck that."

"Rick!"

"Forget about that fucker." He wraps his hand around both of her wrists.

"Give me my phone!" She jerks back but can't break free.

"No! I'm sick of hearing about that asshole. It's you and me. No more dicking me around." Rick's eyes turn steel. He hauls her to the closest bedroom, bangs the door open. "Get the fuck out of here," he yells at the couple writhing on the bed. "This is my room now. Get the fuck out!"

The girl pulls on the boy's shirt and the boy drags on his boxers, grabs his clothes and his girlfriend's. They scurry out of the room.

He slams the door shut, rips open her shirt, throws her on the bed.

"Don't, Rick." She crawls away.

"No more. We're doing this. You're mine."

He tugs at his belt, unzips. She scrambles off the bed, darts around him. He yanks her wrist, flings her on the bed, knees her legs apart.

"No, Rick, stop."

"No fucking way." He pushes her skirt up.

She scratches his face and he backhands her. She bites her lip to stop from crying out. Her eyes are wet. He tears off her thong, pushes into her, over and over again, grunting. She bites her lip until it bleeds. Then she is no longer there. She is in the playground. The swing is covered in shiny red paint. She is flying up into the blue sky and reaching for the clouds. Higher. Higher. But they are too far away.

Allie grasps the sheet, feels self-conscious in her nakedness, self-conscious with her eyes rimmed red. She watches Jack dress. He is nothing like Doug. Jack is confident in his skin, his movements easy, not a moment of doubt in his abilities. His shoulders ripple in his tight blue T-shirt, his hair curls wildly just above the collar. He is no Doug. And he is no future.

"We can't do this again," she says firmly, keeps her eyes fixed on the curve of his spine.

"I know," he says.

She does not want this. She will scrub this, this rashness from her brain, scrub Jack from her memory. It will never have happened. She needs to go back and be with Doug. This, being in someone else's bed, this is not her. And being alone is not for her either. Doug has been her past and he will be her future. Doug and Delwood are all she knows, all she has. She will forgive Doug.

There is no more to say. There has been no pillow talk, no sharing of her girls or Jack's boys or what has brought either of them to this point. The ride back to Delwood will be a quiet one.

Jack sits on the edge of the bed, back still to her, laces up his broken-in Reeboks. He turns around. He is a handsome man, but oh, God, so damaged. And she can no longer fool herself. She is broken, too.

She puts on the same smile she wore when she sat in her Malibu, waiting for Jack to open the bay door, for him to take her on this journey. "Check us out. I'll meet you down in the lobby in fifteen minutes."

He leaves without a word.

Glory runs across the yards, tears streaming from her eyes. She can't think. She can only feel.

She slams through the front door, is vaguely aware of Becca and Ben playing Uno, of them yelling at her. She keeps going, throws herself on her bed. Now her brain kicks in, screams at her. How could he do that? He was supposed to love her! Her world has shattered into a million pieces. She is so ashamed, humiliated. Not wanted.

"What happened, Glory?" Becca's voice keeps repeating, rising.

She pulls the pillow over her head to drown out her little sister. But the pillow doesn't drown out anything. "I thought he loved me," she says. "I thought he loved me."

"He does love you." Becca shifts next to her. "I've watched you together. And I see how he looks at you, Glory. Matt does love you. He does." She rests her hand on Glory's shoulder.

She draws in the warmth. "No, he doesn't." She looks at Becca then Ben. The stricken expression that crosses Ben's features forces more tears.

"It's my fault," he says sharply.

Glory raises her head.

"I told him if he really loved you he wouldn't . . . do it with you."

"Why did you say that?" she asks.

"I told him you were special, different than the girls he's always with." Ben plays with the sheet on Lyne's bed. "That you were my friend and I didn't want him to hurt you. That he needed to treat you better."

"He does treat me better!" She sits up suddenly, almost pushes Becca off the bed.

Ben jerks back. "I know. I know he loves you. I shouldn't have said anything. I didn't think he'd listen to me!"

"He loves you, Glory," Becca says.

"Then why doesn't he want to be with me?"

"I told him not to." Ben looks wretched. "He said it was different with you. He did. He promised me."

"I love him. I want to be with him."

"I don't understand why you have to go home now. Glory's old enough. Fuck it. She can take care of Becca. Jesus, it's not as if you've ever put her to bed before. And where the fuck is your mom anyway?"

Rick's bitching cuts over the low thrum of the car's engine. It is all background buzz in her head. His hand is on her leg, just below the hem of her skirt. He hasn't tried to inch his fingers up. He has to know. He has to know.

"C'mon, babe. Let's turn 'round and go back. C'mon. Night's just begun. Lots of partying left to do."

Buzz, buzz, buzz. None of his words have been an apology. She certainly would have heard that. Not a single sorry for hurting her, for forcing her, for ploughing into her over and over. And then he just lay there, breathing heavily. Smug and fulfilled and so, so proud. Like she was a prize and he had won her. She inched away from him, could barely move. She pulled down her skirt, found a boy's T-shirt in one of the drawers. She bunched her ripped panties and torn shirt, stuffed them in the beautiful gold evening bag.

There are bruises between her legs where he forced her, on her hips where he held her down. Her lip is bloody where she bit so hard to stop from crying out.

"Jesus, fuck, Lyne. Say something!"

"What do you want me to say?" She can't even be angry. She is too numb for that.

"It was good, babe. C'mon. You know it was."

She shifts and Rick's hand drops to the seat. His fingertips burn her thigh.

"Fuck it, Lyne. You're still pissed because I talked to McDermott about Humphreys? The guy's a prick. He'll be gone soon anyway. You said so yourself. Just what the fuck is your problem?"

They screech to a halt in front of her townhouse.

She turns to him. "I don't ever want to see your face again." She yanks the pendant from her neck, throws the broken piece of jewellery at him.

"What the fuck?"

She watches the chain slips through his fingers, then she is out of the car, slams the door. She clutches the evening bag and her stiletto shoes tightly, forces herself to walk barefoot, straight-backed into the house. When she hears the Camaro peel out, she slides down the wall, sticks her fist into her mouth to muffle her cries.

There is a reason why he tries not to hook up with first-time adulterers. And this is it. Allie is pushed into the corner of the front seat of the BMW, body firmly melded to the door. She should have gotten into the back seat. It would have added to her illusion. Or resolve. Or whatever the hell she is calling it. Because regret and guilt are rolling off of her. But if he reads that scent correctly, it's mixed with the hard-learned lesson never to stray again. Doesn't matter that Rutger is screwing another woman. He toys with the idea of saying that to her. But what's the point? It's not as if he wants her to leave her husband. And, small mercies, she isn't asking him for a commitment.

He should have turned on the radio as soon as they got on the road. This silence is stifling.

When he clears his throat, she jumps.

"What?" she demands.

Maybe the wildcat in bed still has some wildness left in her. A passing car lights up the interior and he turns to look at her. Her face is stone. If he says the wrong thing, she will crack. And at this point it's hard to know if the fissure will come in tears or in vitriole. Neither appeals to him.

"Nothing," he mumbles.

Allie shifts so her back is against the seat. When another car passes, she says, "You know your boy is dating my middle daughter. Glory."

It is his turn to jump. "Met her once. They were together." And he told his boy to break it off. Obviously he didn't. "Met your youngest, too."

"Becca." Allie rubs her wedding band. He hadn't seen her put it on. "She and Ben are good friends."

He grunts. He figured that out already. He knows what Allie knows and he isn't even around. What kind of mother is she anyway? Miriam would have been a better mother. Miriam was a better mother.

"Glory's in love with Matt," Allie says.

He presses down on the accelerator and the car lurches forward. He eases off.

"I think Matt's in love with Glory," she says, dropping her hands from the dashboard.

"Not possible. My boy doesn't do love."

He feels her eyes on him. She says blandly, "Like his father?"

"Yes," he says, voice hard. "Love gets you nowhere."

Allie says nothing.

"Look at you," he says and his voice is still hard.

"You're a prick," she says and the energy is back in her words.

"So I've been told."

Time slips away for Lyne and she can breathe again. She digs through the purse, pushes aside her shirt and underwear, lets her fingertips guide her past the condoms in search of soft Kleenex. Her fingers close over a ball of paper. She pulls it

322

out, flattens it. A receipt. Lace babydoll. From La Senza. Mom hasn't been out of town in ages to go to a La Senza. And Lyne didn't find the babydoll when she was dressing for . . . when she was dressing. That is Dad's signature. Dad's signature. Dad's condoms. Oh my God. Oh my God. Her brain is screaming. No. That is not her brain. That is something else. Someone else. Glory.

She drops the purse, crushes the receipt again, drops it, too. She pushes herself up the wall, follows the heartbreaking sobs to the bedroom. She clings to the doorjamb.

"What's going on?"

"Lyne!" Becca yells.

"What's going on?"

"What happened to you?" Becca whispers.

Glory raises her head, gasps. "Oh my God, Lyne. What did he do?"

She pulls her T-shirt down below the hem of her skirt. "Boys are dicks," she says. "Men are dicks." She crosses the room, sinks down between Becca and Glory.

"What did he do to you?" Glory asks.

"It doesn't matter. I'm done with him." She threads her fingers through Glory's hair. Her voice is ice when she asks, "Is this because of Matt?"

"He doesn't want me. He doesn't love me."

"Stay with her," she says to Becca. Then she stalks out.

Matt pulls at his hair. This is not what he wanted. He can't get Glory's face out of his head. She will never talk to him again. But maybe he can try. Maybe he can get her to understand. He still has weeks, maybe even months. He can work with that.

He can get them back to a better place. Make her understand how much he loves her.

But right now he is so hard he hurts, he can't think straight. He is going to have to relieve himself, work himself. He hasn't been with a girl for over two months and he feels it all between his legs. He had wanted Glory so badly. God, he still does. He is going to die of blue balls. Oh, fuck! He flops over, drives his groin into the mattress.

The screen door slams. Ben is home. Ben can help him make things right with Glory again. He has to make things right with her. But Ben can't see him this way. He should call out, tell Ben not to come back here, but he can't do more than grunt. And then the bed dips and there are soft hands moving under the waist band of his boxers and Glory is back and he won't be able to say no again and he is so hard and he can't think, can't think, just wants relief, needs relief, needs release. Needs, needs, needs.

"Is this what you want, Matt?" Lyne says. "This is it, isn't it? This is the only thing guys want. Any girl will do."

Her hard voice mixes with his desperation. And when she tugs down his boxers, rolls on the condom, and slides on to him without removing her skirt, he stops worrying about her words, her tone. He can smell Rick on her but he doesn't worry about that either. It doesn't matter. None of this matters. He just feels so good. He grabs Lyne's hips, startles when she gasps. But then she is moving along with him, faster and harder.

"Oh, fuck, fuck." And he explodes.

Lyne cries out. It is sharp and angry and nothing about fulfillment. It cuts through his high.

"Lyne?"

She rolls away, back to him.

The screen door slams again. It has to be Ben this time. If Ben sees him with Lyne, the kid will never forgive him.

He stands, drops the condom in the garbage can, pulls up his boxers. "Don't come back here, Ben. Wait." His eyes are drawn to the doorway. Glory stands there.

"It's not what you think, Glory," he says. He tugs on his jeans.

"Did you just fuck my sister?" Her blue, blue eyes are clouded.

"Please . . . "

"Then it is exactly what I think." Her face hardens then crumples and she is gone.

Matt sinks down next to Lyne, stares at the empty doorway.

"I told you to give her a Harlequin romance," Lyne says. "But you couldn't, could you? This is all boys want. This is all boys are about. Getting fucked. Well, at least I saved her from that." She stands, straightens her skirt, pulls down her shirt. "She's better off without you." And she follows Glory out the door.

Oh, God! What has he done? He has broken everything. He surges up, fights the sheets off his bed, throws them on the floor. But now he can't breathe. There is no air. He is drowning. He crashes onto Ben's bed.

Jack pulls up at the front of his townhouse. Allie can walk the two doors down. It is three in the morning. Nobody will see her.

She reaches into the back seat, pulls her bag over and leaves. She doesn't look back. Jack grips the steering wheel, watches her hips sway in her tight skirt. When she has crossed the street, he heaves himself out of the car. He opens the back door, pulls out his bag. He rests his forehead against the cooling metal of the car's roof. Christ. What a life.

"Long night?"

He jerks around, drops his bag.

"Mr. Humphreys. You're a hard man to get a hold of," McDermott says. "See you quit Rath's."

"Career move," he says. Did something happen to the boys? Did Matt get into trouble? Did someone call Children's Services? Christ. He wraps his hand around the top of the still-open door. "Why would you be trying to get a hold of me, Constable?"

"Constable McDermott."

"I remember." He evens out his breathing.

"You leave your boys alone an awful lot, Mr. Humphreys." McDermott keeps his voice light.

"My oldest is sixteen. He can handle himself," he says. His tone is guarded, not quite defensive. This is no fucking friendly conversation.

"Yeah, your boy handles himself real well."

"What does that mean?" he shuts the door, leans up against it. The metal is warm but it sends a shiver through his body.

"He didn't tell you about the fight he got into with the Jeffries boy a few weeks back?" McDermott steps closer.

The last time he and Matt talked about anything it was about Allie Rutger's middle child. The one Allie says is in love with Matt. The one Allie says Matt is in love with.

"The Jeffries boy? No idea what you're talking about," he says. He slides his hands into his front pockets, fingers a soft box. Christ. The playing cards. He crosses his ankles.

McDermott bristles. "Your kid's a menace."

"One fight, Constable. Don't think that makes my boy a menace."

"Maybe if you were around you could keep him on a tight leash," McDermott says, calmer.

Jack knows this dance. He takes a deep breath, speaks calmly, too. "You're right, Constable, I need to keep him on a tight leash."

McDermott looks hard at him, flexes his hand that hangs by his nightstick. "Let him know I'm keeping an eye on him."

"I'll do that, Constable." He picks up his bag, steps around McDermott. "Thanks for stopping by."

He keeps his steps unhurried as he makes his way to the townhouse. The door to the police car creaks, slams shut. The street quiets. His heart is beating in his throat. Christ, Matt! The boy knows better than to keep things like this from him. It's because of that girl. Wasn't Matt listening to him? *This* is what love gets you. He steps into the house, drops his bag in the mudroom. He slinks to the front window, keeps hidden behind the curtain until he hears the engine. He inches forward enough to see McDermott pull a U-turn, the cruiser slowly make its way down the street.

Christ. How long has this man been watching? What does he know? They need to move. Now.

Matt feels as if he is surfacing, fighting up through water, buffeted by a rolling tide.

"What the hell, boys?"

He lifts his head. Dad is in the doorway to the bedroom and the rolling tide is Ben pushing at him. "I'm awake, Benny."

"Why are you in Benny's bed?"

It is a simple question and it all rushes back and he is being pulled underwater again. And he can't breathe, can't breathe. Doesn't remember how. And then Ben touches him, small hand splayed across his heart. Warmth. And he remembers. He pushes up against the wall, takes a deep, deep breath.

"He spilled water all over his bed last night so I told him he could sleep with me," Ben says.

"There's a couch, you know?" Dad says. He squints. "What the hell is wrong with you, Matt?"

"What do you mean?" He pulls his legs up to his chin, hugs them tightly. Breathe. Breathe.

"Your eyes are all red."

Matt closes his eyes, rests his cheek on his knees.

"Does it have anything to do with the cop that just greeted me?"

Breathe. "What?"

"What?" Ben echoes.

"Just now. There was a cop parked on our street. Came over to talk to me."

"McDermott."

"Yeah, that was his name. What the hell, Matt?"

He feels the tug of Ben's hand fisted in the back of his T-shirt. If he tells Dad now what he knows, they will leave tonight. He will never get a chance to set things right with Glory. Breathe. If he tells Dad. But if he doesn't tell Dad, he could lose Ben. McDermott will phone Children's Services.

"I had a run-in with the cop a few weeks back."

"A few weeks back! Christ, Matt! You know you're supposed to tell me about these things!" The doorjamb groans under Dad's grip. "It's about that girl, isn't it? That's why you didn't tell me, isn't it?"

"Dad," Ben says. He lets go of Matt's T-shirt and shifts in front.

Matt wants to hug the shit out of the kid. So small yet he thinks he can protect his big brother. "What did he say?"

"He said he's been watching you, watching us. That I was hard to find. That you had a fight with a boy. That you've been getting into trouble."

"That's not true!" Ben yells.

"Ben." He lightly kneads his brother's neck. "I didn't get into a fight with anyone, Dad. Just had words with someone and he knows the cop."

"You need to tell me about these things, Matt, you know that!"

"I know that, Dad," he says. "I'm sorry."

"They could take you and Benny from me!"

"I know that, Dad! I'm telling you now, right? I'm telling you everything now!" He struggles to breathe again. But he can do this. He needs to do this. He pulls Ben in. He will never let go. Never.

"Get your asses up. Get packed."

"We're leaving? Now?" Ben says.

"We don't have a choice, Ben," he says. "I screwed up,"

"But what about Glory? You have to set things right with her!"

"It's too late," he says. "I can never do that. I did a horrible, horrible thing."

"Matty," Ben says.

"It's too late." His breath hitches. He studies the ceiling and breathes, breathes, breathes. "I've made my choice."

"Matt," Dad says and he is no longer harsh.

"Just . . . " He looks at Dad. "You were right. Guys like us don't get girls like that."

"Matty," Dad says.

"Just . . . we need boxes, Dad."

"Yeah, okay." Dad lingers a moment. "Come with me, Benny, I've got boxes in the trunk of the Beemer."

Ben follows without a word.

He fucked up. He has nobody to blame but himself. How could he have done that to Glory? If this is what being in love is all about, he doesn't want this. He is not cut out for this. He pushes off the bed, starts dragging his and Ben's clothes out of the dresser then moves to the closet. His knees buckle and he slides down the wall. His eyes come to rest on the end of the Dempster's bag sticking out from between the mattresses of his bed. He crawls over, works the bag loose, fingers the ten and twenty dollar bills inside the plastic. Taking care of Ben. This is what he needs to focus on. Nothing else. Nothing more. He stuffs the bag into the front pocket of his jeans.

"Matty," Ben says from the doorway, a box in each hand.

"What?"

"It's not your fault. None of this is your fault."

"It's my job to look out for you, Benny."

"That's not on you," Ben says. "It's not supposed to be on you."

He drags a suitcase out from under his bed then Ben's bed.

Dad comes back. "Here." He shoves *The Grapes of Wrath* at Ben. "This was on the kitchen table. Thick book. Got to be yours."

Ben takes it, opens the front cover. A piece of paper flutters to the ground. Matt recognizes the bookmark. Glory left it behind. She wants nothing to do with him. She doesn't ever want to remember him.

Ben scoops up the bookmark, puts it back in the book. "I'll be right back."

Then he is gone and the front door slams. Matt sinks down on the bed, pulls his legs to his chest. He can't breathe. He can't remember how.

Allie is shocked to see Ben crossing the yards at nearly four in the morning. He is clutching a thick book to his chest. She should meet him at the door. But she doesn't want to face him. She stays hidden behind the curtain, tracks his progress. He bypasses the steps, heads for the side of the house. Then she hears voices. He sneaked into the girls' bedroom, went through the screenless window. She quietly makes her way to the bedroom door, inches it open. When she checked on the girls earlier, Becca had been sleeping with Glory. Now, Becca is crouched with Ben on Lyne's bed. But Glory is not alone. Lyne is sleeping with Glory. What is going on? Allie's stomach clenches.

"You have to give this to Glory, Becca." Ben's voice is thick.

"What is it?"

Ben opens the book, pulls out a bookmark. "She gave it back to Matt when she left the book."

"Oh."

"But she wrote in the book for him so I think she's really going to want that bookmark," Ben says.

"What did she write?"

"Look." He opens the front cover, angles it toward the light from the streetlamp.

Becca reads aloud, "'*Man, unlike any other thing organic or inorganic in the universe, grows beyond his work, walks up the stairs of his concepts, emerges ahead of his accomplishments.' This is us, Matt. So much more than where we've come from, so much more than who we've come from. Love you always, Glory.*"

Allie flattens her back against the wall, feels the heavy weight of the wedding ring she shoved back on her finger when she escaped the hotel room. *She* has not come out ahead of anything. She has come back to where she has started. She will stay in this town, stay with Doug. This is all she knows. This is all she has.

"You have to give her the bookmark when she doesn't hate him so much. He really tried, Becca, he did."

"Why doesn't he give it to her? Talk to her? She loves him. She'll listen to him."

"We're leaving," Ben says.

"I know," Becca says.

"Now. Tonight."

"What?" Becca sits up straight. "Now? Tonight? Why?"

"Dad says there was some cop waiting for him when he got home. Threatened him. We have to go."

"No, Ben." Becca is crying.

"I don't have a choice," Ben says.

The relief Allie feels almost replaces the guilt. She can try harder. She will try harder. And Jack won't be here, her constant reminder of the way she has let Glory down, let her family down.

Ben rests his hand on Becca's. The girl is still holding the bookmark. "Please give it to her. Tell her Matt is sorry, that Matt loves her, that he really, really wanted things to be different."

Becca nods. She hugs Ben desperately. Then the boy is out again into the early morning.

Allie backtracks to stand by the living room window, watches the weary steps of the small slumped-over boy. When she turns, she catches a glimpse of something gold on the floor against the wall, a crumpled piece of paper lying next to it.

Jack makes room for one more box in the trunk of the BMW. It's probably Matt's box he's waiting for. Benny pulled an impressive vanishing act and left Matt to do the packing, which means Matt packed Benny's box first and will force whatever books he couldn't get into Benny's box into his own. And Benny had a shit-ton of books piled along the wall behind his bed. His boys don't think he knows these things. But he does. He just doesn't know what to do with this knowledge.

"Here, Dad," Matt says, nudges his elbow with the small cardboard box.

He almost drops the damn thing it's so heavy. "Christ, Matt."

Matt shuffles his feet, keeps his head bowed.

"Where'd your brother disappear to?"

Matt looks quickly down the street before returning his gaze to the fascinating gravel road.

"Hey?" he says. He has never been comfortable with a silent Matt.

Matt looks at him and the boy's eyes are bloodshot, his face pale and drawn. "He had to talk to Becca."

"Talk? Is that what kids are calling it these days?"

"Jesus, Dad."

And there is finally heat in Matt's words, a bit of life in his face.

"You were making out with girls when you were in grade six," he says. He would much rather be dealing with a pissed-off boy.

"Ben's not me," Matt says. The heat is still there. Good.

He sighs. "Go do a final sweep of the house."

"Okay, yeah," Matt says. His steps are unhurried.

"Christ." Jack holds tightly to the still-open lid of the trunk, stuffs his other hand into the front pocket of his jeans. He jams his fingers against the pack of cards. He pulls them out, flips them over and over before fumbling them between two suitcases. "What the hell?" he says. Matt's box, Benny's box both sit exposed, closed only by folded-over flaps. He gropes for the cards, manages to shoot the small deck into the darkened wheel well. "Fuck it."

He slams the trunk and there's Benny frozen under the streetlamp. The kid's face is in shadows, but his eyes are wide. Caught. Trapped. Fear. Always fear.

"Fuck it," he says and stalks to the driver's side of the car.

Matt slides his back along the front seat, farther away from Dad. All he wants to do is curl up in the back with Ben. Hold the boy close like he hasn't held him close for a very long time. Delwood pushed them apart. Glory pushed them apart. He was stupid enough to believe that his world could include more than Ben. But he knows better than that now. Ben is it. Ben is all he needs.

The low beams of a passing car wash over the wet windshield. It has begun to rain, the summer heat finally cut. Glory would say the sky is empathizing, opening up and crying with him. But he knows. The sky is mocking him.

"Hey," Ben says softly.

Matt turns around. "Yeah?"

"I have the book Glory left for you. Do you want it?"

"No."

"She wrote something in it for you."

"I know."

"Have you read it?"

"No."

"Don't you want to read it?" Ben shoves the thick book over the seat.

He pushes it away, speaks to the grey distance. "There is no Promised Land."

"What, Matt?" Dad says.

"Nothing." Dad is like the turtle. Always going some place, but never arriving. No, there is no Promised Land for Dad.

"Matty?" Ben says.

This is all Dad knows. Dad cannot start over. If he wants more for Ben, they will have to start over without Dad. There can be a Promised Land for him and Ben.

"Hold on to it, okay?" He is so, so tired. "I'll ask you when I want it, okay?"

"Okay, Matty," Ben says. He huddles between the backpacks.

Matt closes his eyes, blocks out his father at the wheel, listens to the swish, swish, swish of the windshield wipers, the whir of the tires eating up the wet road. Moving. Moving. Moving ahead.